Judge Me Now

—

Rewritten Edition

By Cheurlie Pierre-Russell

Publishing Information

Printed in the United States of America

Table of Contents

About the Author

Cheurlie Pierre-Russell is a proud U.S. Navy veteran, passionate children's advocate, and acclaimed author dedicated to telling stories that illuminate the beauty of blended families, personal resilience, and the search for identity. Born and raised in sunny Miami, Florida, Cheurlie brings a rich cultural background and lived experience to every page she writes.

She holds a Bachelor of Arts in Sociology from Georgia State University and a Master of Science in Psychology from Walden University. With a deep understanding of both societal structures and the human mind, Cheurlie crafts narratives that inform, educate, and empower—especially for young readers navigating complex emotional journeys.

Through her work, she aims to uplift people of all ages with diverse backgrounds, encouraging them to embrace their own stories, rise above challenges, and believe in the power they carry within.

My Book List

For Younger Readers:

Little Kitty Goes to School
Sheila the Shy Shark
Alani Story ABC Book A Princess is Born

Picture Books:

Broken before the Storm
The Beauty of Love in Those we Shame
Save the Missing Penny
Making Dollars Make Sense:
Business Ownership at Any Age
Butter Me Fly: My Way Home
The Special Little Sister
Friendly Monsters: Behind the Computer

For Older Readers:

The Love of Likes
The Better Betty
Teens Soar in Their Credit Score
Judge Me Now
Hear to Heal
Luxury Travel on a Budget

Prologue: Truth on Trial
The Weight of the Bend

Silence carried its own temperature inside Courtroom 4B. It was cold—not the kind that crept along skin, but the kind that lived in the marrow, a cold that settled between the ribs and pressed against the heart. Judge Dallas Jackson felt it long before the room filled, long before the bailiff called the morning docket to order. It was the kind of cold that memory brings—the kind that warns you the past is closer than it appears.

The fluorescent lights hummed overhead, an anxious, ceaseless drone. A row of attorneys shuffled papers with crisp urgency. The gallery buzzed with uneasy whispers as spectators leaned forward, eager to position themselves for the spectacle the morning promised. Every breath held a subtle tremor. Every face, a quiet expectation.

But none carried the weight of the man seated behind the elevated bench.

Dallas kept his expression steady—practiced, measured. His robe, pressed with clean lines that morning, felt suddenly heavy against his shoulders. His hands rested on oak worn smooth by decades of verdicts delivered by judges whose lives were easier than his. Judges who did not wake with the memory of a baby's cry stitched into their bones. Judges who did not spend nights swallowing ghosts with the same discipline they used to uphold the law.

His gavel lay to his right, polished, ordinary. But to Dallas, it was beginning to feel like a detonator. One strike could shatter the very foundation he'd spent a lifetime rebuilding.

The clerk called the next case.

"The People versus Lake Miller."

A tremor flickered through Dallas's jaw before he could stop it.

Lake Miller.

His brother.

The first hand to ever hold his without letting go.

The first boy who shielded him from cruelty when they were too young to understand what cruelty was.

And now—here.

Accused of taking a life.

Dallas inhaled slowly, letting the air settle his pulse, but the moment he lifted his gaze and found Lake standing at the defense table in a county-issued suit, something inside him buckled. Lake looked older than Dallas remembered—tired, unshaven, eyes dark with months of sleepless nights. Even from the bench, Dallas could see remnants of the boy he once followed through foster home hallways like a shadow.

But today, there was no brotherhood allowed.

No childhood shared.

No history acknowledged.

Only the law.

And yet, how could anyone expect him to be unaffected? How could anyone imagine a judge could amputate the child he once was from the man he had become?

Dallas tightened his grip on the edge of the bench, invisible beneath his robe.

He was losing control—and he knew it.

He scanned the prosecution's table, forcing his gaze away from Lake. Roman Arnold stood rigidly beside the lead prosecutor, his posture rigid as steel. Roman's expression revealed nothing, but Dallas caught a subtle shift—a flicker of tension tightening his features. Roman avoided his eyes just as deliberately as Dallas avoided his.

Something unspoken passed between them anyway.

A history Roman didn't remember.

A history Dallas could never forget.

And thenMovement in the gallery.

Dallas's breath stalled.

Donna.

His mother.

Her hair, once thick and dark, now threaded with silver, had been pulled into a trembling bun. Her cheeks carried the soft hollows of years spent battling demons no one else could see. And in her hands— shaking, frail—she held a stack of papers she was clearly too emotional to read.

Her eyes lifted, searching.

When they met his, the room disappeared.

It was not Courtroom 4B anymore.

Not a trial.

Not a robe.

Not a gavel.

It was the echo of a baby crying through a crack house floor.

It was the memory of a boy clutching a checkerboard napkin.

It was a mother screaming through a police car window.

It was the smell of mold and fear and hunger and shame.

Memories surged forward so violently Dallas steadied himself with both hands.

He tried to breathe.

Tried to swallow.

Tried to remain the man the county believed he was.

But memories were living things.

They had claws.

And they were hungry.

The bailiff's voice cut through his thoughts.

"All rise."

The courtroom rose. Dallas rose with them, but the ground beneath his feet felt hollow, as though he stood on collapsing earth.

"Court is now in session," the bailiff announced.

Dallas's robe fluttered around him as he took his seat. His knees threatened to lock. His pulse drummed against his ribs like a warning bell.

And as he gathered his breath to speak, the past surged again—this time with merciless clarity.

Before he could stop itBefore he could anchor himselfBefore he could announce the casethe world around him blurred and dissolved into memory.

The Night the Past Found Its Voice

The memory hit Dallas like a collision—violent, uninvited, and unstoppable.

He didn't blink.

He didn't move.

He didn't breathe.

The courtroom, the robe, the polished oak bench—all of it dissolved beneath the force of a single truth resurfacing from the depths:

He had been broken long before he was ever whole.

The Descent — Donna, Years Ago

Long before the world would learn the name "Judge Dallas Jackson," there was only a woman stumbling barefoot along a strip of asphalt slick with night rain.

Donna Arnold's bones ached with hunger. Her hands shook from withdrawal. She clutched her jacket—thin, borrowed, not warm enough—as she raced beneath neon motel signs flickering like warnings.

She was seventeen.

Beautiful in a way that hardship couldn't erase.

Soft in a world that punished softness.

Alone in a world that pretended not to see girls like her.

And she was running.

Behind her, the echo of heavy footsteps grew louder.

"Donna!" a voice barked. "Donna, don't make me chase you!"

Razor.

His presence sliced through the dark like a blade. The smell of gasoline and cheap cologne drifted down the alleyway as his Cadillac rolled to a slow crawl behind her, headlights spilling across puddles.

Donna pressed herself against the wall, chest heaving.

"I told you not to run." Razor's silhouette emerged from the car, slow and deliberate. A wolf approaching its wounded prey. "You know better."

Donna swallowed hard, her throat thick with fear. "I'm not doing this anymore."

"Oh, sweetheart," Razor murmured, his voice dripping with false sympathy as he approached. "You were made for this. You're mine. You know that."

Her breathing quickened. The cold wind bit into her, but it was nothing compared to the chill seeping from the man before her.

"I just… I just need help," she whispered. "I need out."

Razor's expression shifted—kindness evaporating, cruelty surfacing like a second skin.

"There is no out," he said quietly.

His hand shot forward, gripping her jaw with bruising force.

"You need me. You hear me? You don't get to leave me."

She winced, the pain stabbing deep into her cheeks. "Please—please, Razor—I can't—"

He squeezed harder. "You can't survive without me."

Hot tears spilled down her face as he dragged her back toward the car.

The night swallowed her scream.

And fate swallowed everything that came after.

The Child She Couldn't Save

Months blurred into years.

The motel rooms.

The hunger.

The nights she prayed for death.

The mornings she prayed to be forgiven.

The men with the cold hands and dead eyes.

And thenA miracle.

A pregnancy she never expected.

A heartbeat she never deserved.

A child she thought could save her from herself.

Dallas.

She whispered his name like a promise.

But Razor saw him only as leverage.

He controlled her with food.

With threats.

With loneliness.

With love twisted into chains.

The house Donna eventually found herself in—the one soaked in mold and desperation—was no home, but a holding cell. A place she was forced to choose between her next high and her next breath. A place where her body obeyed something stronger than her will.

She tried to keep Dallas clean.

Tried to feed him.

Tried to be the mother he needed.

But the demons always won.

The nights grew longer.

The drugs grew stronger.

And her baby's cries grew weaker.

Until the day everything snapped.

The Realtor Who Didn't Look Away

Jamiah Brown had no idea she was walking into a nightmare.

The city assigned her to inspect the run-down property—a task she'd done a hundred times. She expected rodents, mildew, maybe teenagers squatting inside.

She did not expect the smell that hit her when she pushed the front door open.

Rot.

Decay.

Death.

Her stomach lurched, but then—beneath the stench—she heard it.

A sound so faint she thought she imagined it.

A baby's whimper.

Her pulse spiked. "Hello?" she called out, stepping deeper into the dark.

Her heel tapped something—glass bottles scattered on the floor. Another step, and she nearly tripped over a man passed out against the wall.

The whimper came again.

Jamiah froze.

Then she saw him.

A baby, half buried beneath a pile of dirty clothes, his skin blistered from untreated bites, his lips pale, his tiny chest rising shallowly. Tears smeared the dirt on his cheeks.

"Oh God," Jamiah breathed, her voice cracking. "Oh sweet baby… what happened to you?"

She dropped to her knees, scooping him into her arms. He was limp— too limp.

She pressed her cheek to his forehead, and the heat radiating from him sent her into a panic.

She bolted from the house.

Dialed 911.

Screamed for an ambulance.

Cradled him against her chest like she'd known him her entire life.

"Stay with me," she begged. "Please, baby, stay with me."

His tiny fingers curled weakly into her shirt.

A life holding on.

A stranger refusing to let go.

Donna's Collapse

Sirens wailed as police searched the home.

Donna was found on the floor, unconscious, her lips cracked, skin gray.

When paramedics jolted her awake, her first words were not for herself.

"My baby," she rasped. "Where is my baby? My baby—don't take my baby—"

Officers restrained her as she thrashed and screamed.

"Ma'am, calm down."

"No! Please! Please don't—he's all I have—HE'S ALL I HAVE—"

Her cries echoed all the way to the street as they placed her in cuffs.

Neighbors peeked through blinds.

Phones recorded.

Judgment spread faster than sympathy.

Donna clawed at the air, fighting restraints.

"I'm his mother! I'm HIS MOTHER!"

But no one listened.

And as the patrol car pulled away, she watched through the glass as the ambulance doors shut on the only person she had ever loved.

The world blurred into streaks of red and blue.

Her heart cracked with the force of a shattering world.

And she knew—even before anyone told herShe would never get him back.

A Baby Between Life and Death

Dallas lay beneath harsh hospital lights, too small for the bed that held him, too fragile for the life he'd entered.

Doctors murmured over charts.

Nurses whispered fear into the hallways.

"He's severely dehydrated."

"Malnourished."

"His eyes…"

"The infections…"

"He might not make it."

Yet he clung on.

Some spirit inside him refused surrender.

A quiet strength that would follow him for the rest of his life.

Return to the Courtroom — Present Day

Judge Dallas Jackson blinked hard, gripping the bench as the memory slammed into him like a tidal wave.

He could feel the weight of that crying baby as though it lay in his arms now.

Could hear Donna's screams echoing beneath the courtroom's silence.

Could see Jamiah's terrified sprint toward an ambulance.

And somewhere deep inside him, a truth he'd buried clawed its way up:

He was not just a judge.

Not just a success story.

Not just the man the world admired.

He was the child the world almost left for dead.

The child whose mother lost him to her demons.

The child who grew into a man expected to judge others without confronting the truth of himself.

His fingers curled around the gavel.

His breath turned thin.

And the past—long buried, long denied—continued rising.

Fairview. Loss. The First Brother. A Life Rebuilt.

The memory did not let him go.

Even as the courtroom steadied back into focus around Judge Dallas Jackson, his pulse remained unmoored. The attorneys spoke. The spectators shifted. The bailiff watched him with subtle concern. Yet their voices were muffled beneath the roar of a past he had spent a lifetime outrunning.

He blinked—once, twice—but the past refused to fade.

And suddenly…

He was five years old again.

Fairview Youth Center — Where Childhood Went Missing

The Fairview Youth Center was not a place for children to grow.

It was a place for them to survive.

Its walls were painted the color of old lemons, peeling in large curls that fluttered whenever the air conditioning sputtered to life. The smell of overcooked vegetables drifted permanently through the halls. Somewhere, a television blared cartoons that no one watched.

Dallas entered the building with a small blanket clutched beneath his chin—the same blanket Jamiah had wrapped him in at the hospital months earlier.

A social worker guided him to a bunk with the same tone someone might use to escort a stray animal into a shelter.

"This is your bed now," she said gently, but her eyes carried the weary resignation of someone who had explained this too many times.

Dallas touched the thin mattress. It crinkled beneath his fingertips, plastic beneath the sheet to prevent accidents the staff no longer had patience to clean thoroughly.

He looked up at the woman.

"When do I go home?" he whispered.

The question lodged in her throat. She placed a hand on his hair, smoothing it back with the kind of tenderness rare in Fairview.

"You're safe here for now," she murmured. "That's what matters."

But safety meant nothing to a child who had lost everything.

A Quiet Boy in a Loud World

Fairview was loud—children crying, doors slamming, boys fighting in corners for things none of them truly wanted: dominance, attention, control. But Dallas remained quiet, not because he wished to be invisible, but because the world felt too sharp to touch with words.

He carried his blanket everywhere.

He prayed at night with his eyes squeezed shut.

He whispered scripture he only half understood.

"I can do all things through Christ…"

"…who strengthens me."

He repeated it like a charm, like a lifeline, like a stitched reminder that someone somewhere had once cared enough to whisper it into his tiny ear.

At age five, he did not know the weight of scripture.

He only knew the comfort of rhythm.

Arnold — The First Friend

Dallas was sitting alone during breakfast one morning—legs folded beneath him, hands resting on the table—when a boy slid onto the bench across from him.

Arnold.

Pale skin, freckles, hair the color of dusted wheat.

Bright eyes that sparkled with rebellion.

The confidence of someone who hadn't yet been broken by the system.

"You don't talk much, do you?" Arnold asked around a mouthful of cereal.

Dallas shrugged.

Arnold smirked. "That's okay. I talk enough for both of us."

And just like that, the ice around Dallas's world began to thaw.

They played together in the yard.

Built fortresses of cardboard boxes near the dumpster.

Invented stories of dragons, knights, and heroes who never stayed lost for long.

Arnold showed Dallas how to fold paper airplanes that soared higher than their hands could reach.

Dallas showed Arnold how to draw checkerboards on napkins because it reminded him of the only thing from his early childhood he remembered with clarity.

They were inseparable.

Two boys abandoned by circumstance but held together by imagination.

The Day Arnold Disappeared

It happened on a Tuesday.

A normal morning.

A normal breakfast.

A normal promise whispered between bites of toast:

"When we grow up," Arnold said, tapping his knuckles against Dallas's, "we're gonna be brothers forever. Got it?"

Dallas nodded, the promise warming something inside him that loneliness could not freeze.

But when he returned from lunch, Arnold's bed was empty.

The mattress had been stripped.

The blanket folded.

The name tag removed.

"Where's Arnold?" Dallas asked a staff member.

The woman paused mid-step. Her expression softened, but her tone remained brisk. "He was adopted this morning."

The words hung heavy in the air.

Adopted.

Gone.

Dallas's chest tightened, breath caught between wanting to cry and not knowing how to.

He climbed onto his bunk and hugged his blanket tight.

The room felt colder than ever.

The echo where Arnold's laughter once lived hurt more than any wound.

That night, for the first time since arriving at Fairview, Dallas fell asleep facing the wall, silently repeating scripture until the ache dulled just enough to close his eyes.

Life After Arnold — The Quiet Between

Days folded into each other with aching sameness.

Dallas learned that no one stayed forever.

That friendships ended in the space of a phone call.

That attachments were dangerous.

He learned to move softly, speak sparingly, and hold his heart in careful hands.

But even in silence, he grew.

He learned to read words beyond his age group.

Learned that law books felt more predictable than people.

Learned that justice was something you fought for, not something you received.

And thenOne afternoon, everything changed again.

Sara and Hunter Miller — A New Beginning

The Fairview staff called his name over the intercom.

"Dallas Arnold Jackson, please report to the office."

He froze.

Children rarely went to the office unless something terrible had happened.

Heart pounding, he walked slowly, blanket still tucked beneath his arm.

Inside the office sat a woman with warm hazel eyes and a man with gentle shoulders. They rose when he entered.

"Hi, sweetheart," the woman said, kneeling so her eyes met his. "My name is Sara. This is my husband, Hunter."

Dallas swallowed, unsure.

Sara smiled at him—not the strained smile staff used, but one that felt… human.

"We've been looking for you," she said softly.

He blinked. For me?

Hunter extended a hand. "We read everything about you. We want you to join our family."

Family.

The word hit him like sunlight.

Sara reached for his hand. Dallas hesitated—only for a second—before placing his small fingers in hers.

Hunter exhaled a shaky breath as if relieved.

And just like thatDallas's world shifted again.

The Millers' Home — A House That Felt Alive

The Miller home was nothing like Fairview.

It smelled of cinnamon and fresh paint.

It had carpets that didn't scratch bare feet.

It had warm lamps instead of harsh fluorescent bulbs.

On the first night, Sara brought him to a room with pale blue walls, a small bookshelf, and a bed covered in superhero sheets.

"This is your room," she said.

My room.

Dallas walked inside slowly, touching the comforter, the lamp, the dresser—testing the realness of it all.

"It's okay if it feels strange," Sara whispered. "Take your time. We're not going anywhere."

For the first time in his life, he slept through the night without waking from nightmares.

Brothers in a Borrowed Beginning

The Miller home did more than shelter Dallas.

It softened him.

It unraveled the knots the world had tied into him too early.

It gave him permission—subtle, patient permission—to breathe in ways he had never known to be possible.

And it was there, in that warm, humming house on the corner of Willow Drive, that Dallas met the boy who would redefine what it meant to belong.

Lake Miller — The Brother He Didn't Know He Needed

Lake was eleven when Dallas arrived, older by six years and loud in a way that filled entire rooms.

He was the kind of boy who charged through life as though everything in his path were an adventure waiting to happen. His laughter was wild and unrestrained. His smile was quick and contagious. And when he saw Dallas standing shyly behind Sara's legs, blanket in hand, Lake's wide grin softened with something close to tenderness.

"You're the new guy?" he asked, stepping forward.

Dallas nodded.

Lake studied him—quietly, curiously—then offered the simplest invitation in the world.

"You wanna play with us?"

Dallas blinked. No one had asked him that since Arnold.

"Play…what?"

Lake smirked. "Whatever you want."

And just like that, Lake took him by the wrist and pulled him into a world Dallas didn't realize he had been starving for.

A world of homemade forts and flashlight tag.

A world of shared cereal bowls and whispered secrets.

A world where brothers weren't tied by blood but by choice.

Lake never treated him like a guest.

Never made him feel like an outsider.

Never asked him to earn his place.

He simply welcomed him.

And Dallas—timid, careful Dallas—found himself learning to smile without fear that someone would snatch the moment away.

Sara's Love — A Quiet Anchor

Sara had a way of noticing things before they were spoken.

When Dallas hesitated to ask for seconds at dinner, she gently nudged an extra spoonful onto his plate without comment.

When he stood outside the laundry room gripping his dirty blanket, unable to explain the terror of being without it, she washed it at night and returned it warm to his bed before sunrise.

When he had nightmares—quiet, breathless ones that left him sitting upright with wide, wild eyes—Sara appeared in the doorway within seconds, whispering,

"You're safe. You hear me? You're safe now."

She didn't ask him to talk.

She didn't push him to trust.

She simply held space for the boy who had lived too many lifetimes before the age of five.

And that, more than anything, was love.

Hunter's Lessons — A Man's Steady Hands

Hunter wasn't loud.

Wasn't flashy.

Wasn't the type of man whose presence demanded attention.

But he understood boys like Dallas.

He understood the fear of asking questions.

Understood the weight of silence.

Understood that trust wasn't built through speeches but through consistency.

He taught Dallas chess, explaining patiently, moving each piece slowly and deliberately.

"You don't win by being the strongest," Hunter explained one night as they sat at the dining table. "You win by learning to see the board. Life's the same way."

Dallas studied the knight in his hand, its carved edges catching the golden glow of the lamp.

"Did… did I ever have a father?" he asked quietly.

Hunter met the question with a soft, steady gaze.

"You have one now," he answered.

Dallas swallowed hard.

For the first time in his life, the ache inside him eased.

The Quiet Years of Healing

Life settled into a rhythm.

School.

Homework.

Dinner with the Millers.

Twilight races with Lake in the backyard.

Late-night board games with Steven, who always claimed luck was on his side.

The trauma in Dallas's bones never fully left—trauma rarely does—but it curled into something smaller, something manageable when surrounded by warmth.

Yet every once in a while, when Sara tucked him into bed, Dallas would ask the same question in a soft, hopeful whisper:

"Do you think my mommy misses me?"

Sara's heart broke a little each time.

But she always answered honestly.

"I think she loved you," she whispered, brushing his cheek. "I think she loved you enough to pray you'd be safe."

Dallas didn't know enough to question the subtle difference between love and presence.

He simply nodded and tucked his blanket beneath his chin.

Donna — The Woman Who Never Stopped Searching

While Dallas grew, Donna drifted.

Months in rehab blurred into years of halfway houses, recovery programs, relapses, and repentance. But no matter how many nights she spent crawling through her own regrets, one truth lit the darkest corners of her soul:

Her son was out there.

Somewhere.

Living.

Breathing.

Growing.

She wrote letters she never knew where to send.

She whispered scripture she never fully believed she deserved.

"Lord… please… just let him be okay."

When she eventually grew strong enough to hold a job, she set aside bits of her paycheck in a tin box labeled My Dallas.

Inside were:

A lock of his baby hair.

The hospital bracelet from the day he was born.

A faded photo someone took of her holding him.

Broken pieces of a life she'd thrown away before she even knew how to live it.

She never stopped searching.

Even when hope felt like punishment.

Even when the world told her it was too late.

She searched.

Because despite every failure, every wound, every terrible choiceShe loved him.

Fiercely.

Desperately.

With the kind of ache that sank into bone.

Roman's Path — A Parallel Life

At the same time, miles away, another boy was being reshaped by fate.

Arnold.

Roman Arnold.

Like Dallas, he grew in a home not his own.

Like Dallas, he carried memories he didn't fully understand.

Like Dallas, he whispered the same scripture to calm the fear of losing the only stability he'd ever known.

But unlike Dallas, he was adopted quickly.

Taken into a household that embraced him fully.

Raised with resources that opened doors with little effort.

He forgot Fairview.

Or believed he had.

He forgot the quiet boy who drew checkerboards on napkins.

Forgot the promise they made over breakfast one ordinary Tuesday.

But some part of him—some unnamed part—never forgot the feeling of brotherhood, even if memory buried the details.

Roman became focused.

Disciplined.

Relentlessly determined.

By fourteen, he had declared he would become a lawyer.

By twenty-five, he had sworn he would fight for children who felt forgotten.

By thirty, he was Miami-Dade's most promising prosecutor.

He didn't know his path would soon collide with the boy he once loved like a brother.

Life had a way of bending time back onto itself.

Back to the Courtroom — Present Day

The flood of memories loosened its grip just long enough for Dallas to feel the courtroom beneath him again.

The benches.

The murmurs.

The cameras.

The weight.

Lake stood at the defense table—no longer the boy who pushed him on swings or shielded him from drunken neighbors. Now he was a man accused of murder, eyes hollow from grief the world couldn't interpret.

Donna sat in the back, trembling with every breath.

Roman stood at the prosecution table—determined, poised, unaware of the truth stitched into the same air they breathed.

Dallas swallowed hard.

His vision sharpened.

His pulse steadied.

But inside, the storm remained.

A storm born in a crack house.

A storm raised in Fairview.

A storm soothed in the Miller home.

A storm sharpened through law school.

A storm now awakened by the collision of past and present.

And right here, right nowthe storm was rising again.

The Echo of a Life Reclaimed

The more Dallas fought the memories clawing at him, the more forcefully they rose—like the tide pulling toward a storm.

Every breath tasted like the past.

Every heartbeat thrummed with ghosts.

Every second in that courtroom felt stretched across decades.

But the law did not wait for emotion.

The clerk cleared her throat, shifting uneasily beside the bench. "Your Honor… shall we proceed?"

Dallas straightened, forcing the present back into focus. He lifted his chin with practiced composure, though the weight of every memory felt stitched into the fabric of his robe.

He scanned the room.

Lake—standing stiffly, shoulders tense.

Donna—hands pressed together, mouthing silent prayers.

Roman—staring down at his files, unaware of the earthquake beneath the surface.

Sara and Hunter—absent, but present in the quiet strength in his spine.

The past—looming, relentless, insistent.

Dallas inhaled slowly.

He had built his life on truth.

But some truths waited for the right moment to demand acknowledgment.

This—today—was one of them.

A Brother's Destiny

Lake's eyes lifted, meeting Dallas's with a strange mix of fear and hope—two emotions Dallas knew intimately.

Lake had always been the protector.

The shield.

The one who defended the smaller kids in the neighborhood long before they understood the violence around them.

He wasn't perfect.

He wasn't gentle.

But he had been good.

And he had been loyal.

And he had been the first real brother Dallas ever knew.

Seeing him now—accused, isolated, forced to trust strangers with his fate—felt like swallowing glass.

"Mr. Miller," the defense attorney whispered to Lake, nudging him lightly. "Stand tall."

But Lake only looked at Dallas.

And Dallas—despite everything—understood that look.

I'm not who they think I am.

I'm not a monster.

I'm still the boy you grew up with.

The ache behind Dallas's ribs sharpened.

Part of him wanted to step down from the bench and tell Lake he believed him.

Part of him wanted to abandon protocol and apologize for every distance adulthood had placed between them.

But he was no longer the boy who held Lake's hand in the dark.

He was the man who held a gavel.

A man whose signature could ruin or redeem.

Roman — The Unknowing Brother

Roman flipped through his notes with precision, unaware of the thin thread connecting him to the man on the bench.

Unaware that the boy he once promised eternal brotherhood to was standing before him in the form of a judge he respected and admired.

Unaware that the boy he once built cardboard castles with could decide the outcome of the trial he worked so fiercely to win.

Unaware that fate had closed its circle tighter than any of them realized.

He stepped forward to speak.

"Your Honor, the State is prepared to—"

The words cut off when Dallas raised a hand.

Roman paused, brows furrowing. "Is everything alright, Your Honor?"

Dallas hadn't meant to interrupt.

But something inside him—the child who lost everything, the judge who rebuilt himself from ashes, the man whose past was now staring him directly in the face—needed one more breath.

One more second.

One more anchor.

He placed a steadying hand atop the bench.

"Yes," he said quietly. "Proceed."

But his voice carried an undertone none of them understood.

Yet.

The Mother in the Shadows

Donna's eyes glistened with unshed tears.

She sat on the far end of the gallery as though proximity itself could injure the son she barely recognized but had never stopped praying for.

She had witnessed him from a distance before—television appearances, articles, courthouse photos—but seeing him in person…

Seeing him breathe…

Seeing him stand tall in a robe she could never have imagined…

It hollowed her.

It filled her.

It saved her.

It destroyed her.

Her hands shook as she tried to steady her breathing.

She wanted to run to him.

Wanted to fall at his feet.

Wanted to tell him everything she had never been able to say.

But she could not.

He didn't know her.

Didn't know her voice.

Didn't know her tears.

Didn't know her fight.

Not yet.

Her heart beat a frantic rhythm against her ribs as she whispered the same scripture she had whispered over him in the night he was born.

"I can do all things through Christ who strengthens me…"

Her eyes closed.

"…even see my son again."

The Gavel and the Truth

The room quieted as Roman began presenting the motion before the court. Dallas tried to listen—tried to lock into the cadence of arguments he'd heard thousands of times—but his pulse kept pulling him backward.

Back to a child clinging to a blanket.

Back to a boy watching his only friend disappear.

Back to a teenager learning the law as a shield.

Back to the man he became by refusing to let his past define his future.

But now the past had walked into his courtroom.

Sat in his gallery.

Stood at his defense table.

Argued at his prosecution podium.

And waited—patient and relentless—for him to acknowledge it.

He could run from it no longer.

Not from Donna.

Not from Roman.

Not from Lake.

Not from the truth.

His fingers curled around the gavel.

The weight of it pressed into his palm like destiny.

He closed his eyes.

A beat.

Another.

And thenCRACK.

The sound echoed like a gunshot across marble floors.

It vibrated through Lake's spine.

It jolted Roman's breath.

It shattered Donna's composure.

It froze every spectator in their seat.

And as the echo rolled through the chambersDallas felt something shift inside him.

Something permanent.

Something inevitable.

Something he could no longer contain.

The Moment Before the Storm

"We will proceed," Dallas said, his voice composed, though inside him, tectonic plates were shifting.

The clerk marked the docket.

The bailiff stood at attention.

Roman prepared his opening.

Lake braced himself.

Donna gripped the edge of her seat.

But something in the air had changedA crack in the wall of the man Dallas had spent decades building.

A truth ready to rise.

A collision destined from the beginning.

And though no one in the courtroom understood what was happening, Dallas felt it with bone-deep certainty:

This was not just a trial.

It was the beginning of a reckoning.

For him.

For Lake.

For Donna.

For Roman.

For the boy he used to be.

For the man he had become.

And as he lifted his gaze toward the room that held every shadow of his past—the story began.

Chapter 1: Lost and Found

————————— • —————————

As the echo of the gavel fades, the story rewinds:

From the outside, the neighborhood looked like a picture-perfect postcard—white picket fences, blooming window boxes, children's laughter rising and falling like music in the warm afternoon light. But even in this seemingly safe little world, secrets festered behind closed doors. Only one house—the one the other families avoided—stood out as a reminder that even here, innocence can be shattered.

Inside that forgotten house, Dallas Jackson sat unnoticed in a faded armchair. Five years old, bones nearly lost to threadbare fabric, he clung to the smallest sounds of life outside: a bicycle bell, a distant dog bark, music from an ice cream truck. He was a silent witness to a world that looked gentle, but had never once welcomed him in.

His mother, Donna, lay unconscious on the kitchen floor—surrounded by beer cans and shadows, her dreams long since surrendered to her demons. Dallas felt invisible, but the weight in his chest was heavy—a loneliness and fear so deep it seemed to swallow his small voice before it left his lips. Still, somewhere beneath the hopelessness lingered a memory, or maybe a wish: someone would come, someone would see, someone would rescue him. Maybe, just maybe, there was a better version of his story still waiting to be written.

From the outside, the neighborhood looked like a postcard. White picket fences, window boxes brimming rom the outside, the neighborhood looked like a with colorful blooms, and porch swings creaking in rhythm with the breeze. Freshly painted houses, with potted plants and backyard swings set in concrete, provided a safe place for kids to play after school. And there were so many kids there, of all ethnicities, and some from two-parent homes, some from less privileged ones. Each house was a single-story white building, featuring picket fences, verandahs, and rocking chair on the porch. Outside, the sun beat down as children played, stirring up dry gray dust from the thirsty ground. Kids raced their bikes along the sidewalk, their laughter drifting through the air like wind chimes. This place was the middle of nowhere, everyone said, but to all the kids who lived here, it was somewhere. However, what they all shared was being good, healthy, and happy children. People loved and cared for them deeply.

Except for one house…

One house stood out that didn't belong amid all this perfection. A secluded spot, separate from the others, lacked trees, their leaves gone, leaving a space where a neat white fence was expected. It was more an eyesore than a shelter— its windows boarded up, paint chipped and peeling, vines

crawling up its siding like nature was trying to take it back. Empty alcohol cans and bottles, cigarette butts, and dog feces littered the tiny, paved front and back yards.

The house, a brownish color intended to blend in, stood out. And it probably hadn't matched anything for a long, long time.

It looked forgotten and unlived-in.

The authorities had been around again lately, following more complaints from nosy neighbors who'd objected to a house sitting in empty disrepair.

As two neighbors stood on their porch nearby to gossip about the house that didn't belong in their neighborhood. "Dirty devils, they were," one woman said. "They never used to put any laundry outside, you know?'

"Oh, I know! And I always had to wonder where the little ones were," another woman said, tut-tutting. "She'd got boys, you know."

She nodded, one of those nods that said, "you know what I mean?"

It usually implies something bad, mean, and nasty. This case was no different. "Boys. Little drug dealers, they'd grow up to be. With a start like that…anyway, they've gone now.

Moved on."

The other woman was shocked and could be seen recoiling in horror at her neighbor's words. How could small kids possibly be described as little drug dealers? It was a ridiculous thing to say. She looked about the yard for the signs of drug paraphernalia—paraphernalia just being a big and ugly word that meant smoking stuff, like pipes and bongs, and also injectable stuff, like needles and empty vials.

She looked and she looked.

Nothing.

Just the mess from the dogs, the empty food wrappers, the drink cans, the alcohol bottles strewn about. She shrugged.

Drug dealers, she said to herself. What a stupid thing to say!

But in her mind, it was set, that grain of truth in the neighbor's ugly words. There had to be some essence of truth in it.

No smoke without fire.

She bid goodbye to her neighbor, and they both wandered back to their houses, deciding the woman with the unruly boys had probably sold up and moved on—or, if she'd never owned the place herself, she'd been pushed out, forced to go somewhere better suited to her type, by the state.

But that was the thing about houses.

Houses came with walls, tall doorways, and gates. Houses had these things to keep some people in and others out, just like castles used to have moats.

What none of the neighbors could possibly know was that in a few short hours, the secret—the secret of number 12—was going to come flooding out.

And it would be worse, far, far worse, than anyone thought. However, there were going to be no little drug dealers, because the boy who'd been old enough to be a hooligan had been taken away by the state, long ago.

Now, only one boy was remaining.

A baby.

* * *

Inside, the silence was heavier than any storm. It wasn't the peaceful kind of quiet; it was the thick, suffocating stillness of abandonment and despair. The boy who would one day be known as Dallas Jackson sat unnoticed in a corner of that house, his tiny frame nearly swallowed by a stained armchair. He was five years old, underweight, and covered in insect bites. His diaper hadn't been changed in days. His mother,

Donna, was unconscious on the floor, surrounded by others just as lost as she was—littered beer cans, dirty needles, and the remnants of hope scattered across the linoleum.

Donna hadn't always lived like this. There was a time, long ago, when she dreamed of better. But her dreams were small compared to her demons, and addiction had stolen everything. Her firstborn son, Roman, had been taken from her at the hospital. She had not even held him long enough to remember his cry. All she could recall was a faint birthmark on his cheek and the way her body ached when he was gone. That pain never left her. Years passed, and she had another son. This time, she swore she'd do better. But swearing was easy. Recovery wasn't.

However, the system had been watching for a long time, and neighbors had made one too many calls.

It was a Wednesday in September and early afternoon.

Real estate agent Jamiah Brown hugged her clipboard close to her chest and grabbed her elegant black purse from the passenger seat of her car before hopping out onto the dusty, windblown sidewalk.

The local authority had just released Number 12, Acers View for sale. It had been empty, the officials said, for years, hence why it looked dirty, yellowed, and brown instead of crisp white.

It had been emptied since authorities evicted the illegal squatters.

Nobody had been back to check. But Jamiah didn't know that.

Jamiah wore black, flared pants, nicely pressed, with tiny diamantes around the waistline and the pant legs, looking a little like a cowgirl— well-suited to this arid and water starved place. When real estate agent

Jamiah Brown arrived to inspect the abandoned property, she thought she'd find nothing more than mold and trash. What she discovered instead changed her life—and Dallas's.

The story went that the house had once belonged to an elderly lady who had passed away in a nursing home, and whose relatives from overseas could never be located.

And so, the old single-story house fell slowly into disrepair, and then into a total ruin, ignored and overlooked and belonging to nobody. Then, some individuals the neighbors had complained about had taken possession, only to be kicked out by the court and a condescending, uncompassionate judge. The law was like that. Those who didn't have, would never have—could never have. The law would ensure it.

Now, that house was a pitiful eyesore, so it had to be moved on.

Jamiah rummaged through her purse for the house keys she'd received, found them at the bottom of a jacket pocket, and retrieved them. She squinted at them and worked out which one was which, then inserted the key into the stiff lock.

It needed brute force to get it to turn, but turn it eventually did.

The black door with its layers of peeling paint creaked open, and she pushed, and she shoved, and she pushed and shoved again, now setting her delicate shoulder right up against the door and exerting her full body force against it, so the dirty paintwork left a dusty mark on her clothes.

The door gave way and was flung wide. When you open a gift box and have no idea what's inside, there's always that moment of awe, wonder, and excitement.

It was like that for Jamiah when she first went into a house that had been closed up for a while, a house that no one other than her had seen for years. It could be a fantastic surprise, and was always 'something else', as she often described it…

One thing about number 12 is that it was a surprise.

And you can be sure it was something else.

Her heartbeat is fast. The stench hit her like a wave, and she gagged, covering her nose. The malignant odor of a stinking, rotting something or other grabbed her nostrils like the putrid stench of a dead rat.

She reeled backward. But she had to go in. Sorry, but I couldn't go in because it stinks was not on the menu as something she could say to the authorities who needed it removed.

Her responsibility was to go in. Jamiah stepped slowly forward, pushing the mail on the floor out of the way. To her right was a room with a creamy-colored door, and she huffed and puffed, barged and shoved at it, and it too flung open wide…

Inside, the scene was almost too much to process—bodies strewn across the floor, motionless. "Oh my God! Oh, my good God!" and "Oh, oh…oh!" she exclaimed as the sight of bodies sprawled on the carpeted floor met her gaze.

Bodies, dead and rotting, bodies, left there, bodies…BODIES!

Bodies of whom?

Whose bodies?

Who had killed them all?

Why?

When?

How?

They appeared to be the bodies of three women in their early thirties, a stick-thin man… and a kid. Only a little kid it was, too—no, a baby, about six to nine months, that was all—but small and underweight, with his jutting bones and… Her eyes took it all in, and her body backed away toward the way she'd come in…

Police, she thought, must ring the police.

She fled… and then, once on the path outside the house again, she stopped. She rethought the scene, replaying it in her mind. She knew she must take another look, because it couldn't be those bodies that stank; they were all still covered in skin.

There were no flies, or not many.

Jamiah had watched all the police shows; there were always flies where there were dead bodies. So, these were not bodies at all.

Couldn't be!

She slowly edged her way back in, trying not to gag because of the smell.

Oh, my God!

They were not bodies at all. They were alive. Just. Or maybe they were—under the influence of something, a substance?

At first, she thought they were dead. They were certainly all sick. Their glazed eyes, cracked lips, and pale, gray skin revealed their illness. Their clothing was filthy and smelled, and they appeared to have lain on the grubby, disgusting brown carpet for a long, long time.

Around them were more remnants of stuff, drug stuff, smoke stuff, drink stuff… she didn't even know the words for the things she could see, as Jamiah was a clean-living woman from a God-fearing family.

She had heard about such things but never seen them with her own eyes.

But she knew enough to recognize this as a drug house—a dilapidated squat, or one exactly as rumored.

* * *

But then she heard a faint, gurgling cry. The kid looked like a baby boy, with a brown skin tone and a beautiful complexion, and already he had a fine mop of curly, thick black hair.

Fleas, lice, or similar insects bit him, and small white creatures wriggled in the child's hair.

He writhed about, squirming, but his eyes were tightly shut.

It seemed someone had tried to prop him in the corner away from the needles and things—at least that was some small blessing, Jamiah thought—but he was too tiny, too small and too weak to have any sitting ability, so he'd flopped forward, waving his little arms around.

His lips were pale and cracked, dry just like the adults scattered about him. He was in a bad way.

Real bad.

Jamiah dashed to the corner and picked up the baby, ignoring the smell and the filthy baby clothes and the days-old diaper he seemed to be wearing, and she cuddled him to her, feeling a tiny heartbeat that came through from his body despite all the odds.

The others in the room were gone, too far gone to know she was even there.

"Shh," she said to the baby, "shh. Mama's poorly, and Auntie Jamiah's going to get you right out of here. You see… you see, baby."

The child managed to open one eye weakly, but both eyes appeared to be infected. Jamiah's heart was breaking. She didn't hesitate. She grabbed her purse again and fled from the house, dialing 911 with trembling fingers, with the babe in arms. Outside, she sat on a neighbor's wall and called the police, not sure what else to do. And anyway, she had the child wriggling in her arms, but nothing like a baby should. It was weak but tried to nestle into her side to get to her body heat, like a baby bird.

By the time the paramedics arrived, she was cradling him like her own. The cops came in record time, taking away the drugged-out adults and calling in the authorities. Paramedics received the baby, administered an intravenous drip, and transported him to the hospital.

And so began the pitiful life of baby Dallas, Dallas Jackson, nine months old when someone discovered him in a disused crack house where they found his mother, Donna Jackson, stoned and incapacitated, as usual.

That kid would soon become the talk of the town. The kid with no diaper on, but who, when Jamiah had found him, had somehow appeared to be wearing one.

Weeks of mess had formed a kind of diaper of its own around his bottom and, hidden by just an undershirt, no one could tell any different until the paramedics got the child seen to at the county hospital emergency unit.

Dallas was underweight, like a baby from a third-world country, and he was full of infection and malnutrition, but aside from all of that, he was otherwise normal.

Otherwise, he was just a small kid for his age, but surely one who, tragically, could never catch up. He had no hope of making it in life.

As it turned out, Donna Jackson, the baby's mother, had been addicted to crack for years. It was a tiny miracle of God that she'd even gotten pregnant and given birth to a baby that didn't have many health issues. Donna was taken to jail for possession of narcotics and child neglect and endangerment. Donna screamed herself helpless for her baby with a pool of tears running down her face as they handcuffed her and placed her in the police car; it was a shock to everyone that she even had enough fluid in her rake-like body to cry real wetness down her pallid face.

The neighbors stood by, gathered around, their eyes wide and their hands in front of their faces as they whispered and gasped to each other.

How did the woman have the gall to live like that? And with a baby, too!

Donna's screaming was devastating, heart-wrenching, and sad.

But most of all, Donna's screaming was in self-admission that what she had done to Dallas was criminal neglect.

She had almost killed her precious boy by making all the wrong life decisions.

Donna knew the uninhabitable conditions in which she'd lived with her son were precarious, but she felt she had no other choice.

It had become a way of life.

Jamiah Brown had always been more than just a realtor. While her stylish wardrobe and quick-witted confidence made her a standout in Miami's competitive real estate scene, her true ambition reached far beyond closing deals and collecting commissions. Helping families find a place to call their own was her way of healing the world, one home at a time. Raised by a single mother who'd rented for most of her life, Jamiah grew up seeing how instability gnawed at a child's sense of safety. She swore that, one day, she would do something to change that—she would help others find not just houses but havens.

Her colleagues often joked that Jamiah was too sentimental for her own good, lingering with clients long after signing, bringing housewarming plants and handwritten notes, volunteering on weekends to help local shelters and reading to neighborhood kids. They thought her need to fix the world was naïve, even a little desperate, but it was rooted in a deeper ache: Jamiah's quiet, private heartbreak that she could not have children of her own. After years of fertility treatments and tearful nights, she realized that if she couldn't nurture life in the traditional sense, she would give love wherever she could—in every set of keys she handed over, in every lost soul she set on a new path.

That day at Number 12 Acers View, when she found Dallas curled in the corner of the crack house, her resolve to do good—and her longing for a child to save—came together in a way she'd never imagined. She'd walked in expecting filth and vacancy but found a child, shivering and small, whose vulnerability pierced straight through the walls she'd built around her own disappointment. Kneeling amid the debris, Jamiah felt something inside her give way—a tidal surge of purpose and sorrow, a realization that every life she could touch, every home she could repair, was a chance to make the world a gentler place. She cradled Dallas in her arms as if he were her own, promising herself that, if she could not be a mother, she would still mother the world in every way she could.

* * *

Donna's boyfriend, David Kimmel, was a man who had grown roots in the cracks of Miami's underbelly long before addiction swallowed Donna's world. He wasn't born a monster—just shaped into one by a life that taught him survival was louder than morality.

His childhood was a blur of evictions, missing fathers, mothers who worked two jobs and prayed three times a day, and older cousins who gave him lessons no child should ever receive.

By thirteen, David already knew how to run a package from one block to another without being noticed.

By sixteen, he knew how to disappear when sirens wailed.

By nineteen, he had inherited a piece of a small-time street corner from a man who'd overdosed, and from there, he built a reputation no one questioned.

It wasn't power that drove him.

It wasn't ambition.

It was loneliness disguised as loyalty.

And there was another truth—one David never knew, but one Donna carried like a bruise beneath the skin:

David was the son of the man who once trafficked her.

She recognized the connection long before she admitted it to herself.

It was in the way David walked—confident, careless, shoulders rolled forward like he owned a space even when it wasn't his.

It was in the way he said her name—slow, slick, almost familiar.

But the moment that truth punched through her denial was when she saw the tattoo.

A serpent winding behind his ear, inked in the same sharp strokes as the one she remembered on Raymond "Razor" Kimmel—the man who pulled her into exploitation at seventeen and claimed her suffering as his profit.

The man who controlled her.

Who taught her fear.

Who taught her pain disguised as attention.

Who called her "sweetheart" with a voice that made her want to vanish.

And now here she was, standing in the living room of his son.

Donna never told David the truth.

Couldn't.

Wouldn't.

To say the words out loud would force her to relive a past she was barely surviving in silence. And David—broken, aimless, aching for belonging—had no idea his own father had been a monster shaping Donna's nightmares.

So when he met her, he thought fate had been kind.

When she laughed, he felt chosen.

When she leaned on him, he felt valued.

When she needed him, he felt whole.

She reminded him of everything soft he had lost long ago—her laughter came easily then, her beauty still bright beneath the tiredness, and her hunger for love was so raw, it made him feel needed in a way nothing else ever had.

He had never been needed.

Not really.

Not by anyone who wasn't transactional.

So when Donna spiraled deeper into addiction, David mistook enabling her as love.

If she cried, he brought her a fix.

If she shook, he doubled the supply.

If she said she couldn't get through the night, he stayed awake with her—smoking beside her, whispering promises neither of them could keep.

In David's broken mind, he wasn't destroying her.

He was rescuing her the only way he knew how.

"Don't worry, baby," he would say, placing a bag in her palm like it was a kiss. "I got you. I'll always get you right."

He didn't know better.

No one had ever shown him what real love looked like.

He had grown up watching men say "I love you" with their fists, their supply, or their silence.

He had grown up believing provision meant affection.

So when he put a pipe in Donna's hand, he thought he was offering comfort.

He thought access meant connection.

He thought chemicals were care.

But to Donna, every time he offered her a fix, she saw Razor's shadow behind him.

Every time he whispered "you're safe with me," she felt the lie burn.

Every time he embraced her, she remembered the monster whose blood ran in his veins.

David wasn't malicious.

He wasn't cold.

He was broken in familiar ways, shaped by generational pain, street rules, and the systems that failed him long before he failed Donna.

But broken love is still dangerous.

And in trying to keep Donna close, he dragged her into a darkness so deep, she might never have escaped.

The tragedy lay in one simple truth:

David loved Donna.

But he loved her the way wounded people love—desperately, blindly, and in ways that destroy.

The tangled roots of Dallas's family tragedy reached back through the cracked linoleum floors of Number 12 all the way to the man whose shadow loomed over Donna's life. David Kimmel, Dallas's father, was no ordinary supplier; he grew up on the streets the same as Donna, running with dangerous men and getting swept up in the economy of addiction before he ever learned the price. Their relationship started recklessly—drawn by hunger, escape, the fleeting warmth of someone who understood what it meant to want and never have. When Donna fell pregnant, David promised it would be different. But his promises were easily broken, washed away in powder and pipe.

At first, Donna had managed to resist spiraling with him. Even as David brought drugs into the house—at first for himself, but eventually for both—she clung to her baby, dreaming of doing better, escaping the cycle her own mother hadn't escaped. But love wasn't powerful enough to combat addiction, especially with a partner slipping her the very temptation she was trying to outrun. The more David provided, the more Donna slipped, her dreams dissolving into desperation and haze.

It wasn't just the drugs that ruined her—it was the betrayal. Knowing the man who should have protected their family instead became the architect of its ruin haunted Donna in her lowest moments. Each handoff, each fix, pulled her further away from Dallas until all she could offer her son was a half-remembered lullaby and the faint comfort of her body. In the end, it was David's carelessness, just as much as his callousness, that condemned them. He was the reason the authorities kept coming, the reason hope was as scarce in that house as food or laughter.

For Dallas, discovering the truth about his father was like picking scabs off old wounds—painful, necessary, and revealing of just how deep the rot had gone. In the wreckage left behind, Donna carried her guilt like a shroud, and Dallas carried the scars. But Jamiah's intervention—and her understanding of how a child could be lost, and a parent could fail—helped Dallas begin the journey back from that darkness.

He was not supportive of his son's life, but was supportive in keeping Donna doped up. And so, the baby Dallas was taken from Donna and away from the clutches of David Kimmel and placed in child protective services.

Forever.

The baby was freed now, and Jamiah, the sales agent, could breathe again.

She could sleep and breathe, but for a long while after, she was haunted by the thought of what would have become of baby Dallas if she had not shown up that day. And she was going to wonder forever what became of him.

* * *

FLASHBACK — When Donna First Met Razor

Donna was seventeen the first time she saw Raymond "Razor" Kimmel—a name she would one day pray to forget, and a face that would haunt every dark corner of her memory.

It was late—later than a girl her age should've been out.

Miami's night air was thick with humidity, clinging to her skin like a warning.

Her stomach growled with the kind of hunger that came from more than missed meals. It came from years of neglect, loneliness, and desperation to belong anywhere.

She had run from home two days earlier after her mother's drunken boyfriend slapped her hard enough to split her lip.

Her mother didn't defend her.

She didn't even flinch.

The silence was louder than the slap.

Donna walked until her feet blistered.

Until the streetlights blurred.

Until she couldn't pretend she knew where she was going.

That's when she saw him.

Razor stepped out of a corner store, the glow of a neon sign flickering over his shaved head. His presence swallowed the sidewalk—commanding, confident, dangerous. He was older, maybe mid-30s, but carried himself with the cool ease of someone who feared nothing.

His sharp eyes scanned her—her disheveled clothes, the swelling around her lip, her trembling hands.

Predators always recognized pain.

"You lost, sweetheart?" he asked, voice smooth like warm honey hiding a blade.

Donna froze. Something instinctive told her to run—but where? She had nowhere left. No one left. Hunger ate her courage.

"I—I'm fine," she lied, hugging her arms around her thin frame.

Razor chuckled, low and knowing.

"A girl alone this late? You ain't fine."

He stepped closer, and she inhaled his scent—cologne layered over cigarette smoke and danger. He tilted her chin gently with a tattooed knuckle. The serpent ink wrapped around his hand glinted under the streetlight.

"There's fear in those eyes," he murmured. "And pain. Someone hurt you."

Donna's throat closed.

No one had ever noticed her pain before.

Razor nodded toward a black Cadillac parked nearby.

"You hungry?"

Her stomach answered for her.

"Come on," he said softly. "Let me help you."

It was the first kindness she had been shown in months.

Maybe years.

Donna followed him.

Inside the Cadillac was warmth.

A sandwich.

A bottle of water.

A blanket.

And Razor's eyes, watching her with a calculation she didn't understand until much later.

"What's your name?" he asked.

She hesitated.

"Donna."

"Pretty name."

He leaned back, smiling.

"You stick with me, Donna, and you'll never be hungry again."

At seventeen, those words felt like salvation.

The next few days blurred together.

Razor bought her clothes, let her sleep on his couch, fed her meals she hadn't tasted since childhood.

He asked her questions—but not the kind that showed care; the kind that measured ownership.

He never touched her at first.

He didn't have to.

His generosity was a leash.

His smiles were chains.

His concern was a trap.

Donna didn't see it until it was too late.

The first time he placed a small bag in her hand, she hesitated.

"What is this?" she asked.

"A way to feel better," Razor promised. "A way to forget."

She should've run then.

Should've tossed the bag at his feet and bolted into the night.

But she was seventeen.

Scared.

Alone.

Exhausted.

Broken.

Razor pressed the bag gently into her palm.

"You can trust me," he whispered.

And because no one had ever said those words to her before, she believed him.

She took the hit.

Later, when she was numb—when her body floated, when her thoughts slowed into syrup—she saw Razor leaning against the wall, arms crossed, smiling like victory.

"See? I take care of you," he said.

Donna drifted into sleep, unaware she had stepped into a cage she wouldn't escape for years.

* * *

FLASHBACK — Part 2: The First Time Razor Broke Her

Donna woke slowly, as if rising through thick water. Her head felt heavy, her limbs warm and disconnected from her body. The cheap motel room around her swayed in a soft, dizzying blur.

The first thing she saw was the light—yellow, weak, flickering from a crooked lamp.

The second thing she saw was Razor, sitting in the corner silently, elbows resting on his knees, cigarette smoke curling from his lips like a quiet warning. He watched her with an expression that wasn't quite affection, not quite possession, but something darkly balanced between.

Donna rubbed her eyes, confused.

"How long… how long was I asleep?" she murmured, her voice thick, dry, unfamiliar.

"A few hours," Razor said, standing slowly. "You needed it."

He moved toward her with a calculated calm, as if each step was measured. Donna pushed herself up against the headboard, dizzy. "Why am I here?"

"You passed out on my couch," he said casually, lifting his chin. "Couldn't leave you there. Brought you somewhere safer."

Safer.

The word tasted wrong.

Donna's heart pounded. She remembered pieces—him handing her the bag, the warmth spreading through her chest, the way her thoughts softened… and then darkness. She hadn't expected to wake up somewhere else.

"Razor…" she began, her voice trembling. "I don't feel right."

He smiled, slow and patient, the way a spider might smile if spiders could smile at all.

"That's just the first time. It hits harder when you don't have much in your system. You'll get used to it."

Her stomach dropped.

A cold truth whispered into the back of her mind:

She wasn't safe.

She wasn't protected.

She was being groomed.

Razor sat beside her. Too close. Close enough that she could smell the nicotine, the cologne, the threats wrapped in sweet promise.

"Listen," he said softly, touching her knee. "You're with me now. I'll feed you, clothe you, keep you off the streets. But I need you to trust me."

Donna froze as his hand slid higher on her leg.

"I helped you," he continued, "and you're gonna help me."

Her breath stuttered.

"Help… how?"

He didn't answer.

He didn't have to.

He leaned in, brushing a kiss against her cheek—soft, slow, suffocating. Donna's body tensed. She turned her face away, but Razor's hand gripped her jaw, firm enough to make her whimper.

"Don't fight me," he whispered. "Every girl needs someone to take care of her. You said you had nobody."

"That's not what I meant—" she backpedaled, her voice cracking.

Razor's smile vanished.

His eyes went cold.

"You owe me," he said—not loud, but low, like a sentence handed down.

Donna felt the room tilt. Felt panic claw up her throat. Felt her future slipping into the hands of a man who had no intention of letting her go.

Razor pushed her gently back against the mattress—not violent, but firm, as if she were an object he'd already claimed. The softness of the push was worse than force; it meant he'd done this before.

"I promise," he murmured, brushing hair from her face, "it'll get easier. You're home now."

Home.

His weight pressed down on the mattress.

Her fear swallowed her scream.

Her innocence dissolved into the stale motel air.

Donna closed her eyes.

She remembered her mother's silence.

She remembered the slap.

She remembered the cold Florida night she fled into.

And in that moment, Razor rewrote her story into one of captivity.

Long before she met David.

Long before she became a mother.

Long before she lost her son to the system.

This was the night her path bent toward tragedy.

This was the night her addiction found its roots.

This was the night she learned love could be weaponized.

And when it was over—when Razor stood up, pulled on his jacket, and tossed her a towel like an afterthought—Donna curled her knees to her chest and whispered:

"I just wanted to be safe."

Razor didn't turn around.

"Stick with me," he said, "and you will be."

But Donna knew then—knew deep in her bones—that she had traded one hell for another.

* * *

The day the baby broke free from the incarceration of that stinking house should have been the best. The baby was swaddled and carried out of the rat's nest in a soft blue baby blanket before being bundled into a social worker's car and driven away to the hospital and to safety.

Or that was how things initially went.

But as everyone knew, the good foster placements were too scarce, and the number of needy kids was far too great.

Now, after spending a few weeks in the hospital pediatric unit, Dallas was found a place in a group foster home, somewhere in the suburbs, somewhere where life was busy and the kids had been placed there in droves, and where good intentions of the foster parents were often overtaken by the stresses and strains of caring for a whole heap of unruly children of different ages and social behaviors, and special needs.

Dallas's arrival at Fairview Youth Center marked the beginning of a new chapter, though at the time, it felt like exile. Sterile walls, squeaky linoleum floors, and buzzing fluorescent lights replaced the chaos of his former home. Here, he was supposed to be safe at least.

Supposed to be.

But this wasn't peace—it was just another kind of noise. There were too many kids, not enough caretakers, and even less love.

But soon, after the false sense of security of sleeping in a warm cot had worn off, he would not flourish here either.

Here was the place where the memories that would later come back to haunt him would be created and formed, and here was where, within his first five years of life, he would come to be neglected worse in foster care than with his biological mother. At least being with his drug addict mother had made him feel more protected because he'd always been in her presence.

He remembered that time only very vaguely, as he was—of course—under a year old when taken from her and when their contact had been forced to cease.

But baby Dallas had been born with a good brain, even if his body and looks weren't much to talk about, and he remembered some things from the closeness of his mom.

Over time, as the boy grew, he noticed how the memories of his original home faded, as if they had never existed at all, but some things—a few special things—were deeply ingrained in his young mind.

He somehow remembered how it felt always to have her at his side, to know how her skin had smelled, and her hair had felt.

He somehow remembered how it'd been to nuzzle into her side for warmth and comfort, and how she used to pull her sweater down over his small frame to try and keep him warm, because she had no heating, since all the money that came in from welfare was lost on drink and drugs.

He somehow remembered that she had loved him in her way, the only way she knew how to. Anyone on the outside looking in would say that it was a selfish kind of love, because if she had only stopped her filthy habits, she could have supported her boy a whole lot better. But Donna had been in a constant haze, her head somewhere else, and she just got by, like so many American moms.

She just got by, trying her best, even in that drugged-up, fuzzy-minded state.

Although she'd never had much to offer him, she had provided what she thought was quality time to her son, at least when she wasn't sprung on the wicked coke. And— despite rumors that said otherwise—she hadn't always been doped up on drugs because, quite simply, drugs cost money, and money had been in perilously short supply. So sometimes, when the drug supply had run dry and the money had all gone the same way, Donna had taken to passing the day by playing with the boy. Well, the plain truth was that there was nothing else to do.

But for Dallas, it was something, at least.

It had been a small show of affection for him.

But now, in the communal foster home, Dallas was lost.

Dallas didn't talk much. He was a shy boy, one who did not know how to ask for anything for himself, because he was used to not getting anything even when he did ask for it, so what would be the point?

It was inbuilt in him that nothing would ever be available, so a child should just go without and make the best of what he had—or what he didn't have.

Now, Dallas would sooner sit underneath the hallway table of the group home and hide beneath the draped cloth, playing quietly with a toy all on his own, even if he missed mealtimes. And of course, the house was so busy with other kids, so noisy and filled with drama, that hardly ever did anyone say, "Now, where is Dallas?" and go look for him. Why would they?

There was so much else that needed to be done.

They had already given him warmth and shelter, washed him, clothed him, and offered him food at the table.

It was surely a child's fault if he was naughty and chose not to take it.

One carer, Millie, would come and go, but she did notice him. There was one time she had pulled the reluctant kid out from under the table by his legs and put him firmly on her lap. She brought a tiny book out of her purse; a book of children's poems her mama had given her when she was small.

She felt Dallas's bony body and started to read as he wriggled, trying to get away.

'Augustus was a chubby lad,

Fat ruddy cheeks Augustus had,

He always did as he was told

And never let his soup get cold…'

That was the beginning of the rhyme, and after that, it only got worse. It was a scary one designed to make unruly, unwilling, and uncooperative kids eat their food! In the end, in that rhyme, Augustus carried on pushing all the soup away, and he got thinner and thinner… and thinner.

'And on the sixth day, he was dead.'

She clapped the book shut with a loud noise and stared at him.

"So, you're going to start eating soon, little man? We don't want to be force-feeding you, you know? No one wants you ending up like naughty Augustus."

He had just looked up at her, and his face had broken out in a contorted grimace. He was about to start wailing again.

Still writhing in her grasp, he'd been put back on the floor and scampered away, back underneath the safety of his tablecloth.

Millie was the only carer or visitor who really paid Dallas any attention.

The others came and went. Came and went.

One said, "So, that little thing still hiding under that table there, is he?" and lifted the corner of the cloth to stare at him. Then she laughed about it.

The others joined in.

"He's fine," someone said. "Just fine in his sweet way. That boy can't be helped. Lord knows, we try…oh, how we try."

* * *

And when he turned five, one of the owners of the foster home came to find him. He was in his room, just lying on the bed, doing nothing.

"Dallas, so now you are five, we're going to read you a letter," the woman said.

"A letter?" the small child said, sitting up. "What's a letter?" He had never received one before.

The woman sat on the side of his thin mattress and began to unfold a pink sheet of paper with handwriting on it, written in purple ink.

"Someday, you're going to want to read this for yourself, boy, so we'll keep it for you in a special box. But right now, and what with the handwriting on this here thing, I guess I'm going to have to read it for you."

She opened her mouth with a deep breath intake.

Dear Dallas,

It's Momma here. Today, you are five.

You are a big boy now, and I am happy and proud to know you are in a safe, caring, warm home with people who love you.

You are in the perfect place!

Well, Happy Birthday and that you can be anything you want to be when you grow up.

Just don't be like Momma. Don't waste your life.

Fill your life with pleasant thoughts and sweet dreams, work hard and earn some money, and don't spend it on drink and drugs like Momma did.

That way, you'll grow up into a fine young man with a future, and it will all be sweet, real sweet.

Because Dallas, the good Lord looks after you and He will provide whenever you need him, if you do everything Momma says.

So, I love you, Dallas, I love you, millions and trillions.

And I love you more than you can ever know, and I will write again when you're bigger, when I'm allowed to contact you a second time. Kisses and hugs,

Momma Donna.

The letter was a bit too grown-up for such a little boy, but a few things sank in:

He was in the best place, Momma said.

Momma loved him millions.

Or whatever the other word was.

Momma would write again when he was big.

And he could be anything he wanted to be when he was a big boy, and he only had to have sweet dreams and work hard to make it happen.

In any case, the good Lord would look after him if he did what Momma told him.

Oh, and drugs and alcohol are harmful to you.

Very bad.

Donna, meanwhile, had hit rock bottom. Jail was cold and lonely, but it was also where she got clean. For the first time in years, her mind began to clear. She remembered the child she had named Roman, the baby taken from her arms, and the one she'd nearly lost again—Dallas.

She prayed. She wept. And when she was released, she didn't go back to the streets. She walked into a rehab center, enrolled in GED classes, and began the long, painful climb toward redemption.

Years passed.

Dallas would continuously find fear in small things that were supposed to be good, such as food and a hug. He was now sometimes living off bread and water only. There were days he wanted a refreshing fruit juice running down his throat, but it seemed impossible to get hold of one because all the other kids got to the fridge first, and they were bigger, older, and more confident.

So, he settled for tap water.

Some days, he only really got to eat when he sneaked down the stairs after bedtime, in the dark, to steal bread. Dallas ate so much bread his stomach began protruding from his shirt, and so that just added to how he looked like a malnourished child in a third world country, and gave everyone more to talk about. He chewed on his fingers and on his long curly hair that he plucked from his head in boredom.

He would spend his entire days back under that table or in a corner playing with his fingers. Because he was hardly ever seen, nobody acknowledged he was even a family member anymore.

No one would engage in conversation with him except for his one friend.

He would see people passing right by him without saying a word.

The adults did it, and the kids too.

Dallas felt lost both on the inside and outside, as a child confined to the foster system.

* * *

So, Dallas found it very normal to hate himself. He saw the other children leaving the home, getting adopted, and he would smile when they went because he knew it was the right thing to do. But inside, his heart broke every time and that made him feel selfish and mean because he was supposed to be happy for all the good things that happened to any kid in the same situation as himself.

The adopters would walk about the group home, scanning all the children as if they were lollipops in a candy store or toys in the toy depot.

"See that one, oh, my! She's so cute!"

"Look at his little face, bless him…"

"Chubby little cheeks, like a cherub…"

"I would love one I can just take everywhere with me…"

"He got to have my personality, you know…be just like

Daddy. Jus' like Daddy."

"You just got to dress him up! Just like a little doll!"

They would look at Dallas and yet not look all at the same time, as if they wanted to ignore the fact their eyes had seen him, and he wasn't there.

That boy looked too ill, and that spoiled everyone's day if they acknowledged they had noticed him. If they admitted they'd seen him, they would have to do something about it. He was the sickly puppy in the window of the pet store, the one nobody wanted to go in and complain about or adopt because they didn't expect the puppy to live, and it would be too upsetting to lose it so young.

The adopters visiting the home all wanted to believe in a world where everything was pink and fluffy and perfect, where the children were chubby with dimpled cheeks.

To see Dallas simply reminded them how it wasn't.

So, they looked away. Well, it was all they could do.

Dallas felt like a little ghost.

The adoptive parents came and went, came and went, and each time chose and adopted and then collected all the other kids, taking them home to have a new Mom and Dad.

He looked on, watching them go, and then within a few short days, their rooms would be cleared out and other new kids would come to take their places.

But Dallas was going nowhere. He was the shy one, the nameless one, the disinterested one who would not make eye contact with anyone.

And mostly, he had no name.

He was "that boy in the corner".

And that would carry on until he was about to turn six.

* * *

As he approached his next birthday, that's when things changed.

Because life—good, bad, or in-between—never does stand still. The world turns, the sea ebbs and flows, the stars come out each night and the sun each morning, and with all these changes, every human life too would find new turns.

Even for a kid like Dallas, who was nobody's favorite or wanted.

And if you're a kid like Dallas and feel life is mean and cruel, keep reading because you never know. You never know…remember how the world keeps turning, and the good Lord keeps on providing. Yes, despite everything!

* * *

Dallas's gray and lonely and cruel existence flew by, and a week before his sixth birthday, deep in the fall season when all the leaves were dropping from the trees, someone—a woman he knew from the foster home—came to Dallas's room where he lay again in his bed in the early morning. And she spoke softly to him.

"Dallas, little man, you better get your sweet little behind out of that bed, because we got something' real good lined up for you today. And I mean, real special."

Something good? Really special? Dallas wondered. Is there anything excellent to be had in the world? He asked himself, confused.

He saw all the good things float right by his eyes daily and come to land on another little boy or little girl, never on himself.

Good things floated on by like butterflies. They were things he could see and appreciate for a fleeting moment, before they went away somewhere.

As for that, well, it was unimaginable, even in his dreams. The truly good or truly special in the world never happened to Dallas because, just like everyone said, he was not a kid anyone saw as valuable.

The only good thing that would happen was when he was a big boy, and he would receive another birthday letter from his mother. That was what he believed and waited for.

"Dallas!" the woman's voice came again.

It was Shania, his care worker, and now she was shaking him by the shoulders, in an affectionate and excited way. He thought it was a bit weird, like she must have had a funny turn in the night or something! Shania was never friendly.

"Come on, Dallas! You don't want to miss this! Believe me." She pushed back the blankets and tugged on his arm and upper body. It was only seven a.m., too! Usually, he was allowed to sleep for half an hour later.

But he gave in to the commotion.

He threw his skinny little bony pigeon legs out of the bed and sighed.

For one thing, ever since getting the letter from his mother, he would eat now, eat everything he was offered, and that'd taken off some of the pressure in the foster home. He was still considered special needs, but everyone knew he was making headway.

But his build had never caught up with the early malnutrition, so his knobby knees stuck out, and his arms were still like matchsticks, while his ears seemed just a little too big for his oddly misshapen head. No matter.

Momma had said to him quite clearly that he should have sweet dreams, that he was to hold onto them, and that he must work hard.

And he already was doing all that every day.

And the good Lord would provide if he kept on doing it all. He was so sure of it, and that drove him on.

* * *

Dallas grew, passing through the terrible twos, and then he was three and finally turned four.

After four long years, he no longer knew how to begin. Everything about the world seemed too loud, too fast, too unsafe. He flinched at the slam of doors, clung to the edges of rooms, and stared at his plate instead of eating.

And yet, during that confusion, one boy noticed him.

Arnold was two years older, with a quick wit and even quicker fists when needed. He had been bounced from one home to another like a pinball, but he'd learned how to survive. Where Dallas was quiet,

Arnold was fearless. But he wasn't mean. When he saw Dallas sitting alone in the standard room, barely breathing, he sat next to him like it was the most natural thing in the world.

"You're too small to be sitting here all alone," Arnold said, nudging him gently. "What's your name?"

Dallas hesitated, then whispered, "Dallas." Arnold tilted his head. "Have you ever played checkers?"

Dallas shook his head.

"Good. I'll teach you." It was the beginning of something sacred. Surprisingly, he now had a friend, too, Arnold.

Arnold was just like Dallas, another skinny little boy about the same age but with a different skin color, pale as far as Dallas was concerned. Too pale. It was good for Dallas to be with Arnold, not least because now it was Arnold who looked sick, not Dallas. And together, they had great fun. They both liked reading and writing more than anything.

"Two peas in a pod," the carers said.

"Twins separated at birth, but something went wrong with the color selections!" other staff laughed, affectionately.

"Boring little bookworms," a mean one said. "Just glad my kid didn't turn out like those."

Arnold was the only friend Dallas had ever had.

The rest of the kids had seen Dallas growing up to be stronger, more capable, and self-assured, but because of the way he looked and how he'd isolated himself during all of his time there. Because he never joined in on anything the other children did, he was always laughed at.

And worse, he was constantly picked on and bullied in the foster home.

Pushing and shoving were the norm. Stealing his books or his glasses was the norm. Telling tales on him, reporting him for stuff he hadn't done anyway—and never would do, like stealing or picking fights or swearing—were the norm, too. Of course, in their hearts, the staff all knew Dallas would not have done the naughty things. He was just not that kind of kid. He was a good kid. It was probably too good, and that annoyed everyone.

But the good Lord brought Arnold to his rescue, allowing him to open up his personality and beliefs. Arnold taught him the rules of checkers using bottle caps and a checkered napkin. He protected him from the older kids, shared his snacks, and told him stories about the moon, escape plans, and a secret treehouse where no one could ever find them.

"You're smart, you know that?" Arnold would say. "One day, you're going to do something big." And Dallas believed him.

For the first time in his life, he felt seen.

But the system didn't reward connection. One morning, Arnold's bed was stripped empty with a flying hug on the way out. No warning. After the staff worker prepared Arnold for adoption, he made one request: to go and give his friend Dallas a goodbye hug. It was a good thing. But it felt awful. The worst. The boys went to Arnold's room and hugged and cried. "I'm so sorry, Arn, I'm so sorry. I will come and see you."

"All the time?"

"All the time," Dallas said.

He took hold of the storybook they had begun together and opened it on his lap, showing it to Arnold. "We'll finish writing the story someday…". His voice trailed off as he was crying too much.

"You are like my brother," he said.

They cried some more, big blobs of tears running down their faces and wetting their shirts.

"Well, the people coming for you won't want you now anyway," Arnold giggled through his tears. "You messed your shirt!"

They laughed and cried until they could laugh or cry no more.

They had all cried out.

After the boys hugged, they parted ways with great remorse.

Dallas was all cried out. He just folded the paper napkin checkerboard Arnold had made and hid it under his mattress.

He stopped talking again. Stopped hoping. The boy who had once clung to the edge of the world by his fingertips had now let go.

* * *

Sara crouched beside him, holding out a hand.

"We heard you like to read," she said.

Dallas blinked.

"We do too" she added, smiling. "A lot."

And somehow, that was enough.

Dallas felt the rush of cold and windy air come swirling around his feet. The black pants were too thin for wearing in the fall. But it meant someone had flung open the big wooden front door to the home and that some visitors had arrived.

He looked outside to the gravel driveway and saw a parked SUV; it was a deep black, a shade like no other, shiny and well-polished, with a personalized license plate. It must hold at least six people, Dallas thought, and he was sure it looked like an SUV from one of those bodyguard movies, the cars that were used to transport VIPs.

He had caught glimpses of trailers for those movies before the staff would whip the TV remote control away and change channels.

"You can't watch that," they'd say. "Look, here's Disney

Channel."

Disney. Huh.

What would an almost-six-year-old bookworm want with Disney movies?

Dallas read encyclopedias, history books, science and math, astronomy, and even the shipping forecast and the world weather. He read law. Anything he could get his tiny handson, he would devour it, seeing all the big, fat words in law that made no sense whatsoever. But he liked to look them up in an Oxford English dictionary someone had donated to the home's library and speak to them out as if he were a lawyer. He would push his black-rimmed glasses back on his little head and liked using big words so that people would have to ask him, what does that even mean?

He just loved knowing things no one else did.

He was working hard just like Momma had said.

And he was still waiting on the good Lord to notice him and make a man of him, just like Momma said. And when the Lord made a man of him, that'd mean he would be big, and so Momma Donna would reappear in his life. He missed her.

As he approached his next birthday, that's when things changed.

Because life—good, bad, or in-between—never does stand still. The world turns, the sea ebbs and flows, the stars come out each night and the sun each morning, and with all these changes, every human life too would find new turns.

Even for a kid like Dallas, who was nobody's favorite or wanted.

And if you are a kid like Dallas and you feel life is mean and cruel, keep reading, because you never know. You never know…remember how the world keeps turning and the good Lord keeps on providing. Yes, despite everything!

Dallas was eventually placed with a foster family—one that saw beyond his silence. The Millers were a white, wealthy, and deeply religious family. Sara was a doctor, and Hunter was a pharmacist. They had two sons of their own, but believed their family wasn't complete. When they saw Dallas alone in the corner of the group home library, they didn't see a lost cause. They saw a calling.

Dallas went home with them that day. They gave him clean clothes, a room with his name on the door, and permission just to be himself. He was diagnosed with Asperger's shortly after, but instead of seeing it as a problem, the Millers saw it as a gift.

"You're not broken," Hunter told him. "You're brilliant."

They taught him how to ride a bike, how to pray, and how to hope again. Sara wrote Bible verses on sticky notes and placed them on his mirror.

"I can do all things through Christ who strengthens me," one reads.

Dallas whispered it to himself every morning.

Slowly, he began to believe.

Chapter 2: Second Chances

The morning sun filtered gently through the curtains of the Miller home, casting soft patterns on the wooden floor where Dallas now stood—a boy marked by past shadows but stepping hesitantly into light. The house was quieter than the bustling group home he'd left behind, and yet, a strange new silence filled the rooms, thick with the weight of unspoken hopes and fears.

Dallas inhaled deeply, testing this new world with every breath. He touched the worn edges of the checkered napkin in his pocket—Arnold's gift, a tangible link between the past and this fragile new beginning. No one else saw the war waging inside this small chest, but Dallas knew the battle wasn't over yet; it had only just begun.

As the day stretched ahead, filled with strange faces and unfamiliar routines, Dallas clung to a single prayer whispered every morning, "I can do all things through Christ who strengthens me." It was a lifeline thrown across the years of neglect and pain, promising that maybe, just maybe, he could grow beyond the boy who once hid in silence.

Dallas sat by his new window, sunlight streaming across the floorboards of a room that finally bore his name. The air was warm, filled with the scent of laundry soap and fresh paint. The Miller house thrummed with gentle order—Sara humming over dinner, Hunter's laughter echoing off the walls, Lake and Steven crashing through the hallway with sibling ease.

But for Dallas, every kindness felt borrowed. He wore clean clothes and memorized his address, but at night he whispered "I can do all things through Christ who strengthens me," promising a future Momma once said he deserved but feeling, in his bones, the chill of exile. He hid Arnold's checkered napkin in a wooden box, tracing the faded squares, reminding himself there were people worth missing—and promises yet to keep.

When Jamiah, the woman who'd found him as a baby, came to visit, the house brimmed with joy. Dallas smiled, joining laughter at the table, but always kept one eye on the door—as if worried this miracle life could vanish as suddenly as it arrived. Surrounded by love, he still rehearsed his gratitude, saying "thank you" and "yes, ma'am," but deep down, he wondered if the happiness would last, or if he'd be forced to pack his hopes back into a suitcase, just like every other time.

As the family prayed together after dinner, Dallas repeated the Bible verse, his voice trembling at first, but growing steadier with each night. Still, he lay awake, missing his mother and Arnold, haunted by dreams of the group home's shadows. Yet every dawn brought the promise of something new—a letter, a kind word, a hand on his shoulder— nudging him, slowly, toward belief in belonging.

Jamiah's arrival at the Sara household felt like sunshine after a long rain. From the kitchen window, Dallas watched her car pull into the driveway, heart skipping as memories of that first rescue day flickered across his mind. Sara, ever gracious, welcomed Jamiah with hugs and laughter, ushering her into a home alive with the aromas of dinner and the gentle buzz of family. Dallas trailed behind, both drawn to Jamiah's warmth and hesitant, as always, to trust that good things would last.

As Jamiah stepped over the threshold, her eyes softened at the sight of Dallas sitting at the dining table, flanked by siblings who'd become fast friends. She knelt to his level, her voice low and full of encouragement. "You look happy, sweetheart," she commented, ruffling his hair. Dallas's smile wobbled, gratitude and longing tangled in his chest. This was what he'd prayed for on all those lonely nights in foster care: to be seen, to be wanted, to be part of somebody's world.

The Sara home, with its photo-lined walls and gentle chaos, brimmed with an energy Jamiah delighted in. The family insisted she join them for dinner, where laughter came easily and stories tumbled one over the next. Dallas joined in, mimicking his siblings' easy banter, sneaking glances at Jamiah as if asking, "Do I belong here now?" Even with joy all around, old habits lingered—he watched the door, wary as a sparrow, rehearsing "thank you" and "yes, ma'am" so nobody ever regretted letting him stay.

That night, after dinner, in the circle of hands bowed for grace, Dallas's voice quivered but steadied as the family recited their favorite verse. Jamiah squeezed his shoulder gently, radiating pride. Dallas cherished every sign that this happiness might last. Still, sleep came slowly. His mind drifted to memories of his mother, to Arnold's friendship at the group home; shadows haunted the quiet, but new comfort glimmered in the everyday dawn—the Sara family's love, a letter on the nightstand, Jamiah's promise that rescued children could find real homes.

Each morning, Dallas tested the boundaries of hope, inching closer to believing that this life—and the people in it—were truly his to keep. Jamiah's visits marked milestones in this journey: gentle affirmations that his suitcase could finally stay unpacked, and that he no longer had to rehearse his belonging—it was real, and it was his.

Dallas sat by the window, fingers tracing the rim of his across the hardwood floor.

Southwest Ranches, Florida, was where Dallas now lived. He practiced writing his address with the fountain pen the couple had bought for him and setting out the words on the fine writing paper they'd also given him as a Welcome Home gift. It was a predominantly white neighborhood and here, he stuck out like a sore thumb. But they had come for him, regardless. It was unbelievable.

It was out of this world.

He learned that the couple, Mom and Dad, were now called Sara and Hunter Miller. They had been married happily forever, Dad said, like "longer than you'd be in jail!" He had laughed when he'd said it, and his wife had playfully bashed him around the head with a newspaper.

"Shut up, Hunter!" she had chided. "Don't talk about jail to a little boy of six."

They really, genuinely loved each other and lived a clean and wholesome life, with their boys, Lake, ten, and Steven, eight.

And they were educated, holding degrees from universities and all that.

In time, Dallas learned that Sara was a medical doctor at the local hospital and Hunter was a pharmacist. They had met at college.

So now Dallas had a mom, a dad, two great amazing brothers who helped him out in everything they could, and he lived in a home…and what a home it was!

But money meant nothing to Dallas.

Nothing at all.

His currency was love, and only love.

But the story had reached the local newspapers, and someone special had come to visit him. At least, Mom and Dad had said they were inviting someone really special, but when the doorbell rang and Dallas opened the massive white door himself, standing on his tiptoes, he saw a woman standing there and had no idea who she was.

"Dallas," Mom Sara said, "you don't know who this is, do you?"

He squinted at the woman.

She was tall, pretty, and well-dressed, with an exotic scent. "Hi," she said to him as she held out her warm and gentle hand. "I'm Jamiah. I am the one who found you when you were such a little tiny baby…"

And everyone had a wonderful afternoon together.

Everyone ate, drank, and laughed, and Dallas was in heaven. This…this was what life was all about. You could keep your riches and your black glossy SUVs. Love was what made life work.

Love and righteousness.

But despite everything, he would always hold a place in his heart for his mom, Donna. He did not know where or how she was. He hoped to be reunited one day.

He would bring her into all his dreams and hope she had the same good Lord on her side.

He was still deficient in confidence and self-esteem and felt a piece of him would always be missing until Momma Donna came back into his life. He still had self-doubts and felt unworthy and invisible.

Everyone tried their best to buoy him up and bring him out of himself.

Slowly, slowly, progress was made.

He was ten years old now, and the Miller household had become a place of quiet routine. School, church, therapy, dinner. Repeat. It was peaceful. But peace, for Dallas, came with a strange emptiness—like something important was missing, and he didn't know how to name it.

His new white brothers instantly embraced him by sharing all their toys with him. They also contributed a lot of time in helping him with his homework as they noticed he struggled massively, not with the work itself—because he was little short of a child genius, people said—but he struggled with not feeling as if he belonged.

The Millers did everything right. Sara packed him healthy lunches and prayed over him each morning. Hunter drove him to every appointment and taught him how to change a tire. Their sons, Steven and Lake, included him in games of basketball and family movie nights. But Dallas often felt like a guest in a life that belonged to someone else. The first thing the Miller family did for Dallas was to help him believe in himself. Dallas's parents told him to look in the mirror every morning and repeat Philippians 4:13 Bible verse five times: "I can do all things through Christ who strengthens me."

This was the same his momma had tried to say but had put more eloquently.

He faithfully obeyed his parents' orders and recited the Bible verse to himself every morning in the mirror. When he first started saying it, his voice was calm and undeniably soft, showing signs of confusion.

He had watched his mouth moving in the mirror as he spoke the words.

I can do all things through Christ who strengthens me.

I can do all things through Christ who strengthens me…

After about a month, Dallas began displaying positive signs of adjustment in his new environment, as he continued rehearsing the verse very loudly; now, there seemed to be a great deal of confidence coming through the bathroom door.

He smiled when he was supposed to. Said "thank you" on cue. But there were nights he lay awake, eyes wide in the dark, thinking of Arnold and that checkered napkin chessboard. It had long since torn at the edges, but Dallas kept it in a small wooden box under his bed like a sacred relic.

In therapy, Ms. Felton—an older woman with soft hands and a calming voice—once asked him what he missed most about his past.

"Nothing," he said without emotion.

But she waited. After a long silence, Dallas added, "I had a best friend once. He taught me how to think."

She nodded. "What was his name?"

"Arnold."

"Do you remember his face?"

"Every line."

"What happened to him?"

"They took him. Just like they took my mom."

That was the first time he cried in therapy.

* * *

As Dallas grew, so did his determination. He read constantly—law books, biographies, history texts. Anything that helped him understand power, structure, and justice. He wanted to know why some people got second chances and others didn't. Why his mother was discarded. Why Arnold vanished. Why no one ever explained.

Sara noticed his curiosity and fed it. She brought home used books from the university library, enrolled him in mock trial camps, and encouraged him to ask questions.

His adoptive parents invested heavily in his education now, providing in-home tutoring five days a week that focused on the things he feared doing. They also dedicated five hours a week to help him nurture his reading and writing skills, his special talents.

He could learn well, but what he could never do was show anyone what he had taken on board, because each time he'd been asked a question before he was six, he had been made a mockery of for his answers.

No matter what answers he knew, he was afraid to say them.

"I don't know" was the best answer to give.

But really, he knew everything he was ever asked.

He still hated making eye contact, too, and was wary of hugs and cuddles, unless he was in severe distress; even then, he could tolerate them only for a short time. He had been assessed as having Asperger's syndrome, a mild form of autism. He wasn't worried about that as he knew kids like him were very clever in specific ways. But he would keep these ways all to himself, thank you very much.

Still, his brothers continued to help and encourage him. Sara and Hunter—Mom and Dad—invested in him and encouraged him, as well.

"Your mind is your greatest tool, Dallas," she said one day as she handed him a worn copy of *To Kill a Mockingbird.*

"Use it wisely."

He devoured the book in three nights. Afterward, he wrote a letter to the author, even though he knew she was gone. He just wanted someone to know he understood.

* * *

The good Lord, though, was disappointingly not always right there. There were times, Dallas thought, when the Lord God must have been asleep or in the bath, or having his dinner or something, because the good Lord occasionally seemed to have abandoned not only him, but the whole Miller family.

The children at school and in the neighborhood bullied and name-called him shy, dumb, dirty Dallas because of his African American ethnicity and the color of his skin, and because of the fact he rarely joined in with anything all the local kids did in the neighborhood.

All the teachers displayed some type of racism toward him as the school was again predominantly white. Dallas was feeling all alone again, remembering the horrid past he'd had at the group home, and feeling as if he was back all alone in the corner. He felt hopeless and neglected by everyone except his family.

On his first day at Emerson Park Elementary, the hallway felt longer than any corridor he'd ever walked. The floor tiles were polished so clean they shone like mirrors, reflecting rows of backpacks and swinging ponytails and clusters of children who already belonged to someone.

Dallas kept his eyes on his shoes.

Lake walked beside him, bumping his shoulder gently every few steps, as if to say, You're not alone, little bro, without having to use the words. Steven walked on the other side, loud and chatty, trying to distract him with talk about lunch menus and which teachers gave too much homework.

To Dallas, all the noise blurred together.

When they reached his classroom, Lake squeezed his shoulder one last time before peeling off toward the fifth-grade wing. Steven turned back three times, checking on him. Dallas stood in the doorway, feeling every pair of eyes turn toward him.

"Class, we have a new student today," his teacher announced. "This is Dallas… Miller."

The pause before the last name felt like a question mark.

Dallas shoved his hands deeper into his pockets. The room went quiet in that particular way children fall silent when they are measuring someone new—skin, hair, glasses, posture, everything tallied and labeled before he even sat down.

"Say hello, Dallas," the teacher encouraged.

He opened his mouth, but the words tangled somewhere between his chest and throat. A barely audible "Hi" slipped out, almost lost in the rustle of notebooks.

A boy in the front row leaned toward another and whispered loudly enough for everyone to hear, "He's the kid they adopted. From the news."

Dallas pretended he hadn't heard.

He took the empty seat in the back, the one near the window and far from everyone else. It should have felt like a safe corner, but instead it felt like the old group home all over again—like he had been pushed to the edges where no one would see him if he disappeared.

The school days fell into a pattern that was both predictable and exhausting. In the mornings, he lined up with the others, but no one stood behind him or in front of him by choice. Children found excuses to shuffle to another place in line rather than end up next to "the new boy."

At recess, he drifted along the fence while the others played kickball or chased each other across the field. The ball never rolled his way. When teams were chosen, his name was never spoken; he was added as an afterthought, if at all.

"Just let him sit out," one boy muttered once. "He doesn't even talk."

Dallas heard. He always heard.

When the bell rang for lunch, he carried his tray carefully, afraid of dropping it under a hundred watching eyes. On the first day, he sat alone at the end of a long table, picking at his food while chatter swelled around him like a distant radio.

On the second day, when he sat in the same place, Lake and Steven wordlessly joined him. They ignored the strange looks from other kids and laughed loudly about silly things—video games, cartoons, Lake's terrible attempt at making scrambled eggs that morning. They did it every day after that.

"If they're not going to sit with you," Lake had told him that first week, "then they don't get us either."

The brothers' loyalty wrapped around Dallas like a shield. Even so, he could feel the invisible line drawn around him. Other kids took the long way around their table. Some stared. Some whispered. Some just avoided looking at him at all.

In the classroom, things were no easier.

Dallas was bright—painfully bright. He could finish worksheets in half the time it took everyone else, and most days, he had already read the book the teacher assigned. But saying the answers out loud felt like walking barefoot across hot coals.

Once, his teacher called on him to read a paragraph aloud.

"Dallas, why don't you take this next section?"

His heart hammered against his ribs. The letters on the page blurred. He knew all the words; he had read ahead the night before. But as he began, his voice got stuck on one difficult-sounding word. Children snickered behind cupped hands. Someone whispered, "He can't even read," and the shame burned brighter than all the fluorescent lights in the classroom.

The teacher, tired and impatient, misread his silence as defiance.

"Dallas, we've talked about this," she said, tapping her foot. "You need to participate. I don't want to have to write another note home."

He wanted to shout that he could read just fine, that he could probably read better than half the class. He wanted to tell her that every time he opened his mouth at the group home, kids had laughed at him, or worse. Instead, he stared at the desk.

"I don't know," he said.

The words had become his armor. Three small syllables that kept him from showing how much he really did know.

After class, while the other kids ran to the playground, he stayed behind to straighten his papers, giving them time to clear out first. As he gathered his books, the school librarian, Mrs. Kenney, appeared in the doorway, holding a stack of worn paperbacks.

"I'm starting a reading group at lunch," she said, her tone light and casual. "For students who want extra credit. You seem like someone who likes books."

Dallas shrugged, unsure if it was a trick.

"I see your library record," she added with a small smile. "Somebody's checking out more books than the teachers."

He flushed, looking down at his shoes.

"If you want to come by the library during lunch one day, there's always a chair open," she said simply. "No pressure."

It was the closest thing to an invitation he'd received from any adult at school that wasn't another evaluation or meeting. He didn't go that week—or the next. But by the third week, on a rain-soaked Tuesday when the field was closed and the cafeteria felt too loud, he found himself walking toward the library instead.

Mrs. Kenney didn't say anything when he came in. She just nodded toward a table where two other quiet kids were already reading. It wasn't friendship, not yet. But it was a room where no one laughed at him for turning pages.

Not every adult at school was cruel, but the ones who were indifferent hurt almost as much.

Dallas was sent to the guidance office once after snapping his pencil in half when a boy behind him called him "charity case." The counselor, Mr. Hart, scanned his file, asking questions that sounded like they'd been pulled from a script.

"How are you adjusting?"

"Do you feel angry often?"

"Are you having trouble controlling your emotions?"

Dallas wanted to ask, Wouldn't you? But he just shook his head.

"I'm fine," he said.

The word tasted like dust.

When Mr. Hart checked the box next to "no concerns at this time," Dallas realized that being quiet didn't just keep him safe—it kept him invisible.

The testing came later.

After too many days of him staring at the floor and too many notes that said he "refused to answer questions," the school recommended an evaluation. The Millers agreed, hoping for answers, not labels.

Dallas sat in a small room with a woman who smelled like peppermint and chalk dust. She handed him blocks and puzzles, asked him to find patterns, to finish stories, to remember lists of words. On those tasks, he excelled.

"You're very smart," she said.

He didn't know what to do with the compliment, so he filed it away in the same mental box as his mom's Bible verse and Arnold's last hug.

When she asked him to explain how he felt when the other kids laughed at him or when the teacher called on him unexpectedly, his mind went blank. Feelings were harder than puzzles. Feelings were messier.

In the end, they called it Asperger's syndrome and wrote it in black ink at the bottom of a thick stack of papers. To Dallas, it just felt like someone had finally given a name to the invisible wall between him and everyone else.

Only the wall didn't shrink just because it had a name.

School wasn't just a place where Dallas learned math and reading—it was where the battle between who he had been and who he could become played out every single day.

Bullies rolled their eyes when he raised his hand.

Teachers sighed when he hesitated.

Kids snickered in the hallway when he walked past with his lunch tray.

He carried his books close to his chest, head down, memorizing the pattern of floor tiles instead of the faces twisted in amusement. At the same time, somewhere deep inside, another part of him was watching everything—analyzing, recording, understanding.

He saw which kids picked on the smaller ones and which teachers pretended not to notice. He watched who lied smoothly and who flinched when confronted. He started to see that the world wasn't divided neatly into good and bad; it was infinitely more complicated than that.

In class, when the teacher talked about rules, Dallas thought about fairness. When they talked about consequences, he thought about second chances. As the months turned into years, his pain at school slowly began to harden into something else:

A quiet, relentless sense of purpose.

He was battling the confusion of being so obviously and deeply loved by his family but hated by everyone else and abandoned sometimes by the very good Lord his mom, Donna, had promised would always be there for him as he grew, if he worked hard and held firmly onto his values and dreams.

His adoptive parents were board members in their community.

After people in the community heard about their adoption and the race of the child they had adopted, the community members started to make strange complaints about things they were supposed to have done. Eventually, they found some excuse to have them removed from office.

So, the Millers were now being singled out at community meetings because they had adopted an African American boy.

They were no longer invited to their community meetings. But the Millers were strong and good people who did not let that bother them, as they knew what they had done was absolute right thing, the very specific thing their God had asked them to do. They wanted to follow God's order and do right by him. They would never let bullies frighten or alienate them. That would be a terrible message to give to their precious boys.

The Millers quickly learned that adopting Dallas had made them stand out in Emerson Park—and not in ways they'd imagined. At first, their neighbors smiled awkwardly and offered clipped greetings, but after Dallas's arrival, a tide of small grievances began to wash up on their doorstep. The city sent warnings for their compact car parked (legally) along the curb, issuing fines week after week for "out of district" parking, despite identical vehicles left undisturbed on the same block. Someone in the neighborhood association called in a complaint about stray leaves gathering on the lawn. Next came written citations for a single strip of newspaper poking from the edge of their green recycling bin and for the jagged cracks long since present in the concrete at the driveway's edge. The minor details—once ignored by everyone— suddenly mattered immensely.

Behind the facade of "civic pride," it was easy to see the pattern. At community meetings, the Millers found themselves sidelined—no longer greeted, excluded from sidewalk chats, left off the invite list for the annual block party. The unspoken accusation was clear: they had adopted a Black child, and for some, that was an act of rebellion, something to punish. Whispers in the crowd grew louder with every citation, some neighbors more emboldened each month the Millers refused to move.

But the Millers would not be intimidated. Guided by their faith and the conviction that raising Dallas was their calling, they met every penalty with purposeful resilience. "This is our home—and yours, too," Sara told Dallas after yet another parking ticket, pulling him close. "Doing what's right is never easy, but that's what makes it worth it." They refused to shrink from the stares, never letting Dallas see the pain in their own hearts. For him—and for their other sons—they would model courage, compassion, and the certainty that you never let bullies decide where you belong.

Each Sunday, as the family knelt to pray, they held fast to their belief: true belonging runs deeper than approval from any board or neighbor. And in Dallas's eyes, lit gently by love and hope, they found confirmation that there are battles worth fighting, and some families are forged as much by courage as by blood.

* * *

Donna was making her own journey.

Clean now for three years, she was working as a janitor at a community center. It wasn't glamorous, but it was honest. Each day she arrived early, stayed late, and took pride in her work. She kept a picture of Dallas in her wallet—his school portrait, age eight, wearing a red polo shirt and unsure smile. She stared at it during lunch breaks, whispering prayers to God.

"Please let him be okay. Let him grow. Let him know I love him."

One night after her shift, she passed a flyer taped to the bulletin board: "Paralegal Certification Program – Now Enrolling." She paused. Her hands trembled.

Could she? Could someone like her learn the law? Understand justice? Fight for something bigger?

She tore off a tab and took the first step toward changing her future.

* * *

Despite being singled out by the community, the Millers were willing to fight to regain their respect within the community. They felt as though they were fighting against the world to let their voices be heard, telling Dallas's story. And why should they not be heard telling his story?

Who would stop them?

What kind of vile prejudices still existed in 21st-century America, that a wonderful family such as the Millers was being virtually ostracized by the fact they'd adopted a needy little boy of a different race and color?

And yet—that was precisely where they found themselves, and it was shameful.

"But there are thousands of white kids needing homes too, you know?" said one neighbor when the Millers threw a party to welcome their new little boy. And everyone nodded, their eyes boring accusingly into Mrs. Miller. Nobody wanted to show much interest in the child either, preferring to look at the white kids.

"What is your Lake doing, Sara?" asked one woman, Mrs. Hill, over the fence one day. "Haven't seen him around lately?" she added, talking about Dallas's older brother.

"Oh, he's around…and our Steven too," said Sara. "They're good boys, you know, they are usually busy with Dallas, with helping him do his homework and everything," Mrs. Miller said, smiling, thinking of all three boys and how much she loved them all.

"Well, maybe Steven and Lake might like to come play with my Logan and Jasmine," said the neighbor. "You know how they all get along together."

Sara Miller did not know how the kids got along together.

That would be nice…she thought.

"I think that's a great idea," Sara Miller said. "All three boys would surely love to come play with your two."

"Oh, sorry," the woman said. "Just Lake and Steven, please, if you don't mind." She turned away as if there was some secret message written in the sky and the clouds. "Just the boys we know. Not the…not that new one. Not that one. Not again."

It was as if she could not even say Dallas's name.

No matter. In that case, none of the boys would be going. This was how it would always be. It was utterly ridiculous— and sinister. In truth, Mrs. Hill had once even accused Dallas of making up nasty stories about her boy, Logan Hill.

One day, when the boys had only just met over the garden fence as they'd all wandered home from school, Dallas had been heard shouting and then crying.

"What on earth happened?" Sara had asked, rushing out of the front door to see Dallas sprawled on the garden path, rubbing at his scuffed and bloodied knees.

"Where is your schoolbag?"

Dallas had rubbed his scuffed knees even more, blood rubbing off on his palms, and then he'd gotten up from the ground to point across the garden hedge.

"He took my backpack, Mom!" he cried, sniffling but trying to be brave.

"Who did?"

"The boy from next door…Lo…Logan. Logan Hill. He's a big bully."

Sara Miller had gone across and banged on next door, after retrieving her son's ripped backpack from the hedge in between the houses, where she had found it emptied but covered in soda that'd been poured all over it. Dallas's schoolbooks and pencil case were all blowing about the street.

The boy, Logan, had answered the rap-rapping at the front door but had just shrugged. His mother hadn't come home yet, and he swore he hadn't even touched Dallas—and of course, later that night, he told his mother that Dallas had made up a story to get him into trouble, and that he'd seen the colored boy rip up his schoolwork and throw his bag into the hedge.

That was to be the end of any friendship between the white boy and the little colored boy; now, everyone in the road thought Dallas was vindictive and horrible, and a little liar to be avoided at all costs.

A whole pack of lies was being spread about Dallas at school now too, because this boy, Logan, had now even been telling everyone the story was the other way around, and that Dallas had set upon Logan as he'd walked home, jumped on his back and had stolen Logan's school bag.

At school was a whole group of vicious bullies, some boys, some girls. Unbelievably, the girls could be much worse than the boys.

There was one who was a ringleader, Molly Clark, such a pretty and intelligent little thing—a model, everyone thought she would be. She was good as gold to everyone. Except for Dallas. One day, she sneaked up behind him and tore his knitted hat from the very top of his head. She raced off to the other kids, and threw it in the biggest, blackest puddle of mud she could find, showing off. Everyone joined in. To them, bullying that weird African American kid was great fun.

And so, he played with only his own brothers.

The family was destined to fill Dallas's dream of happiness anyway, as—quite simply—no one else's prejudiced opinions mattered in their family's decisions.

However, they could not simply ignore it all when they were torn to find out that their adopted son was also being bullied and singled out by the staff and students at their boys' school. Word of Dallas's supposed attack on Logan had spread to the school, and now every kid and every teacher seemed to single him out as no good.

Boys would be boys, kids would be kids, sure. That was what people said, and to some degree, Sara believed that too.

Kids did evil things to each other.

Bullying would always exist the world over, and one small, individual family could hardly make a colossal impact on eradicating it.

But when it came to the actions and decisions of all the staff at the school, that was something else. Dallas's teachers would assign him a seat right in the back of the class, even though he had poor eyesight due to a lack of vitamins as a baby and a growing child. They knew very well he could not see perfectly and that he would also be too quiet, too diligent, and shy to speak up.

And this was all although he was mildly autistic and would find school hard enough already.

The teachers would deliberately overlook him whenever he attempted to raise his hand. Thankfully, Dallas was very comfortable confiding in his brothers, who then shared it with their parents. Their parents wrote a letter to the school's principal letting her know that this kind of behavior from kids and teachers alike would not be tolerated, and the media—the vicious and persistent TV and news people who could make a huge deal of such things and make things incredibly awkward for a school—were but two seconds away from being contacted.

However, threats against the school were not going to resolve matters; if anything, they would make the situation worse. Nobody liked a snitch, and it was clear Dallas had whined to someone, and word had gotten around.

The boy—one of a different race and color, and with special needs— was bad news for the school's clean reputation.

The weeks passed by, and nothing got any better.

In addition to Dallas feeling sorely isolated in his environment at school, he had to face the same vicious kids in his very own neighborhood. The kids never wanted to play with him and his brothers now, because the boys came as a threesome, and it was as if Dallas had a contagious disease.

Dallas's parents worked extremely hard to make sure he would not be treated differently or be singled out because of his race. Mrs. Miller ensured that he received the same love and acceptance that her biological sons received from the community, or that if this were lacking, at least he wouldn't notice it, because she wouldn't expose him to situations and places where prejudice prevailed.

Her biggest fear was that Dallas might be affected psychologically, as—on top of all the boy's other problems—it had been determined that he already suffered from posttraumatic stress disorder from his early years.

But despite it all, Dallas continued to apply himself and to try hard to be the boy worthy of the Millers' kind adoption, and to be worthy of God's praise. He was a trier and an achiever despite his setbacks, his bullying, and his autism and PTSD, yet at the same time, he stayed humble.

* * *

And slowly but surely, the years all merged one into the other, the seasons changing, the school years flitting by, and the bullies coming and going, coming and going. Many things changed, and the boys all grew older, with the school years ending and then restarting afresh— but one thing never altered, and that was young Dallas's lack of popularity among his peers.

He was not popular at all, not one tiny bit.

The years could make him look bigger and less like a boy and more like a teenager, then less like a teenager and more like a man. They could bring muscles to his upper arms and tiny hairs on his chin and make his voice deeper.

But what the years could not do on their own was to bring Dallas any friends. He was always going to remain the strange boy, the odd teenager, the weird young man with autistic behaviors who always had his nose stuck in a book as if he thought he was going to be someone special, but who didn't know how to play sports, laugh at a movie or skive off for a secret smoke and a drink with the other boys. He also would not make eye contact with people he didn't know, and this never helped anyone to like him.

"He's real shifty, that one," they would say. "Can't give anyone a straight look in their eyes. Looks off in the distance like he's about to rob you blind or shoot you. Well, he probably will. It's what kids like him do, you know."

With the help of his devoted adoptive parents' support, despite the wagging, malicious tongues and the rumors and spite, time went on, and years passed, and all the boys grew. Dallas somehow managed to stay focused and rise above everything, from being selectively mute or stammering at five years old to excelling and serving as the spokesperson for the Speech and Debate class, and then later pursuing work experience at a firm of well-known lawyers.

It was tough to understand that in so few years, the little boy who had not known his numbers from 1 to 10 at the age of five had turned into the same child, then kept a 4.6 grade point average during his senior year of high school.

And the same boy who had suffered eating issues and anxieties from food being placed in front of him, and had become the little family chef, excelled in the home kitchen during the holiday season.

And he was the same boy whose work experience with the firm of city attorneys went not just well, but brilliantly. The odd teen with the thick, black-framed glasses resting on the bridge of his nose, and who would not take lunch breaks because he was too engrossed in case work, was turning into the perfect embodiment of a teenage lawyer—whoever would have thought such a thing?

Everyone in the firm laughed about it but admired Dallas. Some called him the Boy Barrister, while others referred to him as the Juvenile Judge.

Somehow, even in team meetings, the shy boy always managed to say something profound and unexpected about a case, and to notice the little nuances that everyone else had missed. "Autism does that," one attorney had said. "I have a brother who has Asperger's, and he's amazing with numbers, and our Juvenile Judge here evidently has a brain the size of a small planet."

"Mark my words," another said, "If this lad becomes a lawyer, let the criminals be on their best behavior, as there's nothing he won't notice!"

Dallas's teenage years were marked by transformation. The shy boy became a confident speaker. The foster kid became the class president. By the time he was a senior in high school, he was known for his sharp intellect, calm demeanor, and unwavering discipline. People still whispered about his past, but he didn't flinch. He had goals.

Dallas was good at everything academic, quietly confident, and silently rebellious. Unlike the other boys in school or the neighborhood, Dallas had rebelled inwardly, with a wordless, soundless resolve to do well, to outperform even the best of the other kids, to rise above everything and to stand firm— and to become someone his parents would be proud of. To become a great attorney, no less.

He still adored his books and still loved the darkness of the nights when the world slept, and when a small light from an even smaller battery torch shone underneath his bedsheets, as he read up on the issues that afflicted the world, and all about the English language, and about criminal justice and the legal system.

One day, Dallas might finally get to use all his knowledge. The thought lingered as he buttoned his gown, echoing in his mind like a promise just out of reach.

Philippians 4:13—he repeated it, like a mantra:

"I can do all things through Christ who strengthens me."

The words rolled softly beneath his breath, repeating again, steadying him. God willing, the chance would come. He already knew how he would grasp it with both hands and thank the good Lord for everything—everything he had achieved, and everything his parents, the Millers, had poured into his life.

The day shimmered with promise as Dallas stepped onto the stage. His cap sat slightly tilted, his gown rustling with each careful step—a quiet applause of destiny greeting him. The arena overflowed with families, mentors, and students, a sea of faces blurred by tears, pride, and possibility. Dallas's heart pounded—not with fear, but with the weight of how far he had come.

He graduated with honors—the first in his family to walk across that stage. Then came college. Then law school. Each step had felt like a mountain, steeper than the last, but Dallas climbed them all without complaint, driven by something deeper than ambition—a refusal to be forgotten.

When his name was called, the cheers seemed far away, distant echoes in a monumental moment. He caught sight of his mother in the crowd—hands pressed together, eyes glistening with pride. For a heartbeat, time folded: he saw the boy who studied by candlelight and fretted about leaving his hometown behind. Now, here he stood—bright lights above, microphone in hand, ready to speak the words that had lived in his chest for years.

At graduation, Dallas gave the keynote speech.

His voice trembled at first, then steadied, filling the auditorium. "I was a boy forgotten by many," he began, gaze sweeping the packed hall, "remembered by few. But I was loved enough to believe in myself. And sometimes, belief is the beginning of everything."

A hush swept the crowd, then applause rose and swelled until it crashed over him in waves. Dallas exhaled, feeling a single tear trace his cheek. For the first time, he didn't feel like just a survivor—he felt like a testament.

Below, Sara and Hunter wept. Their tears weren't just for his achievement, but for the battles they'd witnessed and the hope they had nurtured with him. In the very back row, hidden behind a crowd, Donna watched. She had not told anyone she was coming; she stayed in contact with Jamiah, who provided updates about Dallas. When she heard about graduation, Donna needed to see it for herself. She slipped in quietly, her shoulders hunched, her presence hidden. She slid into the auditorium and out again without a soul noticing.

He looked like a man now.

Strong. Focused.

Safe.

★ ★ ★

He was nineteen now, standing taller than either of his adoptive parents, and standing firmer in his beliefs and convictions than anyone Sara Miller, his adoptive mom, could ever know. His mind and his body were all grown up, but his attitudes remained the same. He was still calm and gentle, and studious—and more than anything else, Dallas still loved books.

Big books, the bigger, fatter, and heavier the better. Most nights, Dallas's head was bowed over his law study books.

Law.

Law was what bound people together, and a lack of lawfulness was what drove them apart. Dallas had decided to be a lawmaker, not a lawbreaker—and he would try to bring the good and just legal system of America into the homes of the lawless.

That was now becoming his dream: to be not just a criminal lawyer, but the absolute best. Dallas had his head down in the books again on this night, a Wednesday night, when it was dark and raining outside.

Dallas passed the bar on his first try. He became an assistant district attorney, then rose through the ranks. His cases were tough—murder trials, drug rings, juvenile justice reform. He handled them all with precision. But what people admired most was his empathy.

He listened.

He saw the person behind the crime.

He showed mercy when others wouldn't.

One of his first major cases involved a teen accused of robbing a gas station. The boy was nervous, barely seventeen, with shaking hands and eyes filled with regret. Dallas saw something familiar.

He visited the boy's mother before the trial.

"She's in rehab," the grandmother said. "Trying to get it right for her son."

That night, Dallas couldn't sleep. He thought about Donna. He thought about second chances.

The next morning, he offered a plea deal with mandated counseling, probation, and community service.

The boy took it.

Later, the grandmother mailed a thank-you card to Dallas. It read: "You saved him."

Dallas folded it carefully and placed it in the same wooden box that still held Arnold's checkerboard napkin.

* * *

Dallas felt his phone vibrate inside his pocket and pulled it out, laying it face down on the couch next to him. The distinctive Facebook ping echoed faintly, but he ignored it. Hours later, after shutting his law book and letting out a long sigh, he flipped the phone over—and froze.

"Mom!" he called. "MOM!"

Sara entered, wiping her hands on a dish towel, startled by the sharp tone in his voice. "What's wrong?"

He didn't answer, only held out the phone like a piece of evidence in a courtroom. Sara squinted, blinking as she read the name blinking back at them: Donna Jackson.

Her breath caught. "Oh, Dallas." Her tone softened, layered with emotions he couldn't quite decipher. "We knew this might happen someday." She set the phone down gently, as if it might break under the weight of the memory. Then she ruffled his hair—an old habit—and smiled through watered eyes. "Whatever you choose, we're with you. Always."

Dallas nodded, though his eyes stayed fixed on the glowing screen. Donna Jackson wants to connect with you.

He sat there for a long time, staring, before finally whispering the name to himself, as though tasting a word he hadn't spoken in years.

Donna Jackson had been clean for eight years. Eight long, carved-out, back-breaking, grace-filled years. She lived in a modest one-story home on the edge of town, where the scent of fresh paint still lingered from the renovation she'd done herself. On her porch sat a chipped coffee mug filled with daisies and a cat named Mercy, who never strayed too far from her lap.

Each morning, Donna wrote the same line in her journal before heading to work: Be who he needs today.

Her journey had been slow and steady. The program. The late-night meetings. The years of walking past temptation without looking back. She didn't pray out loud anymore, but she spoke her gratitude in small ways—a clean kitchen, warm socks, a paycheck that paid for more than survival. Her bracelet, worn and filled with twelve silver beads, marked each full year of sobriety.

She worked for a small legal office downtown—filing, typing, learning. Her supervisor once told her, "You've lived what others argue in court. That's power, Donna. Use it right."

And on one quiet evening, driven by equal parts hope and trembling, she opened Facebook. She typed "Dallas Jackson" into the search bar, then corrected herself. No—Dallas Miller.

The screen loaded, and there he was: broad-shouldered, smiling, alive. She stared until her hands began to shake. She typed a simple message and deleted it. Then typed again. And again. It took forty minutes before she sent three words: It's your mother. She wept afterward, not because she expected a reply, but because she had finally forgiven herself enough to try.

When Dallas accepted her friend request, Donna reread the notification over and over, each time pressing her palm against her heart as if to slow it down.

Their first few messages were awkward but full of light. She shared she'd earned her GED, that she'd found work with a public defender's office. She didn't burden him with stories of hardship, only small wins: new jobs, rescued animals, quiet mornings with coffee.

Dallas wrote back politely at first, then more genuinely as days passed. He began to see her not as a ghost from his past, but as a human being who refused to give up—on herself or on him.

Weeks later, while reviewing resumes for a courthouse intake clerk position, a name stopped him cold: Donna Jackson. His throat tightened. The photo attached showed a face older than his memory but calmer, anchored.

He called the number before his mind could catch up. "Donna?" A pause, a breath. "Dallas?"

Neither spoke for several seconds. Only the shared silence of recognition filled the line.

They met two days later in his office. She looked smaller than he'd imagined, but her posture was straight, her eyes clear. When she saw him, she exhaled—one long, trembling breath.

"I don't deserve this moment," she whispered.

He shook his head. "You earned it."

They hugged, both breaking at the same time. No rehearsed words, no explanations—just two people breaking the seal on years of regret and rebuilding something new.

When Donna came over to meet the Millers, she arrived ten minutes early. Standing on the porch, hands trembling, she practiced her smile in the reflection of her car window. A small bouquet of sunflowers rested in her hand. When Sara opened the door, the tension dissolved almost instantly. Warm eyes met warmer ones.

Mrs. Miller reached forward first. "You must be Donna. We're so glad you came."

Donna blinked, taken aback by the sincerity. "Thank you for raising my son," she managed.

Sara smiled, steady and kind. "Thank you for giving him to us."

For a moment, neither woman spoke—just tears, mutual understanding, and the kind of peace that didn't need words.

Inside, Dallas stood awkwardly, hands in pockets, his eyes darting between the two women who had shaped his world in different ways. Donna noticed the way his hair curled exactly like hers used to, and she laughed softly through her tears.

They sat down for tea and cake. Conversation fluttered easily—stories about work, life, family. Donna listened more than she spoke, absorbing each detail like a thirsty soul sampling sunlight.

For Dallas, peace came quietly that day—not with fireworks or grand confessions, but with the sight of both his mothers in the same room, sharing laughter between sips of tea.

And for Donna, peace came too. Because for the first time, she wasn't running from her past. She was sitting in the middle of it—and it was kinder than she had ever let herself imagine.

Additionally, Dallas's brother, Steven Miller, was currently away at graduate school. She told Donna that Dallas was the only child currently at the home, which would also change once he left for university.

Dallas told how he had received an honorary scholarship as valedictorian of his class. Mrs. Miller turned to Donna and smiled.

"You ought to be very proud of your son's accomplishment," she said, as if relinquishing all responsibility or ownership of her rightful pride for encouraging and aiding the boy through his education.

Now, Sara Miller handed Donna a sheet of white paper.

"Here is his acceptance letter to the university for Law School! And he'll be with Steven, you know. Because his brother's doing his residency to become a medical doctor."

She smiled again, accepting this time that Steven was her son by blood, and so she could take a small bit of credit for this boy doing so well!

"We are so, so proud…and you should be too. Looks like Dallas has your fine brain!" she laughed. Donna laughed too, as if she could barely believe her ears.

A fine brain? Really? Did she seem that way to other people…she, a woman who had made next to nothing of her life but an unholy godforsaken mess?

And at that moment, seeing the Millers so proud and so welcoming, and with the kind words that gave Donna some credit for the boy's success, she felt warmed inside. Something struck deep into her psyche; maybe she, too, could become something, someone… maybe.

Donna held Mrs. Miller's hand and looked fiercely into her eyes, thanking her for raising her child and giving him the most wonderful life that she was unable to give him. Donna turned to Mr. Miller and said, "Thank you for the father figure and the love and guidance you have bestowed upon him."

She then walked over to Dallas, held both of his hands, and said, "I have to tell you… about your father." She looked away, ashamed.

"Your biological father was killed in jail while serving his life sentence."

Sobbing, Donna apologized to Dallas, saying, "I am sorry, I am sorry, I am sorry." Dallas responded with a deep and resolute tone that remained unwavering.

"I am fine, Momma Donna; Mr. and Mrs. Miller—Mom and Dad— never once left my side. I hold nothing against you.

And anyway, I can do all things through Christ who strengthens me."

"You sure can, Dallas…" Donna wept. "You sure can do all things with the good Lord's help."

Her tears rolled down her cheeks.

They all hugged and cried before Sara returned to the kitchen to brew another pot of tea.

Sara disappeared into the kitchen, and soon the gentle clatter of mugs and the bubbling of a fresh pot of tea filled the room. The conversation drifted to softer tones, the kind reserved for late afternoons and unspoken hopes. When Sara returned, the steam from the teapot wrapped the family in a comforting hush; for a while, no one spoke, simply savoring the moment and the kind of peace that had taken years to earn.

As Donna finished her second cup, she set it carefully on its saucer. She looked around at the faces—kind, expectant, a little teary-eyed—and felt something new building in her chest, tender and bright. Rising unsteadily, she reached for Dallas first, pulling him into a fierce and lingering hug.

"Thank you," she whispered, her voice thick, "for letting me come home."

She turned next to Sara, gathering her in a soft, grateful embrace. "Thank you for all of it," Donna murmured—a simple phrase, but heavy with the weight of years.

Finally, she hugged Mr. Miller, who gave her a gentle pat on the back and a warm, genuine smile.

"I hope we'll do this again," Donna said, blinking back grateful tears.

"You're family now," Sara replied. "Anytime."

Donna lingered in the entryway for a last look. Then, with one final smile, she stepped out into the dusk—a little lighter than she had arrived, hope steady at her heels. The door closed behind her, but the warmth stayed, a quiet promise in that home and in her heart.

Donna's Late-Night Reflection

The house was quiet—quiet in a way only Donna's little corner of peace could be. The cat, Mercy, had curled near her feet. On the kitchen table, her journal lay open, half-filled with crossed-out sentences and the faded lines of earlier days.

She pressed her pen to the page, hesitating as she listened to the hush. Tonight, the silence felt gentle, not punishing.

November 18, she wrote in careful script.

Dear Dallas,

Today I saw you. Not just on a screen or drifting through memory, but real and whole. I saw the way your hands shook—just a little—when you opened the door. I saw how you stood between your parents, tall and careful and brave.

Sara hugged me first. I counted breaths until it happened—that moment of forgiveness I could never find for myself. She said, "Thank you for giving him to us." I tried not to cry, but I did anyway. You did, too.

All these years, I carried your name like a secret stone in my pocket. Every day sober, every job earned, every morning I woke up in this tiny house and counted the animals. I kept believing that if I wanted it enough—if I worked and prayed and forgave—all those broken places might feel less sharp.

The pen paused above the paper. Donna's other hand reached out, fidgeting with her charm bracelet. Twelve silver beads. Twelve years since she lost everything but chose herself, and—finally—chose hope.

I watched you laugh at their stories tonight. Saw your eyes light up when you talked about work. For a moment, I almost believed I was part of that world, too. Maybe I am. Maybe I could be, someday.

This peace—it's unfamiliar. Like the soft hush after storm rain. I'm afraid to breathe too loud in case I wake the old ghosts.

But I won't let fear speak for me anymore. Tomorrow, I'll feed the animals. I'll go to work and see the courthouse light in the morning. And I'll remember what Sara said. I'll hold both your names in my heart. Jackson. Miller.

 My son.

Donna closed the journal gently, whispering "Goodnight" to the page. The cat purred, the moonlight pressed through the curtains. In that tiny house, a mother reclaimed her hope—one line, one breath, one day at a time.

Chapter 3: The Case That Cut Deep

The courtroom was colder than usual. As Judge Dallas Jackson adjusted his robe, the familiar routine of Monday's caseload—DUI hearings, petty theft, a custody dispute—faded into background noise. Today, beneath the smooth order of justice, something inside him felt dangerously off.

He moved with habitual authority, yet his thoughts kept drifting to the picture frames on his desk: Donna, finally healed, and Roman, a brother lost and found proof that broken families can stitch themselves together again. But healing, he knew all too well, has a way of unearthing old wounds before it seals them shut. Dallas's gaze lingered on the empty seat in the gallery where his family sometimes sat, a subtle ache blooming in his chest.

This morning, the case that cut deep landed on his docket, unexpected as a knife in the dark. The defendant—Lake Miller, his own brother— stood accused of a crime that could destroy everything. A media circus had descended on the courthouse steps, the echo of camera shutters and murmurs of public opinion growing louder by the hour.

As testimony began, the boundaries between judge, brother, and son blurred. Dallas listened, trying to quiet the storm within guilt for not protecting Lake, resentment at his own powerlessness, the weight of every judgment he had ever made—on others and on himself. Each detail in the testimony cut through the distance he'd built between his bench and his heart, threatening to unravel him in front of a city that expected him to be unbreakable.

Throughout the day, snippets of his youth haunted him: the echo of his mother's voice, Arnold's checkerboard napkin, the Bible verse that once tethered him to hope. "I can do all things through Christ who strengthens me." He repeated it under his breath in chambers, voice trembling, eyes burning, desperate for faith to anchor him in the storm.

As deliberations stretched into the evening, Dallas glimpsed a familiar figure in the gallery—Roman, whose own journey mirrored Dallas's but diverged at every turn. For a moment, the past and present collided: two sons of the system, now men, both fighting for redemption on their own terms. Dallas braced himself. Family, he realized, is a case that's never closed.

The courtroom was colder than usual. Judge Dallas

of case files before him. It was another routine

Monday—DUI hearings, a petty theft plea, and a custody dispute—but beneath the rhythm of justice, something inside him felt off.

Maybe it was because Roman was not in court that day. Or perhaps it was the silence in his chambers that morning, the way his heart skipped when he glanced at the photo of Donna and Roman. Things were better now, yes—but healing, real healing, had a strange way of unearthing old wounds before sealing them shut.

 A few years slipped by in an almost dreamlike rhythm for Dallas Miller—a quiet era of earned peace. His life had settled into a steady cadence: mornings buried in criminal case files, evenings spent with books and symphonies that filled the soft air of his city apartment. His world felt balanced, even idyllic. The once-scattered pieces of his family had somehow found their places, fitted together again.

Most mornings began before dawn, in the half-light when the city still held its breath. Dallas woke to the soft chime of his alarm, rolled onto his back, and stared at the ceiling for a few quiet seconds while he took inventory of his spirit. No matter how late he'd worked the night before, he gave himself that same thirty-second pause—no phone, no files, no noise—just breath and a whispered, "Thank You for another day."

By six o'clock, the ritual was in motion. Coffee percolated on the counter of his small but meticulously kept kitchen—a space that still smelled faintly of the first meal Sara had cooked for him there. While the machine hissed and clicked, he flipped through the morning docket on his tablet: arraignments, probation violations, sentencing hearings. Names, charges, prior records, all neatly organized into columns that would eventually translate into decisions only he could make.

He dressed the same way most days, not out of vanity but out of discipline: crisp white shirt, perfectly knotted tie, polished shoes, robe carefully folded over his arm. There was comfort for him in the sameness—the way each step, each layer, reminded him that nothing about his authority was accidental. It had been earned, wrestled for, prayed over.

On his drive to the courthouse, he rarely listened to the radio. Instead, the steady hum of the engine and the faint rush of passing cars became a backdrop for private prayers and mental rehearsal. He thought of each case not just as a file, but as a person: a man who'd made one terrible choice, a woman clawing her way out of addiction, a teenager whose eyes still held the wild fear he remembered in his own. He asked God not for perfection, but for clarity. For the courage to be both firm and fair.

The courthouse itself had its own rhythm. The security guards greeted him with the same nod every morning—half-respect, half-familiarity. The clerk outside his chambers had already stacked the files in neat piles according to urgency. His bailiff, Morgan, always knocked twice before entering—a small courtesy that meant more to Dallas than the man likely knew.

Before stepping onto the bench, Dallas had one last ritual. He closed his chambers door, stood in front of the narrow mirror on the wall, and met his own reflection. It was a habit born from childhood, now sanctified by vocation.

"I can do all things through Christ who strengthens me," he murmured once, then again, until the verse no longer sounded like something memorized but like something lived. Only then did he lift the robe over his shoulders, smoothing the fabric as if he were putting on both armor and accountability.

By mid-morning, the machine of the court was in full swing. Defense attorneys shuffled papers nervously, prosecutors checked their notes, and defendants shifted on creaking benches, waiting for their names to be called. From the outside, his workday looked methodical, mechanical even. But inside, Dallas weighed each case with a care that never grew easier with repetition. A simple probation violation might remind him of the boy he once knew in the group home. A custody dispute might pull up echoes of the time no one had fought for him.

Lunch, when he took it, was usually at his desk—half a sandwich, forgotten coffee gone lukewarm, a few quiet minutes scrolling through photos of his family to reset his thinking. He sent quick check-in texts to Sara or Donna, or a brief message to Steven asking about a patient or Lake asking for a picture of the kids. These small exchanges threaded his long days with something bright and human.

By late afternoon, after the last hearing closed and the last gavel fell, he often remained in the courtroom long after everyone left. He'd sit in the empty silence, fingers resting lightly on the worn wood of the bench, listening to the echo of footsteps that were no longer there. Some days he felt like he'd done well; others, he felt the weight of every sentence he'd handed down. On those days, the robe felt heavier when he hung it on the hook in his chambers.

Evenings were quieter, a deliberate counterbalance to the intensity of the day. He'd return to his apartment, loosen his tie, and let the strains of classical music or soft jazz float through the rooms. Case law and legal theory books lined his shelves, but there were novels, too—stories of broken families, lost boys, and complicated grace. He read them slowly, recognizing pieces of himself in the pages.

From the outside, it looked like a clean, predictable routine: court, casework, quiet nights. But under the steady cadence, there was always motion—old wounds healing, new questions forming, faith quietly being tested and rebuilt, one ordinary day at a time.

Donna became a constant visitor, her laughter echoing through the hallways of Dallas's memory as much as his home. Sara Miller had begun calling her "Dallas's Other Mother," a title that started as a joke but soon turned endearingly practical.

"How many kids go from having no mom at all in a group home," Sara would say with her half-teasing grin, "to having a Main Mom and an 'Other Mother'?"

Laughter always followed—warm, unrestrained, anchoring them all in a fragile kind of happiness that none of them dared question too much.

Dallas, though outwardly content, carried solitude like a familiar coat. He had everything—comfort, stability, even a measure of respect in his legal circles—but something unnamed haunted him in quiet hours. He watched Lake and Steven with their wives and children and sometimes wondered if life had quietly passed him by.

Marriage.

The idea had begun to nudge at him lately. He did not know where to begin searching for a wife, or if he even should. After all, he had seen enough of marriage from the courtroom bench—the hollowed-out kind that left people jagged inside. Still, watching Steven light up when his children ran to greet him stirred something tender in Dallas. A small part of him hungered for that, too.

That Monday began like any other—tired, gray, and full of deadlines. Dallas had barely opened his briefcase when the old black telephone on his desk began to scream. Not ring, not buzz—scream. Early calls were never good news.

He ignored it at first. It was not even eight yet. The office didn't open till half past, and none of the staff would be there to deflect whatever nonsense this was. Probably another desperate client with too much guilt and too little patience.

As the ringing dragged on, his irritation simmered. He pictured ripping the hardwired monstrosity right from the wall. Then came another shrill burst, and that was it.

"Miller," he snapped, his tone clipped like a judge's gavel.

For a long second, there was nothing but static. Then a ragged voice broke through, trembling, almost unrecognizable.

"Dal…"

The sound froze him. There was pain there—raw, unfiltered, almost animal. Static crackled and a low, ragged sob came through, nearly lost in the hiss.

"Dallas," the voice gasped, so scuffed and broken it barely sounded human. "You have to help me. Please. They got me. They got me—in a jail cell, brother."

Dallas pressed the phone harder to his ear, frowning. The words came in wet, uneven bursts—like someone drowning, fighting to stay afloat. For a moment, he wondered if it was a prank, a scam, or just some glitch.

He heard labored breathing, the kind that made his own chest tighten with unease. "Who is this?" Dallas demanded, his tone less certain than he meant.

The person on the other end made a choking noise, part gasp, part sob. "Dal… it's me. Lake." The name tumbled out in a half-whisper, with the vowels stretched thin by fear.

But Dallas's mind reeled. He couldn't connect the battered voice with any face he recognized. Lake? The sound was unsteady, pitched higher than he remembered, as if scraped raw by panic and exhaustion. The line went quiet for a beat, filled only by the tremor of contained tears.

Dallas pulled the phone away, stared at it as if the answer might be printed on the screen. He racked his memory—he didn't know anyone named Lake in jail, or anyone who'd call him in such a state of utter despair. The uncertainty gnawed at him, even as the pleading voice echoed in his head: "Please, Dallas. Don't hang up. Please. I can't… I can't breathe in here."

"Lake, are you sure you have the right number?" Dallas finally managed, his own voice now edged with worry. Was this a mistake? Or something much worse? The silence that followed seemed to thicken the air around him. Lake—his steady, easygoing brother—the man he had admired since boyhood. A model husband. A father. A man incapable of cruelty, at least in Dallas's eyes.

"Lake? What are you talking about? Got you for what?"

On the other end came the quietest words Dallas ever heard.

"They say I killed her, Dal… Bella's gone."

Time seemed to halt. The city outside continued its indifferent hum, but inside Dallas's office, all sound fell away. He gripped the receiver tighter, too stunned to speak.

Bella-Luna. Beautiful moon. The name rose through his mind like a ghost. He could still see her—gentle skin, easy laughter, hair that shimmered brown-gold in sunlight. The kind of woman whose absence felt like an error in the universe itself.

He wanted to shout that it was ridiculous—that Lake couldn't hurt anyone, least of all her. But even as his mouth opened, doubt whispered its unwelcome logic. Every murderer's family, he knew, swore on heaven and earth that the accused was innocent.

Still, this was Lake. His brother.

When the call ended, Dallas sat motionless for a long time, staring at the silent receiver. He was a criminal attorney. A partner. Theoretically a man of logic. But no doctrine in the law had ever prepared him for this: the call that shattered the illusion of control he had spent years building.

A part of him burned to rush to Lake's defense. Another warned that he could not touch the case—it would be unethical. Yet, he had never felt more helpless, more humanly bound by love and duty.

For the first time in years, Dallas wished he believed in miracles.

* * *

Dallas retrieved the case file, flipping it open with the detached focus of routine. But as his eyes caught the name on the first page, the world seemed to tilt.

He blinked once, then again. That name—he knew it, but not from any file.

"He's being charged with…" Dallas's voice faltered as he looked up at the clerk.

"Second-degree manslaughter," she started, then hesitated. "Correction—first-degree murder."

The words hit like stones in his chest. He straightened slowly, pulse thundering in his ears. The letters on the page blurred, the air around him tightening. This was not just another case.

The precinct clock ticked with surgical precision, carving steady beats through the low drone of keyboards and phones. Dallas stood motionless, a lone figure framed in fluorescent light. His hand hovered above the jagged edge of an open case file, the paper trembling slightly under the breath of an air vent.

One name. Familiar. Heavy. Unforgiving.

This was family.

The world narrowed to that single truth. His pulse thundered in his ears as the hum of the room receded into static. Faded memories slipped through—the sharp laughter of a brother once close, a mother's whisper from a dinner gone cold. He blinked them away, but they clung stubbornly at the edges of his vision.

Then came footsteps. Slow, deliberate, resonant enough to carve silence through sound.

Detective Mason Crowe appeared in the doorway, his outline catching the sterile light. Every step he took carried the calm weight of authority wrapped around quiet menace. Crowe approached until the two men shared the glass surface of an evidence board, their reflections fractured into blurred shadows.

"Interesting assignment, Dallas," Crowe said, smooth voice shellacked with something sharper underneath. "You sure you're the right man for this one?"

It drifted across the room, soft but designed to pierce. Conversations faltered; eyes flickered up, pretending not to listen.

Dallas clenched his jaw, holding to protocol with visible strain. His badge glinted faintly beside the file, a symbol of control he no longer felt.

Crowe's gaze slipped over the paper, recognition flashing in a small, satisfied smirk. He didn't need to say more. His silence spoke louder.

When he turned and walked away, his shoes struck tile with rhythmic finality, each step retreating like a countdown.

Dallas remained still, staring at the name that refused to blur again. Under the sterile lights, the words and his duty tangled into one unbreakable knot.

Family or justice.

One would have to break.

* * *

Back in the room, Dallas sat alone. The file was open before him, but he could not focus on the legal jargon. His brother's name stared back at him, printed in bold black letters. Lake had always been the wild one—charming, impulsive, and full of dreams too big for his hands to hold. But he had a heart as wide as the sky, and he had loved his wife deeply.

According to the file, the incident happened on a night heavy with summer rain. Lake, always meticulous about his firearms, had been sitting at the kitchen table, oil rag in one hand, the family revolver in the other. His wife moved through the back of the house, her footsteps indistinct under the soundtrack of their ordinary life—a radio humming, the clatter of plates. Then, a sound—a single, sharp crack. The kind that ends the everyday and begins a nightmare.

Tragic. The paperwork called it "accidental discharge." The DA called it negligence. Now, prosecutors wanted more than sympathy; they were pressing for prison.

Dallas stared at the facts until numbers and names bled together. The office was silent except for the crackle of the city outside, the soft glow of lamplight turning case files gold and shadow. His jaw was taut, thoughts spinning—judge, lawyer, brother, bystander. He could not try this case. Not objectively. Not ethically.

But could he hand it off? Could he step back, knowing his brother sat in a cell just miles away—frightened, grieving, branded as a killer?

The door creaked, and Donna slipped in, her figure framed in tired light. "I heard," she said, voice threading through the quiet.

Dallas's eyes were ringed with exhaustion. "I can't do it. I'm too close."

Donna shook her head, closing the space between them. "That's not weakness—it's wisdom."

He exhaled, the sound shaky, haunted. "I fought for this robe. I fought for the law. But right now, I want to be his brother." Emotion glimmered at the surface, raw and unguarded.

"You still can be," Donna replied, her hand settling gently on his shoulder. "Let someone else take the case. Be his strength, not his judge."

Dallas nodded, resigned and relieved—but on edge. "Cyrus Pierre?" he asked, naming the colleague he trusted above all others.

"He'll understand," Donna promised, offering a small, steady smile.

News traveled fast. Across town, Roman—Dallas's colleague and close friend—received the call, the weight of it grounding him instantly. The city's legal circles buzzed with speculation as Cyrus stepped into the breach: respected, relentless, known for integrity. He picked up the file, knowing every move would be scrutinized, every ruling a test not just of law, but of loyalty.

In the days that followed, Dallas lived in split worlds—advising at a distance, guiding his family, supporting Cyrus quietly without crossing the invisible ethical boundaries that marked his profession. The court was a stage now packed with all the drama of a public spectacle: headlines screaming, cameras hungry, every moment spent beneath a magnifying glass.

Cyrus led the defense with a steady expertise sharpened by late-night calls with Dallas, the two men speaking quietly about strategy, about faith, about the burden of perfect justice in an imperfect world. Dallas recited his anchor verse in sleepless moments—"I can do all things through Christ who strengthens me"—and poured everything into supporting Lake and their parents from the gallery, never from behind the bench.

When the verdict came, the relief was seismic but not without its scars. Dallas had stood aside as Cyrus carried the case, true to his calling both as brother and as officer of the court. In the echoing hush that followed,

Donna wrapped Dallas in a grateful hug, and Cyrus caught his friend's eyes—a look of shared honor and cost.

The city would remember a trial where justice and family collided, but in the end, Dallas kept both his principles and his colleague's trust. And in a world hungry for heroes who did the right thing—especially when it hurt—he stood a little taller, the weight of the robe now resting on steadier shoulders.

* * *

The best he could offer, especially without in any way prejudicing his hard-earned position, was to be supportive, provide sound advice to Sara, his adoptive mother, and pass the case on to one of the partners in his firm. He is willing to guide his partner on how to find loopholes. More than this, he could not very well do, but he promised Sara everything would turn out just fine if Lake had not done the evil deed.

The law would always prevail on the right side, because God would see to it. They all had to attend church frequently and pray until they could pray no more.

Lake, too, was going to have to pray, and pray hard. He told Lake to remember this, and to repeat it daily two to five times on each occasion every time he was near a mirror, and that he was to believe firmly in it, no matter what:

I can do all things through Christ who strengthens me.

I can do all things through Christ who strengthens me…

Sara was relieved, and after Dallas agreed to hear all about the case and at least offer his opinions and continuing counsel to the family, he was able to continue with his workday. But—Lake—a murderer? His brother and that fine upstanding man? No way. No way. He could barely tear his mind off of it and concentrate on the cases he now had to conclude.

He felt nauseous and tore away to the bathroom.

* * *

The following morning, after a criminal case had just been settled in the court, he headed to the county jail to see Lake. He was still not going to get overly involved in the case but had promised Sara he would look in on his brother and have a man-to-man talk about how this had all happened and about the bitter truth at the core of it all. He still could not believe the adorable Bella-Luna was dead.

And certainly not by his own brother's hands, which he steadfastly wanted to believe had not a single stain of guilt on them.

That morning, he had also dropped by his mother's house and told her what she needed to hear.

He'd told his mother, "Mom, you worked tirelessly on my upbringing and my education, and I promise I will be there for you and Dad on this case. However, you must understand that, although I am a criminal law attorney, my involvement can only be limited to advice, hope, and prayer, as anything more would only work against Lake's case and cast suspicion on it. I can help you find the best lawyer the state has to offer, and I can oversee the case to ensure that nothing is left to doubt—but I cannot personally take it to trial. You understand, Momma?"

She said that she did and hugged him close. But really, her inner voice was screaming out, take it, take it—for your brother! How can you be so selfish?

Despite what Dallas was explaining, in her heart of hearts, she could not believe he was not the right man to take the case to trial, if it came to that.

Why would he not be the right attorney for his own brother's case?

Of course, people rarely understood that one type of lawyer could not do every other kind of law, that a family law attorney could not get a man off the hook if he burgled a store or robbed a bank. A barrister in immigration law did not deal with road accident claims, nor did a criminal law partner personally take on capital murder cases incurred by his brother! To most people, a lawyer was a lawyer, and they could handle all things, regardless of the circumstances.

If you have one in your own family, that could also save a whole heap of money and aggravation. Couldn't it?

That was what they thought, and the good Millers were no different.

Dallas will sort it out was on everyone's lips.

But Dallas couldn't and wouldn't even try, for getting involved to try to get his brother off the hook in a murder trial would not work wonders for him in keeping hold of his position, and nor would it assist Lake. That would be Lake's and his mom's task.

In the end, Dallas lined up the best attorneys with a record of success in similar case histories and helped his mother choose which one to appoint. After reviewing Cyrus's credentials and past familiar cases, he felt confident in recommending him to handle his brother's defense.

Dallas also guided his mother on how to speak to the police and what questions to ask, hoping it might create a window through which a small glimmer of light could shine onto his brother, Lake.

Even though he had extricated himself from any direct responsibility to look after Lake's case, he still somehow felt the whole weight of the world on his shoulders again, because at every turn—even if he'd made his position abundantly clear—his mother or father would cry, what shall we do now, Dallas! Oh, what should we do?

And Lake himself would use every dime he had to call the office again, pleading, "Help me, Bro, you have to help me!"

Now bearing the pressure of his brother's case, whether he wanted to steer it or not, Dallas knew he needed to revert to the mirror to rehearse his verse.

Each day in his offices, he would run into the bathroom and repeat the verse in the mirror.

I can do all things through Christ who strengthens me. I can do all things through Christ who strengthens me… I can do all things through Christ who strengthens me. I can do all things through Christ who strengthens me… I can do all things through Christ who strengthens me.

However, the problem was that he no longer knew if he genuinely believed it was true.

Now, no matter what happened in Lake's case, he knew his family would pin it on him. If Lake lost the case at trial, Friedrichs would be no good, and it would be considered Dallas's fault anyway for not taking the case through to trial himself.

* * *

Cyrus did understand—more than anyone. He had seen too many families fracture under the weight of accusation and grief, and he recognized that same heaviness in Dallas's voice. When Dallas called him that evening, the silence between their words carried years of mutual respect and the quiet understanding that this case was different.

"You made the right call," Cyrus said finally. "You can't carry both the gavel and the grief. Let me take it."

Dallas exhaled slowly, the sound roughened by restraint. "I'm not asking you to go easy on him."

"I know," Cyrus replied. His tone was steady, measured—a man who had argued both mercy and conviction in the same breath more times than he cared to count. "But I won't go hard either. I'll go fair."

Dallas nodded, even though Cyrus could not see him. The words were simple, but they held more weight than a verdict. For the first time in days, Dallas felt something loosen inside—a sense that justice and compassion did not have to stand on opposite sides of the courtroom. And that was enough.

* * *

At Lake's bail hearing, Dallas's firm was able to reduce his bail amount and secure his release from jail until his trial date. Still, due to the capital murder charge and the perceived risk of his absconding, Lake was to wear a tracker tag on his right ankle and could not leave the Miller family home.

It seemed a small price to pay for having him freed, even if the Miller family had been forced to cash in $250,000 of savings for the privilege of it.

During this time, Dallas's chosen lawyer—and, by implication, Dallas too—had their work cut out for them, as Lake's wife, Bella-Luna, had sat on the Board as Chairman in their county district.

As they were driven home by the police, for Lake to then stay under lock and key in the Miller family home, Lake finally explained to Dallas how the death had happened. The couple, he said, had begun arguing over their finances. BellaLuna had delved into the safe and pulled out their 9mm handgun and pointed it at him. He knew she had never fired a gun before, so he had a chance…

He forcefully reacted in self-defense and jumped on her to grab the gun, pointing it away from her as he clasped her hands tightly, with the firearm still in her grasp and now also in his. And as he did so, it went off, shearing the lower part of her jaw, and a single shot making its way up through her skull to embed deep into her brain, behind the right eye.

Dallas returned to the courtroom after hours, his steps slower, his gaze deeper. He ruled with more compassion, now with more humanity. He saw beyond the cases—into the lives.

And he prayed.

Not for clarity, but for strength.

To be a man worthy of the second chances he'd been given.

To be a brother who forgave.

To be a son who is inspired.

To be an attorney who believed.

* * *

After about ten months, the trial began—not short, not simple, but slow and suffocating, every day peeling back another layer of grief.

The courtroom was packed.

Bella-Luna's family filled one side of the gallery—eyes red-rimmed but fierce, her father's jaw clenched tight as if holding back a lifetime's worth of words. The Millers sat on the other side, Sara twisting a tissue between trembling fingers, Hunter stiff and upright like a man holding himself together by sheer will. Lake sat at the defense table in a gray suit that didn't quite fit, a GPS monitor hidden beneath his pant leg, his hands folded so tightly his knuckles blanched.

Friedrichs stood at his side, posture poised but eyes sharp—aware that every misstep could seal a coffin.

Across from them paced the prosecutor: Frederick A.—the kind of attorney whose very presence announced a battle. His reputation preceded him; he rarely lost. Today, he carried Bella-Luna's memory like a banner.

"Ladies and gentlemen of the jury," Frederick began, voice smooth but edged with controlled anger, "this case is about responsibility. A gun. A home. A wife who never got to see another sunrise because the man who had a duty to protect her failed."

His hand cut through the air, slicing invisible lines between negligence and intent. He did not call Lake a monster. He didn't have to. The words reckless, careless, avoidable did the work just fine.

When it was Friedrichs's turn, he stepped forward and let a beat of silence linger.

"This case," he said simply, "is about a tragedy. A terrible, irreversible tragedy. Not murder."

He walked toward the jury, his voice steady. "You'll see the footage. You'll hear the arguments. But at the end of all of this, I'm asking you to remember one thing: sometimes, awful things happen not because someone wanted them to—but because two human beings made a series of mistakes in a single, terrible moment."

Witnesses

The State called its first witness: Detective Harlan Reyes, lead investigator.

He walked through the scene step by step—photos projected on the screen: the kitchen table smeared with oil and gun-cleaning supplies; the wine glasses; the toppled chair; the horrifying stillness of Bella-Luna's body.

"Was there any sign of forced entry?" Frederick asked.

"No," Reyes replied. "No pry marks. No broken locks."

"Any signs of a struggle elsewhere in the home?"

"No. The only signs of an altercation are around the kitchen table."

Frederick nodded. "So all we have is a gun, a husband, a wife, and a deadly shot fired in their own kitchen."

"Objection," Friedrichs interjected. "Argumentative."

"Sustained," the judge said. "Rephrase, counselor."

Frederick smiled slightly. "Detective Reyes, who else was present in the home at the time of the shooting?"

"Just Mr. Miller and Mrs. Miller."

"Thank you. No further questions."

On cross-examination, Friedrichs shifted the tone.

"Detective Reyes, you reviewed the home's security footage, correct?"

"Yes."

"Did you see any evidence that Mr. Miller loaded the gun in order to harm his wife?"

"No."

"Any messages, threats, or prior domestic reports on file?"

"No. None."

"Is there anything in your investigation that suggests this was anything other than a horrible, chaotic moment between two people?"

Reyes hesitated, then exhaled. "That's what it looked like to me."

Next came the forensic analyst, explaining the bullet's path, the angles, the distance. Her testimony was clinical, but the words felt like knives.

"The entry wound was just below the mandible," she said, pointing to a diagram. "The bullet traveled upward and lodged in the cranial cavity. It was a close-range discharge."

"Could this trajectory be consistent with two people fighting for control of the gun?" Friedrichs asked on cross.

"Yes," she admitted. "It's consistent with a struggle."

The medical examiner followed, detailing cause of death. Sara cried quietly into a tissue; Donna, in the back row, silently mouthed a prayer.

Then Bella-Luna's mother took the stand.

Her voice broke on her daughter's name. "She was my baby," she said. "She was the one who held this family together. She loved Lake. She believed in him so much."

Frederick approached gently.

"Did she ever tell you she was afraid of him?" he asked.

"No," her mother answered. "She said they argued sometimes. About money. About the gun. She didn't like it in the house."

"Did she ever say she thought something like this could happen?"

She looked at Lake then, tears streaking down her cheeks. "No. Never. She thought… they'd grow old together."

The jury watched every flicker of her pain. It wasn't evidence. But it was impact.

The Home Security Footage

Finally, the lights dimmed. The large screen lit up.

The den glowed with late afternoon sun. Jazz hummed through the speakers. Lake and Bella-Luna moved through the frame, cleaning up dinner, laughing, bumping shoulders.

Then—the conversation shifted. The body language changed.

Lake checked something on his phone; his brow creased. Bella-Luna's posture stiffened. They moved partially out of frame, voices muffled but tense.

A moment later, she was seen opening the safe. The gun appeared in her hand.

Gasps rippled through the courtroom.

Frederick let the video play without comment. The footage showed Lake stepping forward, hands raised in a calming gesture. Bella-Luna backing up, still holding the weapon.

Then they collided—hands grabbing, bodies struggling, the gun twisting.

One deafening flash of light.

Bella-Luna crumpled.

The video froze on Lake dropping to his knees, screaming her name, his hands pressing desperately to her wound.

The lights came back up slowly.

A solemn hush smothered the room.

Lake Takes the Stand

It was a risk. Friedrichs knew it. Dallas had known it when he'd advised from afar. But in the end, there was no way forward without Lake's voice.

He walked to the stand like a man walking through water. He placed his hand on the Bible, voice rough as he said, "I do."

"Mr. Miller," Friedrichs began, "did you love your wife?"

Lake's eyes filled instantly. "Yes." His voice cracked. "More than anything."

"Did you ever want to hurt her?"

"Never. I would've died for her."

Friedrichs nodded. "Tell the jury what happened that night. From your perspective."

Lake swallowed. "We had dinner. We talked about bills. I brought up an account that had been overdrawn. I shouldn't have said it the way I did. I made it sound like I was accusing her. I was just… scared. We wanted to buy a second house. I was trying to plan."

His hands shook as he spoke. "She got upset. Thought I didn't trust her. She went to the safe. She grabbed the gun. She never… she never really handled it before. I panicked."

"Why?"

"Because I know guns. I know what they do. I thought she might hurt herself by accident. I lunged for it. We both grabbed it. I tried to point it away. Then—"

He closed his eyes, tears spilling over.

"The shot went off," he whispered. "And she was just… gone."

"Did you intend to fire that gun?"

"No," he said, shaking his head violently. "I didn't even know a round was chambered. I would've unloaded it if I'd known. I thought it was safe."

On cross, Frederick's tone sharpened.

"You're telling this jury," he said, "that the chairman of a county board—a man who knows procedure, planning, risk—somehow didn't think to check whether his loaded firearm was safe in a house with people in it?"

Lake's shame was palpable. "I was careless," he admitted. "I thought I had cleared it earlier. I should've checked again. I will live with that forever."

"Exactly," Frederick said. "You will live. She will not."

"Objection," Friedrichs snapped. "Inflammatory."

"Sustained," the judge said. "The jury will disregard counsel's last remark."

But no one truly could.

Closing & Verdict

In closing, Frederick urged the jury to focus on responsibility.

"Tragedy does not erase accountability," he said. "Negligence with a firearm is not a small mistake. It cost a woman her life."

Friedrichs, in turn, walked them back through the footage, the testimony, the lack of threats, the grief in Lake's voice.

"This is not a man who set out to kill his wife," he said quietly. "This is a man who will pay for his mistake every day, whether you lock him in a cell or not. The law does not require you to turn every tragedy into murder."

The jury deliberated for hours that felt like years.

Sara prayed silently. Hunter sat rigid. Donna, in the back, clutched her bracelet. Dallas waited miles away, unable to bear sitting in the pews.

When the jury filed back in, the air itself seemed to hold its breath.

"On the charge of murder in the first degree," the foreperson read, voice steady, "we find the defendant, Lake Miller—not guilty."

A sound escaped Lake—half sob, half disbelief. Bella-Luna's parents held each other, grief unmoved by the verdict but deepened by its finality. Sara covered her face with shaking hands. Hunter bowed his head.

Lake cried openly at the defense table.

Freedom had never felt so heavy.

Dallas broke down—not in relief, but in sorrow. For the pain. For the trauma. For the lives changed forever.

Lake wept in his arms outside the courtroom.

"I never meant to hurt her," he choked.

"I know," Dallas said. "But that doesn't mean you don't carry it."

Lake nodded. "How do I move forward?"

"You live. You love. You never forget, but you never let it stop you from becoming better." Weeks passed.

* * *

And though he didn't know it yet, from his past was about to walk through his courtroom doors—this time wearing the orange jumpsuit of the accused. But that reckoning would come in time.

For now, Dallas stood not as a man undone, but as a man made whole by everything that had once broken him.

And the gavel, when it struck, no longer sounded like punishment.

It sounded like a purpose.

* * *

Dallas worked as a Criminal Attorney while continuing to pursue his education, completing some certifications with the goal of one day being appointed as a judge. Although Momma Donna worked in the same vicinity as Dallas, they hardly crossed paths with each other at work. After about a year, Momma Donna returned to school to pursue a degree in

Legal Studies. I'm coming after you…" She laughed. " Dallas was astounded by the words that slipped from her mouth, "I am proud of you, Mom." And it was true; Dallas's heart swelled with pride to think that his mom, who had such a rough life, was making so much of herself at last. He was sure her achievement was even greater than his own, because she had nobody on her side, supporting her, and he felt as if the whole wide world was on his side, in the form of his adoptive mom and dad, and his brothers.

"Not as proud as I am of you, my boy!"

"I'm prouder than you, Momma Donna," Dallas laughed.

"Well now," she said, "We will soon see who does better at the law, my child! As I said, I'm hot on your tail, boy! You better watch out!"

It looked like it was turning into something of a competition between them, and they both loved every second of it.

* * *

The weeks flew by in a frantic, work-filled, pressure-filled blur.

Dallas's brother, Steven, had heard the news of their brother, and one day, as soon as he could, he drove home to support his parents. As he burst in through the door, though, a sight met his eyes.

The kitchen light was on as usual, but when he looked around, he saw no one. He could hear a helpless sobbing. He looked around the other side of the kitchen island and could see his father down on his knees on the floor, stroking his mother's hair, and sobbing hard.

For a moment, Steven was sure his mother was dead.

Well, why else would Dad sit there doing nothing?

Then he realized it was just shock and probably the whole stress of everything that had been going on. Mom might only have fainted.

"What to do, son? Your mother just fell to the floor," Hunter cried.

Steven immediately ran over to his mother and checked her pulse, calmly. He was a physician, after all! No pulse, but she was warm, so whatever had happened was very recent, and they had plenty of time to work on her.

He began C.P.R. and ordered his father to call the paramedics as he needed a defibrillator to restart his own mother's beautiful heart.

* * *

Dallas reassured Lake that his case was in good hands. He believed in Lake, too.

They were interrupted by the ringing of the phone.

It was Dad calling Dallas to inform him that Mom had gone unconscious from a presumed heart attack, and that Steven was performing C.P.R. on her.

The police driver turned on blue lights and sirens to get them home even faster. After five more minutes of driving, Dallas and Lake were pulling into the driveway at the same time as paramedics, and two officers bundled Lake inside the Miller house. Lake ran over to his mother's side and grabbed her hand as the stretcher rolled past the front door, toward the driveway. Still, he was prevented from following her further by two armed officers at the Millers' front door, pushing Lake back roughly and reminding him about the tracker tag around his ankle.

"One move outside this door, whether we're standing right here or not, and you know you're going right back to the jailhouse. So, don't you try anything," said one police officer, twisting Lake's arm up his back.

Dallas accompanied the stretcher down the driveway and repeated the Bible verse to her five times, louder each time he said it.

"I can do all things through Christ who strengthens me.

I can do all things through Christ who strengthens me…

I can do all things through Christ who strengthens me.

I can do all things through Christ who strengthens me…

I can do all things through Christ who strengthens me…!" Then he shouted, "Mom, Mom… you have to say it!"

That was precisely when Mrs. Miller opened her blue eyes and squeezed his fingers tightly. She did not say the words, but Dallas knew she had heard. Lake reassured her that everything would be fine, and he wanted her to repeat the Bible verse to herself. She was admitted for cardiac checks, and strangely, nothing was found even though she had had no pulse and had been brought back to life via C.P.R. and a defibrillator.

It was as if God had come right then and there to save her, to fix her up and send her home without a trace of what had happened.

Nobody could quite believe it.

They kept her under observation, but her file consistently reported the same medical-speak: NAD.

That meant the Latin phrase, nil ad demonstrandum: 'nothing to report'.

After a week, she was miraculously released and returned home, doing well.

Chapter 4: The Shining Light

———————— • ————————

Dallas stared out the window of his home office, the golden light of late afternoon streaking across old photo albums and piles of open case files. For months, he'd been working behind the scenes to save Lake, his brother, from the brink—juggling the crushing pressure from both families, the Miller household and Bella-Luna's. Every day, as the trial loomed closer, the weight in Dallas's chest grew heavier: Would faith and truth be enough to win against the famed attorney, Cyrus Pierre?

Clutching the edges of the album, Dallas traced his own childhood face—fearful, uncertain, caught somewhere between exile and belonging. He pictured Sara and Hunter praying at the kitchen table, their hope a fragile thread binding the family together despite the threat of public humiliation and heartbreak. Dallas ached to protect them, to prove that even children raised in chaos can shine a light strong enough to lead the way.

The conflicts mounted around him like walls closing in—personal, spiritual, professional, and emotional. What started as one tragic accident had spiraled into a chain reaction that drew blood from every corner of Dallas's life.

Family Conflict — Two Families at War

The Millers and Bella-Luna's family were once inseparable—holidays spent together, birthdays shared, church retreats attended side by side. Now, grief carved a violent fault line between them.

Bella-Luna's mother wouldn't return Sara's calls.

Her father refused to look at the Millers during church.

Family friends whispered loud enough for Dallas to hear.

What hurt worst was knowing they weren't angry out of malice.

They were angry out of heartbreak.

And heartbreak is unpredictable.

Dallas saw Sara silently wiping tears at the sink at night, trying to stay strong for everyone. Hunter tried to act tough, burying his worry under loud humor, but at night Dallas caught him staring blankly at the family photo wall.

The fracture was deep—and widening.

Church Conflict — When Faith Isn't Enough

Church, once their refuge, felt like walking into a courtroom without a defense. One group prayed openly for Lake; another murmured that justice for Bella-Luna demanded accountability.

One Sunday morning, Mrs. Alvarez, a long-time friend of Bella-Luna's mother, stopped Sara.

"Forgive me, but you all need to stop defending him publicly. You're making things worse."

Sara's face crumpled, her faith colliding with pain.

Dallas clenched his teeth.

This was the first time he truly understood:

Faith can be a battlefield.

And not even scripture could prevent people from weaponizing heartache.

Community Conflict — Media & Neighborhood Pressure

As news spread, reporters camped outside the courthouse. Cameras flashed whenever any Miller walked to their car. Headlines questioned Dallas's involvement:

"Rising Attorney Secretly Guiding His Brother's Murder Case?"

"Judge-to-Be Miller Compromised by Family Loyalty?"

Neighbors who once waved across the yard now avoided eye contact. Some recorded the Miller home out of morbid curiosity. Every grocery run became a quiet hell—side glances, hushed voices, judgment disguised as concern.

Dallas felt every stare like a mark on his skin.

Firm Conflict — Professional Doubt & Ethical Tightropes

At the law firm, tension simmered beneath politeness. A few colleagues supported him. Others worried his involvement would taint cases or damage the firm's reputation.

Friedrichs pulled him aside one night.

"You don't understand, Dallas—half the firm expects you to magically solve this. The other half fears you'll sink everything."

Both halves terrified Dallas.

He was doing everything right—staying ethical, staying in the background—but perception was a beast with its own hunger. And Lake's life hung in the balance.

Internal Conflict — Trauma Woken From Sleep

The closer the trial came, the more Dallas dreamed of the group home.

The locked doors.

The cold floor.

Arnold's trembling hands gripping a blanket.

The fear of losing the only person he loved.

Watching Lake in an orange jumpsuit reopened wounds he thought had healed. He found himself repeating his verse in bathrooms, in his car, in the silence of his closet:

"I can do all things through Christ who strengthens me."

Some nights he repeated it until his voice cracked.

Because faith was no longer a comfort.

It had become his survival.

Lake's Emotional Decline — A Brother Unraveling

Lake was deteriorating.

He cried unpredictably.

Argued with shadows.

Stared at walls for hours.

Jumped at sudden noises.

Often whispered, "I'm scared," even when no one asked.

Some days, Lake swore he heard Bella-Luna's voice calling his name.

That terrified Dallas more than anything.

Because he could not save Lake from a grief that lived inside him.

And he couldn't save himself either—not completely.

Who Was Dallas Becoming? — Identity Crisis

Dallas had built himself into a man of discipline, dignity, and morality. But now:

He was angrier.

More restless.

More withdrawn.

More afraid of failure than ever before.

Every headline.

Every news clip.

Every church whisper.

Every sleepless night.

Every pleading call from Lake.

Every prayer from Sara.

They all dug deeper into his ribs until he wondered:

Is this what "shining" feels like, or am I burning alive?

The Turning Point

Then one evening, Donna walked into his office and found him asleep on his desk, face down on legal pads soaked with tears he didn't notice he'd shed.

She touched his shoulder.

"Baby… you're fighting too hard. Don't forget—you're human."

Dallas lifted his head slowly, eyes red.

"I have to do this right. This community judged me my whole life. But this time…"

His voice broke.

"This time I'll show them what God made me."

Donna cupped his cheek gently.

"Your shine comes from within, not from a courtroom."

Those words steadied him more than any legal strategy.

And so when Dallas rose from his desk that night, album under his arm, he walked forward not just as a brother seeking justice—but as a man determined to shine a light no darkness could shake.

The tension radiated through nightly family dinners, silent church pews, and frenetic law firm meetings. Dallas recited his Bible verse every evening before sleep, seeking solace in its promise. But this chapter was about more than faith—it was about actively fighting to keep hope alive, even as the world seemed intent on tearing it away. Dallas realized that "shining light" wasn't about being perfect, but about risking everything to do the right thing, regardless of the outcome.

When Lake's trial day arrived, Dallas walked into the courthouse with his family behind him, photo album tucked under his arm—ready not just to defend his brother, but to expose the truth of their journey for all to see. No matter how hard the world tried to break them, Dallas's story would be the one that lit the way for others lost in darkness.

After months of working and gathering evidence, Lake's case was finally coming together. Dallas was working with great determination on it, but only behind the scenes, alongside another attorney from his firm, Friedrichs, who was leading the case to trial.

Despite this, everyone's nerves ran wild at Friedrichs, and Dallas didn't dare reveal to his mom that he was not even sure the firm could win the case. What nobody else was being told was that Bella-Luna's family had gone and hired the most well-known attorney, Cyrus Pierre.

Cyrus was known to have beaten every opponent in every case he had ever worked on. Dallas wasn't letting that intimidate him, though, and nor was his colleague, as they felt their evidence for the defense was strong enough for an acquittal; only Cyrus's formidable reputation was what shook their confidence a little.

The whole thing was distressing for the boys' mom and dad, too, since they loved Bella-Luna's family as their own, and now it was as if two families who were supposed to love each other had been sent to war.

Life could be so unfair sometimes.

Each family's kid had made a big mistake—the biggest of their lives—and it was everyone else paying the price. Of course, poor Bella-Luna had paid the ultimate…

As Dallas worked these extended hours to thoroughly piece together all the evidence and support his attorney colleagues on the case, and to meet the fees from counsel—the barrister they had hired—he was too drained to drive home.

He nestled his weary head down into the crook of his arms that were folded on the desk late one evening, after everyone else had left for home. He planned to get just a short halfhour nap to ensure he could get home safely.

"Momma, I'm so proud of you," Dallas said.

"Not as proud as I am of you," she answered.

He immediately requested her help to put Lake's case together. Dallas knew he was up for battle against the community once again.

It was the same community that had bullied him repeatedly because of his race.

It was the same community where teachers and students had taunted him, so he felt this was going to be his time to show them precisely what he'd learned from that Bible verse he'd been repeating to himself.

This was his time to shine. And by default, in his doing so, the good Lord Jesus Christ would get to shine too.

Dallas was sure they made a great team.

* * *

Dallas was appointed to his Judgeship just two years after working heavily on Lake's case. The fiasco involving the jailbird in his own family, and the battle against the formidable prosecution attorney named Cyrus, was all settled and put to rest some time ago. It was a relief for the whole Miller family—but, of course, everyone still felt the terrible loss of Bella-Luna.

But at least nobody needed to fret or worry anymore about Lake going to jail.

The sleepless nights had all come to a halt.

The case had concluded in favor of the defense. Lake, Dallas's fine brother Lake, was now a free man once again, with no ugly accusations of murder or anything else hanging over his head.

Over time, it became apparent in the news that although Dallas was not the defendant's lawyer throughout the trial, he worked at the same firm as Friedrichs and had been involved in his own brother's case.

And yet nobody would have known it; he had not jumped up and down, screaming and asserting himself, even when the case was not progressing so well. He had not insisted upon being the big 'I Am' in court and taking the reins away from his younger and less clued-up legal counterpart. Instead, he had passed on as much expertise and confidence to his colleague attorney as he could and had let the other man run the case as he saw fit, with no interference at all.

It was all a real show of what Dallas Miller, Criminal Lawyer, was made of, and the sort of man he was.

"He is made of nothing but impeccable legal knowledge, resolve, fortitude, and ethics," is what the firm's founder had said of him after the case was concluded. The quote was printed up in all the newspapers.

So, although Dallas had always disliked the idea that this involvement might come to light and damage his career, it proved to work oppositely. Everyone in the legal profession respected how Dallas, though significantly more experienced in handling this type of defense case, had handed the reins over to a different and younger, less experienced attorney— and he had done this even though it was his brother.

He had taken the risk, simply knowing that it was the right thing to do.

In the firm and the neighborhood, everyone said it showed integrity, spirit, and ethics. Oh, and someone said, it showed a true faith in God.

America's legal system relied heavily on the Lord to shine through, delivering righteous justice in complex cases. People believed that attorney Dallas Miller had done the right thing by taking a back seat and allowing the law and the Lord to work in harmony.

The fact that justice was served, and an innocent man did not spend his days incarcerated for a mistake anyone could make, was even better, they said.

Dallas was now well-known in the county and continued to escalate in his career.

He was a Judge now, in the criminal court, and wore the wig and the long, black robes that distinguished such fine men from anyone else.

He had aimed high, worked hard, overcome prejudice, attacks, and bullying, to get to where he now sat, up front in the courtroom where he presided over the most heinous and instrumental criminal cases. But he would never, ever forget his past, often looking back and remembering the day when Momma Donna had caught him napping at work. She had playfully chastised him for seemingly forgetting and casting off his background.

He did not forget it.

He would never forget it.

He did not—not for one small moment—set aside in his mind the memories of how he had sat alone in school, at playtimes, when the kids would not play with him because he had a different hue to his skin, or because his hair was curly and black, or because he had no birth mom and dad.

He would never forget how he was torn away from the group home, away from his only friend, Arnold, for whom most days he still shed a silent tear, not knowing what had become of the boy he had left there, all alone.

And he would never stop saying thank you to the Millers for seeing the value in him and picking him out that day, for investing in him, nurturing him, spoiling him, cherishing him…and believing in him.

No, he would never forget his lonely roots, his childhood upbringing, and the struggles he had to endure to see how the Lord loved him.

* * *

Now, Dallas knew everything there was to know about God and faith. He knew that it did not matter what lowly, seemingly 'godforsaken' background any child came from, the squalor and filth they lived in, the foul language their mother or their father spoke, the drugs or the drink their parents indulged in or how they might take the Lord's name in vain by swearing and cussing till they were blue in the face.

None of that mattered to God.

So why would it matter to him?

The only thing of any consequence was for a person—no matter their circumstances—to carry on trying, to carry on fighting, to have ambitions and to be the best person they could, despite everything.

He understood now what it had all been for.

Jesus Christ had been watching him and keeping notes in His big fat notebook about every boy and girl, every teenager, every young man or woman, to see if they would fall off the right path or carry on regardless, and the Lord had seen Dallas carry on. And the Lord had written it all down, and then every year, flicked through his notes to see where Dallas had gone wrong.

It was when Dallas began at the law firm that Jesus decided he had found a young man who had stayed true to himself and his faith, and that it was now abundantly clear Dallas would not deviate from that path, no matter what obstacles were deliberately thrown at him to test him. It was time to reward him.

That was when God and the angels held a conference and looked at Jesus's notes, and said, "We should send Momma Donna back to him, and we should give her another chance, too. Because she is trying to turn around her own life, just like her son." That was what they all agreed on, and that was what happened.

From then on, Jesus walked alongside Dallas Miller in everything he did.

And he had heard Dallas's prayers and heard him when he had stood before all those mirrors and repeated, "*I can do all things through Christ who strengthens me*," five times. And Jesus knew that here was a boy—and then a man—who would make it, and who could become anything he wanted to be in life.

Because of this, it was Jesus Christ who lifted Dallas when he felt low, or when he was on the verge of falling by the wayside.

There was a goodness in Dallas, and he brought that goodness with him into the courtroom. Sometimes, it was too busy there, with so much bad being committed in the world. There were endless trials and hearings.

Chapter 5: Faces from the Past

The morning sun filtered through the blinds of Dallas's office, casting golden bars of light across the worn edges of a faded Polaroid. Structure was his sanctuary, but on days like this, the echo of the past was louder than any gavel could silence. Each diploma on the wall felt a world away from the lonely boy hidden beneath a table, clutching a checkered napkin, hoping someone would finally see him.

Dallas's hand trembled as he reached for that photo. In its frame, an eleven-year-old version of himself blinked back—caught between the promise of belonging and the ache of not quite fitting in. Today, routine would give way to revelation: a knock at the door, three sharp raps that carried the weight of years.

When he opened it, memories rushed in. The visitor bore a familiar uncertainty in his eyes, as if the act of stepping into Dallas's world risked shattering it. It was Arnold—changed by time, but carrying the same quiet strength and sadness that had anchored Dallas through the worst of the group home years. Their greeting was awkward, a handshake that turned into a hug, both men acutely aware of what they'd lost—and what they'd managed to hold onto.

They sat in silence for a long moment, the glass of sunlight inching across the desk, as if time itself needed a minute to catch up. Arnold placed a battered chess piece—the black knight—on Dallas's stack of case files. "You told me to keep it safe," he said, voice thick. "Strength in silence, remember?" Dallas nodded, the old code sparking in his chest like a flare in midnight darkness.

Dallas rose and moved to the window, letting the light wash over his face. He opened his mouth once, then closed it, his throat too tight for words.

"You think…" he finally managed, voice strained, "you think Roman might be your son?"

"I don't know," Donna whispered. Her fingers tightened around the folder she held, the paper crinkling as her knuckles turned white. "But something deep in me says yes."

Dallas turned back toward her, the low hum of the city below no match for the pounding in his chest. Could it be? The odds, the impossibility of it, the quiet, aching hope that rose with the thought…

Roman.

Arnold.

His best friend from Fairview.

The older boy who had taught him checkers on a napkin grid. The boy who slipped away in the middle of the night with a too-tight hug and a promise that felt too big to ever be real.

Was it even possible?

Arnold's reappearance had cracked open a doorway Dallas didn't realize had been waiting for years. But in another part of the city—quiet, precise, and tucked behind the disciplined facade of a rising legal star—Roman Arnold was fighting a storm of his own.

Roman had spent his entire adult life controlling the uncontrollable. His files were immaculate, his dates color-coded, his suits pressed to perfection. Order had saved him. Routine had raised him. Achievement had protected him from asking questions no one could answer.

But inside him lived a boy who never stopped listening for footsteps in the hallway.

A boy who fell asleep gripping a small plastic knight.

A boy who wondered every birthday whether the woman who gave him life even remembered his name.

Roman had mastered the art of being unreadable.

In court, he was stone.

In negotiation, he was fire.

In solitude, he was glass.

And yet, the moment he stepped into the courtroom that day and saw Dallas—a familiar face he couldn't place, a presence that disrupted the borders of his perfectly contained world—something in him shifted.

Something ancient.

Something wounded.

Something hopeful.

Roman had learned to bury feelings so deeply that even memory struggled to find them. But now they came rising like floodwater: blurry echoes of a friend at Fairview, a boy with dark eyes and a trembling voice, a chess game drawn on a napkin, the silent bond two children formed to survive a system not built for them.

He had forgotten the boy's name.

He had never forgotten the feeling.

The courtroom was thick with tension that afternoon, the kind that made every breath slow and deliberate. Overhead lights hummed, throwing a hard glow across polished benches and the dark grain of wood. Papers rustled like whispers. Every cough, every shifting chair echoed louder than it should have.

Roman Arnold stood at the front of the room, spine straight, shoulders set beneath a crisp gray suit. His tie was perfectly knotted, his shoes shined to a mirror gloss that caught the fluorescent light. His eyes—

dark, focused—moved across the room with practiced precision. There was nothing hurried about him. Every gesture was measured. Every pause intentional. He was known for that: quiet authority, meticulous preparation, a presence that never needed to shout to be heard.

Dallas slipped in through the side door, the hinges sighing as he entered. He chose a seat in the back, far enough to watch, close enough to feel every word. He held a folder flat against his chest, though he never looked at it. His eyes were fixed on Roman.

He watched the way Roman's hand moved when he emphasized a point, the way he let silence settle after a question, the way his voice shifted from firm to almost gentle when he wanted the judge to lean in. This was Roman in his element—controlled, persuasive, utterly at home.

Donna sat a few rows behind Dallas, fingers twisting the fabric of her blouse, pulling and releasing the hem until the material creased. Her eyes were locked on Roman's face, tracing the familiar lines of his jaw, the birthmark, the set of his mouth. She watched like she was trying to read a story written in his features, a story only she might recognize. Her breaths came unevenly; she blinked hard whenever tears threatened, swallowing them back before they could fall.

At the front of the room, the defendant's voice wavered as he pled guilty. There was a brief pause, the soft crack of the gavel, a flurry of movement as papers were shuffled and notes were gathered.

Court adjourned.

The words hung in the air a moment longer than usual, as if the room itself needed time to absorb them.

Court adjourned.

But before the usual shuffle toward the exit began in earnest, Roman's voice cut in with measured clarity.

"Your Honor, if the court permits, the victim would like to address the defendant briefly as part of the sentencing record."

Judge Alvarez considered him for a beat. She knew Roman's reputation—precise, prepared, and not prone to theatrics.

"You may proceed, Mr. Arnold," she replied. "Briefly."

Roman turned toward the gallery. "Ms. Cortez," he called softly.

A woman in her late thirties rose from the second row. Her hands shook as she stepped forward, clutching her purse like a shield. She took the stand with visible effort, eyes darting toward the defendant—a slight man in his twenties with tired eyes and the restless posture of someone who'd used chaos as a coping strategy.

"Ma'am," Roman said gently, "I know we've gone over this, but for the record—can you state your name?"

"Gabriela Cortez," she whispered.

"And, Ms. Cortez, you were working at the Evergreen Pharmacy on May 17th of this year?"

"Yes."

Roman nodded, his tone inviting, not forceful. "Can you tell the court what you remember most from that day?"

She drew a breath, eyes unfocusing slightly as she went back there. "I remember the bell over the door. It rang, but I didn't really look up. I thought it was just another customer. Then I heard him shout." Her hands twisted in her lap. "He said to open the register. He had a gun."

Roman stepped closer, but not too close. "And what did you feel in that moment?"

Gabriela swallowed. "I thought I was going to die. I thought I'd never see my kids again. And I… I couldn't move. My legs just wouldn't work."

"Did the defendant fire the weapon?"

"No. But he waved it. At my face. At my chest." Her voice shook. "And I still wake up at night thinking I'm going to see that gun."

Roman nodded slowly. "Thank you, Ms. Cortez. No further questions."

The defense declined cross-examination. The defendant—Marcus Lane—stared at his shackled hands.

When Judge Alvarez turned back to him, her posture softened only slightly. "Mr. Lane, you've pleaded guilty. Is there anything you want to say before I sentence you?"

He swallowed hard.

"I was high," he rasped. "I thought I just… I thought I needed money. I didn't think about her. I didn't think about—about anybody. I'm sorry." His eyes flitted to Gabriela and away again, as if he didn't feel entitled to look at her for more than a second. "I never meant to actually shoot. But I know that doesn't matter."

Roman watched him closely, cataloguing every tremor, every flinch. This was the part no textbook ever fully captured—the thin line between remorse and regret, between someone sorry they did it and someone sorry they got caught.

"Your Honor," Roman said, stepping forward, "the State recognizes Mr. Lane's guilty plea and lack of prior felonies. However, the impact on Ms. Cortez has been profound and ongoing. The use of a firearm, even unloaded, carries a terror that doesn't end when the door closes behind the offender. We're asking for a sentence that reflects both accountability and the chance for genuine rehabilitation."

Judge Alvarez nodded and delivered a structured sentence—years in state prison, with mandated addiction treatment and trauma-informed counseling.

As the bailiff led Marcus away, Roman didn't celebrate. He simply exhaled, a long, quiet release, like someone setting down a weight only to pick up another.

It was then that his gaze drifted to the gallery—and collided with Donna's.

Her expression was unreadable at first, then cracked open with something raw and unguarded. Recognition. Grief. Hope.

Roman's step faltered.

For reasons he couldn't name yet, the case didn't feel finished. A guilty plea had been entered. Sentence had been passed. Justice, by all visible measures, had been done.

And yet, as Donna stared at him from the second row, her fingers pressed to trembling lips, Roman felt a strange, undeniable sense that this had only been a prelude.

Only then did he gather his files and tap them into alignment, the practiced motion of a man closing one chapter without realizing another had already begun.

Roman stacked his files neatly and tapped them into alignment, the simple, practiced motion of a man closing another chapter in a long day. He turned, ready to leave the weight of the case behind.

But his gaze collided with Donna's.

She froze, fingers still curled around the bench. Her eyes, wide and shining, held his with a look that was equal parts hope and fear—and something older, deeper, impossible to name. Roman stopped mid-step. The folder in his hand slipped slightly before he tightened his grip.

For a heartbeat, the noise of the room faded. The scrape of chairs, murmured conversations, the shuffle toward the exit—everything dimmed around them. The air between them seemed to thicken, charged with something neither of them could define.

Roman blinked. Confusion flickered in his eyes. He didn't know why her face hit him like a wave crashing against a distant, forgotten shore. But it stirred something in him—something buried, something that refused to be ignored.

Donna looked away first. She fumbled for her purse and papers, movements clumsy and rushed, her composure fraying at the edges.

Roman turned toward the exit, but his mind didn't follow his feet. The weight of her gaze lingered like a hand on his shoulder long after he stepped into the hallway.

That night, in the soft glow of his apartment, Roman sat at his desk, a half-empty glass of water pushed aside, untouched. The light from his computer screen glowed against the tired lines beneath his eyes.

He opened the courthouse directory. His fingers hovered over the keyboard before he typed.

Donna Jackson. Intake Clerk. Start date: [six months ago].

The entry was clinical, factual. But the name pulsed with something far from neutral.

He stared at it, the room shrinking around him as old shadows shifted in the corners of his memory.

His chest tightened.

Slowly, he opened a new tab. The words came harder this time, his fingers trembling as he typed:

Fairview Youth Center.

He hadn't let himself think about that place in years. The very name twisted something in his gut. He could almost smell the sharp sting of bleach, hear the muffled crying of children who had learned that loud tears brought the wrong kind of attention.

The records were buried beneath layers of outdated systems and broken links. But he kept digging, following the administrative breadcrumbs with stubborn persistence.

And then he found it.

Arnold D. Jackson.

His birth name.

The sight of it jolted him like electricity. Every nerve in his body felt awake and unsteady. He stared at the screen, breath caught somewhere in his throat, the blinking cursor suddenly loud in the silence.

Donna.

He pressed a hand to his forehead, eyes squeezed shut as the fragments of his past shifted and locked into place. The landscape of his life—the story he thought he knew—rearranged itself in an instant.

He didn't sleep that night.

The next morning, Roman requested a meeting with Dallas.

The office was quiet when he arrived. The low hum of the building's heating system filled the space, blending with the steady ticking of the wall clock. Roman stepped inside, briefcase in hand, his steps slow but deliberate. The leather at the edges of the case was worn, softened by years of use.

Dallas rose from his chair, setting a folder aside. It felt unimportant now. Whatever Roman was about to say demanded more space than any case file could hold.

"Roman," Dallas greeted, his voice calm but threaded with something tighter beneath—anticipation, maybe. Or dread. Or both.

"Thank you for seeing me," Roman replied. His voice was even, but quieter than usual. Less courtroom. More human.

"Of course. Have a seat." Dallas motioned to the chair across from him. The leather creaked as Roman sat down, his posture composed but not relaxed.

Roman adjusted his tie, more out of habit than necessity. His fingers lingered at the knot before dropping to his lap, where he laced them together so tightly the skin along his knuckles blanched.

"I won't waste your time," he began, taking in a steadying breath. He let it go slowly, his words emerging on the exhale. "I think… your intake clerk might be my birth mother."

Dallas's breath left him in a slow, quiet rush. The air between them seemed to hold the sentence, refusing to let it pass easily.

"What makes you say that?" Dallas asked. His tone was soft but direct, giving Roman something solid to stand on.

Roman looked down at his hands. "There's a birthmark on my face. She stared at it like it hurt to look at. Then I looked her up. Her name matched the records from Fairview."

Dallas said nothing. He let the silence stretch gently, not as an absence, but as room—room for Roman's truth to settle.

"I've never searched before," Roman admitted, his voice dropping. "Never wanted to. But now…" He swallowed, the word catching. "Now I couldn't not."

Dallas's chair scraped softly against the floor as he stood and walked to the file cabinet. He opened it and pulled out a well-worn folder, its edges soft from being handled too many times.

He returned and laid it in front of Roman.

"My mother came to see me yesterday," Dallas said. His voice was steady but warm. "She told me what she saw. What she felt."

Roman's eyes shot up, widening.

"She thinks you're her son," Dallas continued.

Roman's hands trembled as he stared at the folder. The pages inside were suddenly more than paper. They were proof. They were history.

They were him.

Neither of them spoke for a long time. The clock ticked steady seconds as the truth settled between them.

Finally, Roman's voice broke the silence.

"She named me Roman?"

A faint smile touched Dallas's lips. "She did."

Roman blinked, tears gathering in his eyes despite his efforts to hold them back. "I always thought my adoptive parents chose it. I thought they just… liked the name."

"It was always yours," Dallas said gently. "From the beginning."

Roman leaned back, his grip tightening on the arms of the chair as if the room had tilted beneath him. "Why didn't she find me sooner?"

"She tried," Dallas answered quietly. "They never told her where you went. She didn't know how to reach you. Only that you existed. Somewhere."

Roman dropped his gaze to the floor, his shoulders sagging under the weight of all the years he had spent believing he was alone. "I didn't think I had anyone."

"You did," Dallas said, leaning forward, voice low and sure. "You always did."

Roman looked up slowly, studying Dallas's face. A spark of recognition flickered in his eyes.

"Wait," he whispered. "Fairview. That checkerboard. Dallas?"

Dallas nodded, a small, knowing smile forming. The memory sat clear in his mind, bright against the dark backdrop of the group home.

In that instant, they were no longer two professionals meeting in an office.

They were two boys again.

Two boys hiding in a corner of a crowded home, bent over a makeshift board drawn onto a napkin. Two boys sharing food, stories, strategy, and the silent understanding of what it meant to be unwanted.

"I taught you checkers," Roman said, almost to himself, the ghost of a laugh wrapped around the words.

"You taught me how to survive," Dallas replied.

They sat in a quiet that was no longer empty. It was full—of years, of loss, of connection reclaimed.

Roman let out a small, incredulous laugh, shaking his head. "This is insane."

Dallas leaned back, the tension in his shoulders finally softening into something lighter. "No," he said with a soft, disbelieving smile. "It's a miracle."

Donna was waiting in the break room when Roman stepped inside.

She stood as soon as she saw him, though her movements were stiff, as if her body moved before her mind could catch up. Her palms smoothed down the sides of her skirt again and again. She drew in a breath and lifted her eyes to his.

Roman walked toward her slowly. The hum of the vending machine and the faint ticking of the microwave clock felt too loud, too ordinary for what was happening between them.

He stopped just in front of her. Up close, he could see the faint lines time had carved around her eyes, the tremble in her lower lip, the way her hands shook as she clasped them tightly together.

"My name is Roman Arnold," he said quietly. His voice trembled but held. "But I was born Arnold Jackson."

For a moment, everything stilled.

The lights hummed overhead. The stale scent of coffee hung in the air. But none of it mattered.

Donna's eyes filled instantly, tears spilling before she could even try to stop them. Her hand flew to her mouth as a broken sound escaped her—a sound pulled up from somewhere deep and long-silent.

Roman reached into his pocket with unsteady fingers and pulled out a small, worn photograph. The edges were softened from years of being handled. In it, a four-year-old boy sat at a foster home table with a plastic spoon in his hand, looking just past the camera—half hopeful, half uncertain.

"I've carried this my whole life," Roman said, his voice thick. "But I never knew who took it."

Donna stepped closer, eyes locked on the photo. The memory rose in her with almost painful clarity—the cheap camera, the stained table, the way she had tried to capture just one moment of her boy before the world took more from her.

"I did," she whispered. Her voice cracked on the words. "I took it."

He nodded, tears now sliding freely down his cheeks. The truth settled around them, fragile and absolute.

Then they moved—at the same time, without another word.

They closed the distance in a few steps, wrapping their arms around each other like they were trying to erase the decades between them.

Donna buried her face in his shoulder, her sobs muffled against his suit. Her hands clung to him desperately, as if afraid he might vanish if she let go.

Roman held her just as tightly. His eyes closed, his forehead resting lightly against her hair as wave after wave of emotion crashed through him—grief for what was lost, relief for what had been found, and something like peace slipping into the hollow places where emptiness used to sit.

Across the building, in his office, Dallas stood by the window, blinds casting narrow stripes of light across his face. From where he stood, he could see them through the glass of the break room door.

He watched quietly, his heart full.

Three lives once shattered.

Now, slowly, carefully, being made whole.

The past had finally collided with the present.

And though it felt like an ending, Dallas knew better.

This was only the beginning.

The city was waking. Miami's skyline climbed through the soft orange haze, windows catching fire at dawn, but inside Dallas's office, the hush was sacred—a haven carved out of chaos. The blinds slit patterns across the furniture, making everything look fragmented, divided between light and shadow. Dallas stood in the stillness, fingers brushing the rough edges of a Polaroid, the old photo both artifact and wound.

He inhaled, felt the dry tickle in his throat, the familiar tension in his jaw. There were days when the law was enough—days when the structure, the calendar blocks and syllabi, the lines of the statute books, would drown out everything. But this morning, every framed certificate seemed to waver on the wall as if doubting the very foundations of his carefully curated life.

He stared at the photo—himself at eleven, a boy of sharp elbows and guarded eyes, smile ghostly and unsure. There was hunger in the gaze, longing for something unnamed. Belonging, maybe. The truth was, all the verdicts Dallas would ever hand down grew in the shadow of that lonely child.

Then came the knock—three clear, deliberate raps. Not frightened, not demanding. Familiar.

Dallas's heart stumbled. His hand hovered, then pressed flat to the surface of the desk as he called out, "Come in." The door swung inward on a draft tinged with the distant salt of the sea, Miami's pulse humming just through the concrete walls.

Arnold stood there. The years had sculpted new lines into his face, silver threading the hair above his ear. He was broader, quieter than the quick-witted, sunburned boy at Fairview. But Dallas could still see the checkered napkin on Arnold's lap, could remember how the older boy had traced game pieces out of nothing, had spun stories of knights and battles that made the world—if only for a heartbeat—gentle again.

The men hesitated, caught on the edge between past and present. A handshake, then a squeeze of shoulders that dissolved, unexpectedly, into a hug. Short. Fierce. Steeped in old codes that didn't need new names.

When they sat, the silence wasn't awkward, just heavy with years. The light climbed higher, spotlighting the chess piece Arnold slid from his pocket. A black knight, battered at the mane. Dallas let out a breath, an embarrassingly small sound. He remembered—how could he not? "Strength in silence," he whispered, and Arnold nodded, the words unlocking a section of Dallas's chest he'd boarded up long ago.

"You kept it," Dallas said, awe mixing with grief.

"It got me through," Arnold replied. He looked down, thumb running the plastic smooth. "On nights it seemed like nobody remembered us, I'd hold it and imagine you did."

Dallas wanted to say a hundred things. Thank you. I'm sorry you left. I needed you. Instead, he asked, "Why now? What brings you here?"

Before Arnold could answer, a new presence filled the doorway— Donna, hair pinned in tight coils, a folder trembling in her hands. She stepped in, shoulders squared, eyes gleaming wet. Breakfast smells— toast, burnt butter—clung to her like armor for a day that could unmake her. Donna's gaze darted between the two men, looking for… what?

"Sorry to crash," she managed, and Dallas stiffened in his chair. His mother was both comfort and unfinished business. Yet beneath her defenses, something raw trembled—a mother's hope burning through time.

She pressed the folder down on the desk, her knuckles blanching. "I need… I wanted to talk to both of you."

Arnold reached out, gentle, not wanting to startle her. "You can. Take your time."

Dallas watched as Donna's composure wavered. In her eyes, he saw the room at Fairview, the smell of bleach and hopelessness, the endless waiting for doors that never opened. He saw a woman who loved messily, fiercely, badly—but always.

She pushed the folder closer. Dallas opened it, his hands careful. Documents, court records, a photograph—a four-year-old boy at a battered table, looking up, captured mid-question.

"My son," Donna whispered. "Roman…" Her voice caught. She tried again. "I think he's here. In this city. I think—God, I know—I think Arnold… Roman… is my boy."

A pause thickened into panic. Arnold, stilled by some force ancient and aching, opened his jaw. "My name was Arnold. I always hated it. I changed it after… after adoption. I became Roman Arnold." His lips trembled, saying the names aloud, seeing them clatter together like magnets he couldn't pull apart.

Dallas felt the hairs on his arms rise. "All these years, Mom. Why didn't you ever tell me you had another son…"

Donna folded in on herself, not from shame, but sorrow. "I lost him before I ever had the chance to be a mother. They took you both. Roman was first… I never even had time to hold him. Dallas, you were born in a storm, boy. But I tried… I tried so hard to hold on."

Arnold—Roman—leaned forward, elbows braced on knees. "What happened, Donna?"

Her story poured out—foster system, decisions made without her, nights of addiction, the mornings spent praying for a sign, a letter, any detail. Just one more chance to know her children.

The silence afterward was complete and unjudging.

Across the city, in a law office boxed in clean lines and glass, another man wrestled with secrets his mind couldn't untangle. Roman, the name he chose, was order itself—a tide of appointments, color-coded calendars, obligations defined down to the minute. But the question left by Donna's folder gnawed at him. There was a birthmark… and her face had softened with pain when he passed her in the hall.

Alone in his apartment that night, Roman let habit guide him—files arranged, suit pressed, but the movements went slack as the memories clawed free. He found himself on a battered website searching for "Fairview Youth Center." He scrolled through outdated PDFs and half-broken links until he found the records, reading the entries again and again. Arnold D. Jackson. His own name. And then Dallas Arnold Jackson—a brother, a line on a paper, a ghost in every childhood dream.

Roman felt his chest tighten. Not with fear, but with hunger—a need for explanation, for the right of reply, for truth to outlast silence.

The next morning, he asked for a meeting.

Dallas's office felt smaller with Roman in it. The judge's gavel, that symbol of power and finality, seemed pathetic against what Roman was about to say.

"I need answers," Roman began, voice tuned lower, less sure. "I think Donna is my mother."

Dallas didn't dispute it. "She thinks so, too."

Roman looked at his own hands, then up at Dallas. "I've spent my life controlling the uncontrollable. But I can't control this. I don't know how to… be a son. Or a brother. Not anymore."

Dallas, who had spent a lifetime burying grief beneath achievement, recognized the plea. "Maybe you don't have to know how. Maybe you just have to try."

A door opened quietly behind them. Donna entered, her eyes rimmed with red, something like hope floating in her bearing. For a moment, no one spoke—the world's noise fell away.

Roman broke first. He pulled out a photo—creased, worn at the corners—of his four-year-old self in a sunlit kitchen, gripping a plastic spoon. "Have you… do you know this picture?" he asked.

Donna cupped her hands around her mouth. The memory was a tidal wave. "I took that. The day they told me I couldn't keep you. You were watching cartoons. I needed one thing to hold onto."

She stepped forward, overcome by a need to bridge the decades. Roman let the photo fall to the desk, rising as Donna crossed the distance. Mother and son found each other in a choked embrace, arms tight, tears wetting skin and silk alike. Every year, every longing, every empty birthday candle found a place in that grip.

For a long while, Dallas watched, his heart full, his regrets dissolving in something like grace.

Not far away, the city thrummed, indifferent, but for the three lives in that room, time bent around reunion.

Outside, a sunbeam split the office blinds, crawling across the desk, warming the photograph, the folder, the knight chess piece—the relics of their shared wounds and found salvation.

This wasn't just a moment of healing. It was a beginning—messy, unfinished, and real.

Chapter 6: Bloodlines and Burdens

The courthouse buzzed like a beehive—footsteps ricocheting off marble floors, phones ringing in clipped tones, and hushed conversations curling up toward the high ceiling lined with portraits of judges past. Interns rushed by with overstuffed files clutched to their chests, attorneys checked their phones between hearings, and the security guards swapped quiet jokes by the metal detectors. The tang of strong coffee and laser printer ink hung in the air like a second atmosphere.

But inside Judge Dallas Jackson's chambers, time refused to move.

The soft tick of the clock above the bookshelf was the only sound, marking each second with maddening precision as if the room itself were counting down. The heavy door was closed, the blinds half-drawn, slicing pale light across the walls and cutting through the framed degrees and family photos.

Dallas sat at his desk, elbows braced on the polished surface, staring at the letter Donna had slipped into his hand just minutes ago outside the courtroom. The paper trembled slightly between his fingers, the edges soft with handling, the ink blurred where tears had fallen.

Her shaky but deliberate script read:

Dallas, I believe Roman is your brother.

He'd read the line twelve times already and it still didn't land softly. It scraped. It tore. It rearranged the past.

It wasn't just a suspicion anymore. Not just an ache or a question buried under years of survival.

It was truth—raw, unrelenting—clawing its way into daylight.

Dallas leaned back in his chair. The leather creaked in protest, echoing the pressure mounting in his chest. For a moment the room blurred, and he wasn't forty anymore, or a sitting judge, or the face of judicial integrity in Miami-Dade County.

He was eleven again.

He was under the cafeteria table at Fairview Youth Center because the noise was too much, clutching a half-torn paper knight, listening to Arnold's small voice whisper, "Strength in silence, D. When the world gets loud, we stay quiet and strong."

He remembered the promise: We'll be brothers forever.

He remembered the day the bed down the hall went empty. The name tag gone. The blanket folded. The word adopted sinking like a stone in his stomach.

Now that friend had a new name.

Roman.

And his old life—every abandoned hallway, every whispered prayer, every silent meal—suddenly had a new meaning.

Dallas pressed the heel of his hand to his forehead, willing himself to breathe through the shock. For years, he had kept the memories of Fairview packed away in tidy boxes in the back of his mind. He let them out only in small, controlled doses—just enough to fuel his compassion, never enough to drown him.

But this letter had torn the boxes apart.

Roman—Arnold. Not just a protector. Not just a friend.

His brother.

His blood.

His fingers loosened and the letter slipped to the desk, landing beside the black chess knight that always sat near his lamp. He traced the familiar grooves of the piece, the plastic worn smooth by decades of turning it over in anxious palms.

"Strength in silence," he murmured.

Only now silence felt heavy, like the wrong kind of strength. The kind that kept truths buried and families apart.

His phone buzzed. A text from the clerk.

Clerk: Judge, counsel are ready on the Miller matter whenever you are.

Clerk: Bailiff says gallery is already full.

The Miller matter.

Lake.

Dallas's jaw tightened. His world wasn't just shifting—it was tilting, shuddering, dragging every fragile piece of his identity with it.

He had built his adulthood on a sturdy story:

He was a foster kid who got a second chance.

He was the boy the Millers chose.

He was the one who outran the statistics.

Now the foundations beneath that story were cracking, and beneath them, bloodlines ran like buried rivers he'd never charted.

He swallowed hard and forced his focus outward.

In a matter of minutes, he would walk back into Courtroom 4B wearing the robe the county trusted and the composure the public expected. On the docket: motions in The People v. Lake Miller—his brother, his shield from childhood, now facing the weight of a homicide charge.

At the prosecution table stood Roman Arnold—his first brother, whether he wanted to claim that word or not.

And somewhere in the gallery sat Donna—his biological mother, clutching papers and prayers.

Bloodlines and burdens, all converging in one room.

Dallas pushed his chair back and stood. His knees resisted, heavy with the years between the boy he had been and the man he had become.

He picked up the letter again and folded it with slow, careful movements. There was something sacred about the flimsy page— terrible and holy at once.

He slipped it into the inside pocket of his robe.

"Alright," he whispered to the empty room. "Let's see what the truth costs."

He reached for the door, took a breath that felt too shallow, and stepped out into the hallway.

Downstairs — Donna & Roman

On the courthouse steps, Donna sat with her fingers woven so tightly together her knuckles blanched white. Each inhale scraped against her ribs. The air held the faint chill of late afternoon, stirred occasionally by passing buses and the murmur of downtown traffic.

She'd been here countless times before—dragged in cuffs, escorted in chains, sitting in holding rooms that smelled of bleach and despair. But never like this.

Today she was here by choice.

Today her hands shook not from withdrawal, but from hope.

Every breath was a silent plea:

Let it finally be enough.

Let him not turn away.

Let God grant me this one thing.

She adjusted her denim jacket, more for comfort than warmth, and wiped her damp palms on her jeans. Her eyes kept dragging to the tall glass doors, expecting Dallas to walk out, expecting security to tap her shoulder and tell her she didn't belong here in his world.

Instead, footsteps echoed behind her.

Roman.

He approached with a confidence he didn't fully feel, his stride measured and calm, but his eyes searching—always searching. The crisp line of his tailored suit, the glint of his badge clipped to his belt, the neatness of his life—all of it trembled around the edges today.

He stopped in front of her.

"Hey," he said softly.

Donna looked up. Up close, she could see it clearly now—the faint birthmark near his jaw shaped like a thumbprint, the slight tilt of his brow, the same curve of lips she had kissed seconds after he entered the world. She had memorized his features in the two stolen days she had with him. Thirty years later, her memory had not lied.

Her voice came out cracked. "Hi."

Roman shifted, the file in his hand bending slightly under his grip. "I, uh… I found the record," he said. "My original birth name. Roman Arnold Jackson." He swallowed. "It was yours. Mine."

Donna's hand flew to her mouth. A small, stunned gasp escaped.

"I… I named you after my father," she whispered. "Roman Jackson. He was the only gentle man I ever knew."

Roman's breath hitched. He'd grown up with adoptive parents who were stable, kind, middle-class—people who packed lunches and came to school concerts, who made sure he wore a seatbelt and saw a dentist twice a year. But gentleness—this holy, trembling kind of gentleness in Donna's eyes—was something else entirely.

"I didn't know," he said softly. "I never knew any of it."

"Well…" Donna's gaze dropped to the concrete. "I didn't get to tell you." She stared at a crack in the step as if the right words might be tucked inside it. "They took you at birth. I… I was using. They said I couldn't keep you. I tried to get clean, but…" She exhaled, a fraying sound. "Addiction chained me hard. It took until after Dallas before I could even breathe right again."

Silence settled between them—thick, fragile, glowing at the edges like something newly forged.

"I used to dream someone out there loved me," Roman admitted, his voice barely above a whisper. "Even if I never met them. I just… I wanted that to be true so badly." He looked at her. "I never knew it was you."

Tears tracked down Donna's cheeks before she could wipe them away. "You were always loved. Even when I was too broken to keep you." Her shoulders shook once. "I carried you every day after they took you. On birthdays I didn't get to celebrate. On Christmas mornings. At every rehab meeting. I prayed Psalm after Psalm and that verse your brother loves—Philippians 4:13—over your name, even when I didn't deserve to say it."

She fumbled inside her bag and pulled out a wrinkled envelope, edges yellowed, ink faded.

"I wrote you letters," she said. "Hundreds. I never knew where to send them, so I just… kept them. This is the first one." She pressed it into his hand. "From the day after you were born. I was still in the hospital. I didn't know they'd take you yet, not for sure. I wrote about your cry. Your little fingers. How you wrapped your hand around mine like you'd known me your whole life."

Roman stared at the envelope like it was something radioactive and sacred all at once.

"Can I… read it now?" he asked.

Donna shook her head, smiling through tears. "You can. Or you can wait. Just… promise you'll read it sometime."

He tucked it carefully into the inside pocket of his coat, next to his phone, close to his heart.

Roman cleared his throat and reached into his own pocket.

"I, um… I brought something too." He pulled out a small black chess knight, edges smoothed by time. "Dallas gave me this the night I left Fairview. We were kids. He said it meant 'strength in silence.' I didn't know why I kept it, but… I guess I do now."

Donna choked out a soft, breaking laugh. "He's kept the board all these years. Folded under his bed at the Millers' first, then in his closets later. That knight's the missing piece."

Their smiles trembled but didn't break.

"Do you hate me?" Donna asked suddenly, the question tumbling out raw. Her voice shrank. "For the life you had? For the questions? For not being there?"

Roman held her gaze. For a moment, the prosecutor—the man who built cases from facts and evidence—struggled to gather words for something that had no clear precedent.

"I don't know what I feel yet," he admitted. "There's anger. And grief. And… something like gratitude. Because if you hadn't… if things hadn't gone the way they did… I don't know who I'd be. Or if I'd even be here." He paused. "But I don't hate you."

Donna nodded, shoulders shaking with relief.

"I just want the chance to know you," he added quietly. "Like… really know you. Not the paperwork version."

She let out a breath that sounded like a prayer answered halfway.

"That's all I ever wanted," she said. "A chance."

A car horn blared in the distance. A gust of wind made her shiver. After a moment, Roman glanced toward the doors.

"They're probably waiting on me upstairs," he murmured. "We've got a full docket. And…" He hesitated. "Lake's case."

Donna's throat tightened. "That's Dallas's brother," she said, almost to herself. "His first family after Fairview."

"I know." Roman adjusted his tie, the prosecutor sliding back into place. "This system has a sick sense of humor."

He started to turn, but Donna caught his sleeve.

"Roman?"

He looked back.

"I prayed for you and Dallas together," she whispered. "For years. I didn't know how God could fix what I broke. But you both made it. Different ways. And you're both up there now—one in a robe, one in a suit." She smiled through tears. "Don't let the system steal what's ours again."

For a man whose life was built on rules and process, the words landed like a verdict.

"I'll do my best," he said. "For both of us."

He squeezed her hand once and headed inside.

Donna watched him go, then bowed her head.

"Philippians 4:13," she whispered. "For my boys. Always."

The Holding Cell — Lake

On a lower level of the courthouse, beneath the polished marble and portraits, the air grew colder and more metallic. Down here, concrete replaced oak paneling, and the soundtrack was a chorus of clinking chains and murmured curses.

Lake Miller sat on a narrow bench in a holding cell, elbows on his knees, hands clasped so hard his knuckles ached. His orange jumpsuit sagged slightly at the shoulders, as if even the fabric had grown tired.

He stared at the small scuffed window on the cell door, where a strip of brighter light bled through whenever someone passed.

The last time Lake had been inside a courthouse, he'd sat in a wooden pew with Sara and Hunter at his sides, watching Dallas take the bench for the first time. He'd joked that his little brother looked like he was playing dress-up. Dallas had rolled his eyes, but Lake saw the pride burning under his calm.

He'd never imagined his next courtroom appearance would be like this.

"Lake Miller," the deputy called, glancing at the clipboard, "you good?"

Lake huffed out a half-laugh.

"Define good," he muttered.

The deputy shrugged, something almost sympathetic in his expression. "Your attorney's upstairs already. They'll bring you up in a few."

Lake nodded absently and let his mind drift, because replaying that night for the hundredth time wasn't going to undo it.

He saw it anyway.

His wife's laugh echoing in the kitchen.

The sound of metal clinking as he cleaned the gun he never should've bought.

The flash. The scream. The silence.

The security footage had shown what he already knew—there had been no fight, no malice, no intent. Just a careless man and a loaded weapon and the cruel speed of tragedy.

The state called it manslaughter. Some of the headlines called him worse.

Dallas had tried to take the case at first. Lake had seen that determined glint in his little brother's eyes, the same look from when they were kids and Dallas insisted he could fix the broken lawnmower on his own.

But judges weren't supposed to preside over their own family's cases. It was almost laughable, how quick the ethics board had moved when it was about one of their own.

Dallas had stepped aside. Another judge had entered. The machine had kept grinding on.

Lake thought about Donna—he hadn't grown up with her, but he'd watched her from afar once Dallas let her in, watched the awkward dinners and long talks and scribbled letters. He thought about Roman, the new variable in an already complicated equation.

Mostly, he thought about Dallas as a kid—small, cautious, eyes too old for his face—trailing after him in the yard of their first foster home.

Stick by me, Lake had told him. I got you.

Now here he was, waiting for strangers to call him defendant and decide his fate while his little brother carried the weight of a gavel one floor above.

He let his head fall back against the wall.

"God," he murmured, the word unfamiliar but not unwelcome in his mouth. "If You're still anywhere near this mess, don't let him break for me. He's carried enough."

His voice was swallowed by the hum of fluorescent lights and distant doors slamming shut.

That Night — Dallas's Townhouse

Rain tapped rhythmically against the windows of Dallas's townhouse that night, streaking the glass and blurring the city lights beyond. The storm outside lent a quiet soundtrack to the hush within.

The living room glowed with warm lamplight. A soft throw blanket was draped over the side of the couch, one of the chess sets from his youth sat on the coffee table—board unfolded, pieces halfway set up as if someone had abandoned a game mid-opening.

Three mismatched mugs of tea steamed between them: one chipped navy mug Dallas had kept since law school, one floral cup Donna had insisted was "too pretty to stay in the cabinet," and a plain white mug Roman had pulled at random from the shelf.

Dallas, Donna, and Roman sat together for the first time—not bound by the sterile formality of a courtroom, not separated by benches and microphones and protocols—but as three people trying to rearrange decades of hurt into something like a family.

The silence between them was thick but not empty. It was packed with unasked questions.

Dallas broke it first.

"So," he said, fingers resting lightly on his mug, "we're all horrible at small talk."

Donna snorted through her nose, a fragile laugh that surprised even her.

Roman's mouth tilted into a small smile. "I cross-examine witnesses for a living," he said. "This is… harder."

Dallas lifted his gaze to Roman. Even now, with the letter tucked in his pocket and the records burned into his mind, it still felt surreal— looking at this man and knowing he was Arnold. The boy who stole extra bread rolls for him at Fairview. The boy who'd promised brotherhood with toaster crumbs still on his fingers.

"So," Roman ventured slowly, "I was your best friend… and your brother. And neither of us knew it."

"Not then," Dallas said softly.

He swallowed, feeling a knot in his throat loosen just enough to let truth through.

"You were the only good thing at Fairview," he admitted. "You taught me how to throw a punch and how not to pick one. You taught me how to make a paper airplane with one hand because the other had to hold your tray." A ghost of a smile crossed his face. "You told me I could be anything. Lawyer, judge, astronaut. All while we were fighting over stale cereal."

Roman let out a breath that trembled at the end. "You were the first person who made me feel like my weird quiet didn't mean I was broken," he said. "You used to sit with me when the older kids picked on me for my freckles. Remember? You'd quote that Bible verse you barely knew—Philippians 4:13—like a shield."

Dallas blinked. "You remember that?"

"I remember you," Roman said simply. "Everything else is pieces."

Donna wiped at her cheeks quietly.

"You boys saved each other back then," she whispered. "And I didn't even know where you were."

Dallas turned to her, something softer than anger settling in his chest. For years, whenever he'd thought of her, it had been through a lens of abandonment and near-death. He'd seen her as the woman who'd chosen a high over a baby.

But now he saw the letters. The tin box. The rehab meetings. The way her hand shook when she reached for her tea, not from withdrawals— but from the weight of finally being here.

"I spent years asking why," he said, his voice quieter than he intended. "Why it had to get that bad before someone intervened. Why nobody checked on the house. Why they took me and never looked back. Why you didn't come." He held her gaze. "I built a whole life on the assumption that you didn't care enough to fight for me."

Donna flinched like he'd slapped her. "I did fight," she whispered. "Just… too late. Too clumsy. Too high. Too ashamed." Her eyes shone with tears. "Every time I tried to clean up, something pulled me back. Your father—David—he kept me using because a sober woman might leave. Razor taught me that love was a leash. By the time they took you, I was half-dead myself."

Roman frowned. "David?"

"Your father, Dallas," Donna said, voice shaking. "Razor's son. The same man who dragged me deeper after Razor ruined me. I didn't know at first. I just thought it was… some curse that I kept ending up with men who treated me like inventory."

She swallowed.

"When I realized David was Razor's son, I panicked. But I was already pregnant. With you."

The room seemed to grow smaller.

Dallas stared at her, stunned. "So the man who pimped you out… his son is my father."

Donna nodded.

"And Roman's father?" he asked.

"Different man," she said. "Different mistake. Same broken girl."

Roman looked down at his hands, as if tracing the lines of his own existence. "So we share a mother and trauma," he said. "But not a father."

"Blood is messy," Donna whispered. "Sin is messy. But love can still be real inside all that mess."

Dallas let out a breath, leaning back. It wasn't absolution. It wasn't erasure of what happened. But it was context. And context mattered.

He looked at Roman. "You resent me?" he asked. "For being chosen by a family when you weren't?"

Roman shook his head immediately. "No," he said. "I was adopted too, remember? Different family, different city. They did their best. They gave me stability, a bed, braces, every advantage they could. But…" He searched for the right words. "There was always this… itch under my skin. This feeling like something was missing. Like a part of my story had been ripped out of the file."

Dallas understood that itch. He'd carried his own version—a blank space where his origins should've been.

"I started working with a nonprofit a few years ago," Roman continued. "Roots & Futures. Helps adults who aged out of the system find their biological families if they want to. I thought it was just a job at first. A passion project." He huffed a small laugh. "Turns out, I was practicing on other people what I needed for myself."

He glanced at Donna. "I've helped teenagers track down parents who got clean. I've stood in living rooms when mothers sobbed at the sight of kids they thought were lost. The whole time, I told myself I wasn't curious about my own file." His mouth twisted. "But I was."

Donna nodded slowly. "And now you've found us," she said. "For better or worse."

"For better and worse," Roman corrected gently.

Dallas cleared his throat, suddenly aware of the file lying open on his coffee table—a printout of Roman's juvenile records, the Fairview intake logs, adoption forms. The judicial side of him had demanded to see proof. The child side of him had just wanted the magic of recognition.

"Do you blame me?" Dallas asked quietly. "For not looking for you? For not going back to Fairview sooner?"

Roman studied him for a long moment.

"You were a kid," he said finally. "We were both kids. Then you were a foster kid trying not to get sent back, then a law student trying to survive, then a Black man in this system trying to climb without getting crushed." He shook his head. "You did what you had to do. We both did."

He reached forward and picked up the chess knight from the table, rolling it between his fingers.

"Besides," he added, voice softening, "you did carry me. Every time you pulled a kid from the edge in your courtroom, you carried me. Every time you gave some scared teenager a second chance, you were keeping our promise: we'll be brothers forever, no matter who's listening."

Dallas blinked hard, his vision blurring. "Damn," he muttered weakly, "you got good at this feelings thing."

Roman smirked. "You should see me in closing arguments."

Donna chuckled through her tears.

"I'll say this," she murmured. "If the devil meant to destroy us, he underestimated my boys. A judge and a prosecutor? That's poetic."

"Trauma's favorite coping mechanism," Dallas said dryly. "Overachieve until people forget where you came from."

They all laughed, and something loosened in the air.

For the first time that night, the silence between them felt less like a wall and more like a bridge being built plank by plank.

A Week Later — A Café Reunion

The café windows fogged with warmth, blurring the city outside into streaks of motion and light. Inside, the air smelled like espresso and cinnamon, and soft jazz hummed from speakers overhead.

Dallas sat at a small corner table, suit jacket draped over the back of his chair, tie loosened an inch. His robe was tucked away at the courthouse, but its weight lingered on his shoulders anyway.

Roman arrived two minutes late, an offense that would've driven him crazy in court but somehow felt human here. He slid into the seat across from Dallas, shrugging off his coat and letting out a breath.

"I almost transferred away," Roman said without preamble, wrapping his hands around his coffee cup as if drawing strength from the heat. "Right after I saw the Fairview files. I thought distance would help me breathe."

"But you stayed," Dallas said, watching him carefully.

Roman nodded. "Yeah. Turns out staying is braver."

Dallas tilted his head. "Or stubborn," he said. "We'll call it brave, though. Sounds better in therapy."

A corner of Roman's mouth lifted.

A waitress dropped off their drinks and a plate of shared fries. The brothers picked at them absently, like two teenagers instead of two high-profile officers of the court.

"You know Sara called me," Dallas said after a moment, surprising himself with the admission.

Roman's brows rose. "Your adoptive mom?"

"Yeah." Dallas toyed with a fry. "She saw the news segments. Somebody dug into my 'inspirational foster care success story' again for a piece on the Miller case." His jaw tightened. "She said she was proud. Then she asked how I was holding up. I almost lied."

"What did you tell her?" Roman asked.

"That I found you," Dallas said. "That I found him."

Roman's expression softened. "How did she take it?"

"She cried," Dallas said. "Said she always suspected there was more to my early records than the paperwork showed. That there had to be a reason I flinched at goodbyes." He swallowed. "She said if I wanted to bring you over, the door was open. That they had room at the table."

Roman blinked. "Just like that?"

"Just like that," Dallas said. "That's who they are."

Roman leaned back, absorbing that. "You really hit the jackpot with them," he murmured, no bitterness in his tone—just a quiet awe.

"I did," Dallas agreed. "And you hit a different kind of jackpot. Two parents who kept every science project and cheered at every debate. That doesn't erase what you lost. But it counts for something."

Roman nodded. "Yeah," he said softly. "They do."

They fell quiet for a moment, each man tracing the paths that led them here.

"You know what's messed up?" Roman said suddenly. "I almost stood on the other side of Lake's case."

Dallas stiffened. "How close?"

"Close," Roman admitted. "The file crossed my desk. 'State v. Miller, Lake.' I saw the name, didn't connect the dots." He shook his head. "I passed it to a colleague because my docket was overloaded. I thought I was just offloading work." He met Dallas's gaze. "If I hadn't…"

"You'd be prosecuting the man who tucked me in when I had nightmares," Dallas finished.

"Yeah." Roman's jaw clenched. "Our lives keep almost crashing into each other without us knowing."

"Not almost," Dallas said. "They keep colliding. We just finally opened our eyes."

Roman exhaled a low laugh. "Fair."

Dallas leaned forward, elbows on the table. "I need to ask you something. Not as a judge. As your brother."

Roman's lips parted just slightly at that word.

"Okay," he said. "Ask."

"Are you angry that I recused myself from Lake's trial?"

Roman blinked, thrown. "You didn't have a choice, Dallas. Judicial ethics—"

"I know the rules," Dallas interrupted gently. "But part of me feels like I abandoned him." He stared at the table. "I keep thinking… if I had been the one on that bench, I would've seen him. Not just as a defendant. As Lake." He swallowed. "And I keep wondering whether my bias would've tilted the scales too far the other way."

Roman studied him for a long moment. "That's the burden, isn't it?" he said quietly. "Of being on this side of the system. We're expected to be more than human and less than human at the same time."

Dallas let out a dry chuckle. "Story of my life."

"You didn't abandon him," Roman continued. "You stepped back so the verdict wouldn't be tainted. That's a different kind of loyalty. Doesn't mean it doesn't hurt."

"It hurts," Dallas said simply.

Roman picked up a fry, then put it down again without eating it. "I visited your courthouse hallway the morning of his last motion," he said. "Watched him being led in. I saw the way you looked at him through the chamber door. I saw the way he looked for you in the gallery, even knowing you couldn't be there."

Dallas's throat tightened. "He still sees me as the kid who needed protecting," he murmured. "He doesn't understand that sometimes protecting someone means stepping aside."

"Maybe he will," Roman said. "Eventually. After all this shakes out."

"How do you do it?" Dallas asked suddenly. "Stand up there and argue for the state when you know how messy people's stories really are?"

Roman thought for a moment.

"I used to tell myself it was simple," he said. "Crime, punishment, deterrence. Then I started seeing the files differently. Twenty pages of record and one missing page no one bothered to ask about." He gestured between them. "We are the missing page, Dallas. Every kid whose file says 'mother unknown' or 'father not involved' or 'removed due to neglect.'"

He took a breath.

"I still believe in accountability," he said. "But I don't trust easy narratives anymore. That's why I joined Roots & Futures. That's why I dig deeper. And that's why sitting with you and Donna in your living room felt like… like the system folding in on itself and opening a small door."

A smile ghosted over Dallas's mouth. "You talk like a closing argument even off the clock."

"I'm a one-trick pony," Roman said dryly.

They lifted their coffee cups.

"To family," Dallas said.

Roman held his gaze.

"To starting over," he replied.

They clinked cups. The sound was small, but it rang with something vast.

Donna's Kitchen — A New Beginning

Donna's kitchen glowed with steam and love.

A big pot of gumbo simmered on the stove, filling the small house with Cajun warmth and the familiar comfort of home-cooked food. Motown played softly from a speaker on the counter—Marvin Gaye crooning under the clink of spoons and the occasional hiss of oil hitting hot metal.

The table was covered in a patchwork tablecloth that had seen better days. At its center, a bowl of cornbread sat like an offering, golden and imperfect.

Dallas leaned against the counter, stealing bits of andouille sausage whenever Donna's back was turned.

"Boy, if you don't get out my pot," she scolded without looking, swatting his hand with a wooden spoon.

He grinned, the movement feeling unexpectedly easy. "Consider it judicial oversight," he said. "Quality control."

Roman stood by the small bookshelf in the living room, scanning the titles—devotional books, GED study guides, a worn copy of a law for non-lawyers book someone had donated to Donna's recovery group.

"You reading all these?" he called.

"Trying," Donna answered, stirring the gumbo. "You two made me want to keep up."

The doorbell rang.

Donna wiped her hands on a dish towel, suddenly nervous. "That should be them," she said.

"Them?" Roman asked.

Donna shot Dallas a look that was half warning, half thrill. "I told you I invited her."

Before either man could ask who her was, Donna opened the door.

Jamiah Brown stood on the stoop, shaking raindrops from her umbrella. She was dressed in a simple blouse and jeans, her realtor polish softened by the familiarity of the neighborhood.

The moment Dallas saw her, his lungs stalled.

He had seen her before in adult life—once at a city event, once in a hallway when she came to testify in a housing case. But he'd always kept a polite distance, unsure of how much he could bear to remember.

Now she stood in his mother's doorway, holding a small gift bag.

"Hey, Donna," Jamiah said, smiling. "I brought dessert. Figured you'd have the rest covered."

"Jamiah!" Donna beamed, pulling her into a hug. "Get in here before the food gets cold and my nerves get hot."

Jamiah stepped inside, her gaze scanning the room. It landed on Dallas, and for a moment, both their faces shifted—past and present colliding.

He saw her as she had been: a young woman in dress pants and a pressed blouse, kneeling in dust and decay, dialing 911 with shaking fingers, cradling a nearly lifeless baby.

She saw him as he had been: impossibly small, burned with fever, eyes swollen nearly shut, clinging to her shirt with a strength that belied his condition.

"Judge Jackson," she said quietly.

"Jamiah," he replied, his voice softer than the title deserved.

Donna gestured between them. "You two know each other already," she said, pride draping over every word. "But you don't know each other like family yet."

Roman stepped forward, extending a hand. "Roman Arnold," he introduced himself. "The long-lost plot twist."

Jamiah laughed, shaking his hand. "I've been following your work," she said. "You took down that crooked landlord on 18th Avenue. My agency couldn't stop talking about it."

"Happy to serve," Roman said with a little bow.

Donna shooed them all toward the table. "Everybody sit. Food's ready. Gumbo on the stove, cornbread on the table, and Jesus in this house whether you invited Him or not."

They took their seats: Donna at one end, Dallas at the other, Roman and Jamiah on either side.

Donna bowed her head.

"Lord," she began, voice trembling just a little, "I don't have fancy words tonight. You saw me when I was on that dirty floor. You saw this boy—" she squeezed Dallas's hand "—when he was one breath away from gone. You saw Roman when they took him from me. You saw Jamiah when she picked up what the world threw away. So tonight, I just want to say… thank You. For gumbo and forgiveness and second chances and… and my family all around this table." Her voice cracked. "Bless this food and the hands that prepared it and the hearts that are trying their best. In Jesus' name, amen."

"Amen," they echoed.

They ate.

Conversation flowed easier as the bowls emptied. Roman told a story about his adoptive mother's obsession with holiday decorations. Dallas shared a memory of Lake teaching him how to ride a bike, complete with the time he crashed into a mailbox. Jamiah confessed she still checked public records sometimes just to see what happened to kids she'd crossed paths with in her work.

"I used to Google 'Dallas Arnold Jackson' every six months," she admitted, laughing shyly. "Just to see if you were… okay. If you made it. The first time I saw your face on the county website, I screamed so loud my assistant thought I'd won the lottery."

"You did," Donna said, eyes glistening. "We all did."

Between stories, Donna disappeared into her bedroom and returned with a shoebox.

She set it gently in the middle of the table.

"What's that?" Dallas asked.

"My receipts," she said.

Jamiah raised a brow. "I hope you're not using that as your accountant strategy."

Donna rolled her eyes and removed the lid.

Inside were folded letters, photographs, small objects—a hospital bracelet, an old pacifier, a dried rose petal pressed between Bible pages.

"Every time I got a paycheck in rehab, I put five dollars in this box," Donna said. "For the day I'd find you. For bus fare, for copies of records, for whatever it took. I didn't know it would take thirty years." She smiled sadly. "But it got me here."

She handed Roman a small stack of letters bound with worn string. Then another to Dallas.

"These are yours," she said. "Just… be gentle with 'em. And with me. I was a mess when I wrote most of them."

Dallas ran a thumb over the top envelope. The date was scribbled in shaky handwriting. Dallas's tenth birthday that she missed. The words blurred as his vision swam.

"I don't know when I'll be ready to read them," he admitted.

"That's okay," Donna said. "They've waited this long. They can wait a little longer."

Roman flipped one open, just a corner.

Dear Roman, it began, today I stayed sober for twelve hours. I did it because I wanted to be the kind of mother you could be proud of, even if you never meet me…

His throat closed. He folded it shut again.

"Later," he murmured.

Later felt like a promise.

Jamiah reached into her bag and pulled out a slim folder, sliding it across the table toward Donna.

"What's this?" Donna asked.

"That paralegal program we talked about," Jamiah said. "Night classes. Financial aid info. Application deadlines." She smiled. "You've been running your own appeals in life for years. Might as well get a certificate for it."

Donna laughed, a full, bright sound that hadn't lived in her chest for decades. "Me? In a classroom again?"

"Why not?" Dallas said. "We're short on good paralegals who understand people like the ones in my courtroom. You'd be lethal in a good way."

Roman nodded. "You'd be dangerous with legal training," he agreed. "In all the right ways."

Donna blinked rapidly. "Y'all trying to make me cry into this gumbo."

"Occupational hazard," Dallas said. "We're sentimental professionals."

Jamiah picked up the Polaroid camera she'd brought—one of those trendy retro ones—and waved it.

"Alright, evidence time," she announced. "Nobody move. Say 'new beginnings.'"

Dallas leaned toward Roman. Roman draped an arm over Donna's shoulder. Jamiah balanced the camera with one hand and reached to squeeze Donna's other shoulder with the other.

The camera flashed.

The print slid out, colors slowly blooming into existence: Roman mid-laugh, Dallas pretending to scowl, Donna's eyes shining, Jamiah caught between photographer and participant.

Donna took the photo with reverent hands.

"I want this life to have receipts," she said, voice thick. "I want proof. For the days it feels like maybe I dreamed it."

She walked to the small shelf that held her Bible and her old tin box. Carefully, she tucked the photo into the front of the album, where it would be the first thing anyone saw.

The outside world faded.

Old hurts waited quietly at the door.

Inside this small kitchen, drenched in Motown and steam and second chances, three broken histories were becoming one imperfect, holy story—with Jamiah's steady presence knitting the edges.

For the first time in decadesRoman was not alone.

Donna was not grieving in the dark.

Dallas was not searching.

Tonight, they belonged.

The Weight of What Comes Next

Later that night, after the dishes were washed and the leftovers packed away and the house returned to its familiar quiet, Dallas stood alone in his townhouse, staring at the Polaroid Donna had texted him a picture of.

His phone screen glowed in the dim bedroom as he sat on the edge of the bed, suit jacket hanging over the chair, tie undone.

He thought about the courtroom.

About Lake's weary eyes in the holding cell.

About Donna's trembling hands on the gallery bench.

About Roman's steady voice at the prosecution table, now colored by history he couldn't escape.

He thought about Sara and Hunter, waiting for a call about how dinner went, eager to know this new piece of his puzzle. He thought about little kids in foster homes across the city, whispering scripture into the dark, not knowing who might be searching for them.

Bloodlines and burdens.

He had spent his whole life trying to separate the two—believing his blood doomed him and his choices saved him. Now he understood they were knotted together. Pain and grace, abandonment and adoption, biology and choice.

His phone buzzed.

A message from Roman.

Roman: Court tomorrow. You okay?

Dallas: No. But I'm ready.

Roman: That's all we get in this life. See you on the record, brother.

Another message popped up, this one from an unknown number Donna had clearly borrowed from someone at her program.

Donna: Philippians 4:13, baby. For all of us. Love, Mom.

Dallas smiled, the word Mom landing in his chest softly but firmly.

He set the phone on the nightstand and reached under the bed, pulling out the old chessboard. He opened it on the mattress, the hinges creaking, and placed the knight Roman had returned to Donna but insisted he keep for now.

He set it in the center of the board.

"Strength in silence," he murmured. "But not silence forever."

Tomorrow, he would enter Courtroom 4B again. The law would demand neutrality. The public would demand clarity. His past would whisper and roar.

But tonight, for one fragile, precious moment, he let himself feel it all—the terror, the gratitude, the grief, the strange, buoyant hope.

A child almost left for dead had grown into a man holding the power to change lives.

A mother once shackled by addiction had become a student of second chances.

A boy lost in the files of Fairview had reappeared as a brother with a badge.

The burdens were heavy.

But the bloodlines no longer felt like chains.

They felt like threads he could finally see—and maybe, just maybe, begin to weave into something new.

Dallas lay back, eyes tracing the shadows on the ceiling, the echo of laughter and clinking dishes from Donna's kitchen still alive in his ears.

For the first time in a long time, the weight on his chest didn't feel like crushing stone.

It felt like responsibility.

And somewhere deep inside him, the boy he had been whispered to the man he had become:

We made it this far. We can carry this, too.

Chapter 7:
When the Past Pleads Guilty

The courthouse buzzed with a life of its own. On mornings like this, even the marble floors seemed to vibrate with anticipation, the echo of hurried footsteps bouncing off high ceilings as lawyers in pressed suits conferred in hushed, urgent tones. The air tasted faintly of burnt coffee and printer ink. Faces blurred past in a river of worry, ambition, resignation—but at the center of it all, behind the heavy oak bench, Judge Dallas Jackson stood like an anchor in a rising tide.

He adjusted his robe, the fabric suddenly feeling too heavy, too warm, as if holding the weight of the past inside its folds. The fluorescent lights hummed overhead, a restless, anxious buzz like insects trapped inside glass.

Then the bailiff's voice rolled across the room:

"The People vs. Logan Hill."

The name hit like a collision. Time folded in on itself. For a moment, Dallas was not a judge—he was a trembling boy in an oversized backpack, clutching books to his chest while a taller, crueler boy slammed his locker shut with the force of a gunshot. Logan Hill. The one who taught him to stutter. The one who taught him fear.

And now?

Logan was the one trembling.

He shuffled into the courtroom wearing a battered orange jumpsuit, wrists shackled, cheeks hollowed. His posture collapsed like a man tired of carrying his own mistakes. Dallas tightened his grip on the bench, breath shallow.

At the prosecution's table, Roman sat stone-faced, organizing files with his usual clinical precision. But he saw it—the twitch in Dallas's jaw, the tightening in his shoulders, the way the gavel trembled ever so slightly in his hand. Roman's eyes narrowed, protective instincts rising like a tide.

In the gallery, Donna watched with her notebook half-open, her gaze flicking between her sons with unspoken worry. She recognized that look. A mother always does.

And beside her—Lake Miller. Not the same man he once was. Not the man crushed by guilt and accusation. He watched Dallas with a fierce, older-brother intensity, jaw clenched, fingers drumming against his knee.

A silent vow radiated from him:

If that man hurts my brother again… I swear…

Dallas's brothers sat behind him like pillars he hadn't asked for, but needed more than breath.

"State your name," the clerk called.

"Logan Hill," the defendant murmured.

His voice was not the cruel, mocking tone that haunted Dallas's memories. It was small, defeated—almost childlike. The courtroom shifted, air thickening with the tension of two timelines colliding.

Dallas forced his gaze downward, fighting the tremor in his chest. But Logan's eyes lifted—and the moment their gazes met, Dallas felt the full weight of years he'd spent trying to outrun that fear.

Roman watched the exchange with narrowed eyes.

Lake watched with rising anger.

Donna watched with a mother's broken heart.

The morning dragged like a held breath. Evidence came in waves—grainy surveillance footage, a witness trembling through testimony, a doctor's monotone describing the aftermath of Logan's actions. Everything painted Logan in stark, damning strokes.

But Dallas barely heard the legal arguments. His mind kept flashing back—shards of memory sharp as glass.

Flash: Logan shoving him into lockers.

Flash: Dallas eating lunch alone, Roman the only boy who ever sat beside him.

Flash: Lake racing across a football field at home, yelling, "Nobody messes with my little brother!"

He had three lives now colliding in this courtroom.

Three versions of himself.

Three versions of what protection looked like.

Recess.

Dallas retreated to chambers like a man fleeing a fire.

He barely sat before Donna opened the door, her presence soft but firm, her eyes studying him with surgical accuracy.

"You knew him," she said.

Dallas nodded, voice hollow. "He made my life hell. Every day."

A soft rustle. Roman stepped in behind her, silent but radiating tension. He closed the door with deliberate care, as though sealing the moment from the rest of the world.

Lake followed, leaning against the bookshelf, arms crossed, jaw tight. "Why didn't you ever tell us?" he demanded gently—hurt and protective all at once.

Dallas swallowed. "Because I didn't want to be weak."

Lake stepped forward. "You're not weak, Dallas. You never were. And you're not alone anymore."

Roman moved to the desk, placing a hand on Dallas's shoulder. "You don't face ghosts by yourself now. You've got two brothers in this fight."

Dallas exhaled shakily, the truth settling into him like warmth after a winter storm.

Three siblings. Three survivors. Three men united by wounds they didn't choose—but were choosing to heal.

**Trial Day.

Inside, the courtroom filled slowly—officers along the back wall, a few reporters near the aisle, scattered members of the public curious about any case with the word armed in it.

Roman arranged his files at the prosecution table, gaze sharp, suit immaculate. Today, he wasn't just Dallas's brother. He was the State's voice.

Logan's public defender, Ms. Chen, sat beside her client, flipping through a worn yellow pad, eyes flicking between her notes and the man beside her—a man who couldn't seem to decide whether to stare at the floor or at the judge.

Dallas took the bench. The clerk called the case. The oath was administered. A jury of twelve strangers watched it all, ready to weigh a life they'd never known before this morning.

Opening Statements

Roman rose first.

"Ladies and gentlemen of the jury," he began, voice steady, "this case is not about who Logan Hill used to be in a high school hallway. It is about what he chose to do on the night of March 12th."

Dallas felt the words land, layered with irony only they truly understood.

Roman clicked a remote. A still image appeared on the screen: a convenience store, fluorescent and sterile.

"At approximately 11:23 p.m.," Roman continued, "the defendant walked into this store, brandished a firearm, and demanded cash. You'll see the footage. You'll hear from the clerk whose life he threatened. You'll hear from the officer who arrested him. And you'll see that this was not a moment of confusion."

He let the silence hang.

"This was a choice."

Ms. Chen's opening was shorter.

"Logan Hill," she said, "is a man with a history of poor decisions, yes. But he's also a man with a history of untreated trauma, addiction, and survival on the margins. You will hear his story, and you will see that underneath the mugshot and the mistakes, there's a human being worth more than the worst thing he's ever done."

Dallas listened to both sides and felt the tension between justice and mercy stretch taut inside him.

Witness Testimony

The prosecution called the store clerk, a young man named Javier Ortiz.

He fidgeted in the witness box, fingers kneading the edge of his sleeve.

"Mr. Ortiz," Roman began, softening his tone, "what do you remember most from that night?"

Javier swallowed. "The gun," he said. "I remember the gun. I remember thinking, 'This is it.'"

"Did the defendant say anything to you?"

"He said… 'Empty the register. Don't make this difficult.'"

"Did you believe he would hurt you if you didn't comply?"

"Yes," Javier whispered. "I believed he'd kill me."

Roman nodded. "You recognize the person who threatened you that night?"

Javier glanced quickly at the defense table. "Yes. He's right there. Logan Hill."

"No further questions."

On cross, Ms. Chen approached slowly.

"Mr. Ortiz," she said, "you testified that the gun was pointed in your direction. Did he fire it?"

"No."

"Did he physically harm you?"

"No."

"Thank you for your honesty," she said. "I know that doesn't erase the fear you felt. But you understand the difference between someone frightening you and someone actually pulling the trigger, correct?"

"Yes," Javier replied softly.

She nodded. "No further questions."

Next, Roman called Officer Daniels, the arresting officer, who described finding Logan three blocks away, out of breath, money stuffed into his pocket, gun tossed in a dumpster.

"The weapon was loaded?" Roman asked.

"Yes. One in the chamber."

"So the threat wasn't hypothetical."

"No, sir."

Ms. Chen used her cross to highlight Logan's cooperation.

"Officer Daniels," she said, "did my client resist arrest?"

"No."

"Did he confess on the scene?"

"Yes. He said, 'Yeah. I did it.'"

"And he never reached for the gun while you were present?"

"No."

She nodded. "Thank you."

Finally, the State rested after playing the store surveillance footage—a flickering video of Logan, hood up, jaw clenched, waving the gun in jerky motions as he shouted at Javier.

Dallas watched it all, each frame overlaying the memory of a locker slamming shut, a young Logan grinning viciously as books scattered at his feet.

Logan Takes the Stand

Ms. Chen made a calculated choice. Logan would testify.

He walked to the stand looking older than his years, suit wrinkled, hands trembling as he placed them on the Bible. "I do," he said, voice barely audible.

"Mr. Hill," Ms. Chen began gently, "do you remember Dallas Jackson from high school?"

A murmur ran through the room. Roman tensed.

Dallas's heart thudded but his expression stayed unreadable.

Logan blinked hard. "Yeah," he croaked. "I remember him."

"Do you remember how you treated him?"

He closed his eyes for a moment. "I wasn't… I wasn't kind," he said. "I was a bully. I was angry at everyone, and he was an easy target. I'm not proud of it."

"Why were you angry?"

He swallowed. "My dad drank. A lot. Sometimes the only control I felt like I had was at school. So I… took it out on kids who couldn't fight back."

"Like Mr. Jackson."

"Yeah," Logan said. "Like him. I was wrong."

She nodded. "Let's talk about the night at the store. Why did you do it?"

Logan's shoulders sagged. "I was broke. I'd lost my job. I was using again. I thought if I could just scare the guy, get some cash, I'd get through the week. I knew it was loaded. I knew it was wrong." His voice cracked. "I'm so tired of feeling like an animal in my own life."

"What do you feel now, sitting here, facing these charges?"

"Like I deserve whatever happens," he whispered. "But I also… I don't want to be this person anymore."

On cross, Roman's tone was firm but not vicious.

"Mr. Hill," he said, "you knew the gun was loaded."

"Yes."

"And you pointed it at an unarmed man."

"Yes."

"And you chose to walk into that store."

"Yes."

Roman nodded. "No further questions."

The facts were not in dispute.

The question now was what to do with them.

Verdict & Sentencing

The jury moved quickly. The evidence was strong, the charges clear.

"On the charge of armed robbery," the foreperson read, "we find the defendant—guilty."

Logan closed his eyes. Ms. Chen put a hand on his arm. Donna squeezed Roman's hand in the gallery. Lake glanced at Dallas, reading the tension beneath his calm.

Sentencing fell to Dallas.

He took a long moment before speaking, scanning the file, then lifting his gaze to Logan.

"Mr. Hill," he said, voice steady, "the law requires punishment for what you've done. You terrorized an innocent man. You carried a loaded gun into a public place. You could have killed someone."

Logan nodded, eyes wet. "I know, Your Honor."

"But," Dallas continued, "this court also recognizes that people are shaped by their past—but not bound to repeat it."

He paused, choosing each word like a stone laid carefully.

"I remember you from high school," he said plainly. "You made my life very difficult."

A ripple of shock moved through the room.

Logan's face crumpled. "I'm sorry," he whispered. "I really am."

"I believe you," Dallas replied. "But sorrow without change is just another performance."

He leaned forward slightly.

"I'm sentencing you to a term of incarceration under the statutory guidelines for armed robbery. In addition, you will complete a structured rehabilitation program, trauma counseling, and educational courses while in custody. Parole will be contingent on proof of meaningful participation."

He held Logan's gaze.

"This is not a free pass. This is a demanding road. But it is a road. And if you choose to walk it, you may leave this season of your life not just as a man who has served time—but as a man who has changed."

Logan swallowed, a tear escaping. "Thank you, Your Honor," he said hoarsely.

The gavel fell.

The courtroom exhaled.

And somewhere inside Dallas, a knot that had been forming since adolescence loosened—not completely, but enough to let grace in.

Logan stood before the bench in a borrowed suit, suddenly looking like the scared child he once was.

His public defender spoke. The prosecution countered. The clerk read charges. Evidence repeated like a haunting refrain.

But Logan's eyes kept flicking to Dallas—guilt and fear battling for dominance.

The gallery sat still as stone.

Roman's jaw tensed every time Logan looked at Dallas.

Lake leaned forward, fingers gripping the pew.

Donna held both their hands, praying silently.

When it was time for sentencing, Dallas removed his glasses. The courtroom stilled.

"Mr. Hill," he said, voice steady despite the tremor in his heart. "The law demands accountability. But justice demands we see the person behind the crime."

He paused. The room leaned in.

"You hurt people. You terrified them."

His voice tightened. "You terrified me."

Gasps. Logan's eyes widened.

"But I will not judge you from the wounds of a boy you once broke. I will judge you from the man you can still become."

The silence was thick and holy.

"I'm sentencing you to incarceration," Dallas said. Lake's shoulders dropped with relief.

"But also to mandatory counseling and rehabilitation. Your punishment will not be just time. It will be transformation."

Logan's lips trembled. "Your Honor… I'm sorry. For everything. I don't know why I did any of it."

Dallas nodded. "Then start by learning who you are—without the rage."

The gavel fell like a benediction.

Roman exhaled slowly.

Donna wiped her tears.

Lake looked at his brother with awe.

That evening, the three brothers gathered in Dallas's office.

Rain tapped the windows like a soft memory.

Roman sat across from Dallas, tired but proud.

Lake leaned against the wall, arms relaxed now.

Donna sat on the couch, watching her boys—her sons—with a heart full of both scars and gratitude.

Dallas finally spoke. "I didn't think I'd survive that."

Lake stepped forward. "You didn't just survive. You grew."

Roman added, "You broke the cycle, Dallas. That's something only a strong man can do."

Donna whispered, "You judged him as a man—not a monster. That's grace."

Dallas looked at them—the brother he grew up with, the brother he finally found, and the mother who chose him twice.

"This," he said softly, "this is what saved me."

Roman lifted a cup of coffee. Lake lifted his water bottle. Donna her tea.

Four cups lifted together.

"To breaking the cycle," Roman said.

"To family," Lake added.

"To healing," Donna whispered.

"To justice with mercy," Dallas finished.

The clink of their cups echoed through the room.

And for the first time in years, Dallas felt the past loosen its grip.

Not erased.

Not forgotten.

But rewritten—with brothers by his side.

245

Chapter 8: The Weight of the Robe

—————— • ——————

The flashbulbs were relentless.

Each step Dallas took down the courthouse stairs brought him deeper into a storm of questions, camera shutters, and grasping hands. The black robe that draped over his shoulders—a symbol he'd once craved—felt impossibly heavy this morning, its shadow stretching ahead of him, chased by rumors and hope in equal measure. For almost a decade, he had worn that robe with pride. But now, as the city's attention pressed in around him, he was reminded that every thread was stitched with someone's suffering—and someone else's hard-won reprieve.

He ignored the barrage of voices, the accusing and the exultant, relying on the rhythm of his footsteps: left, right, left, right. Each beat a defiance against the chaos. Each echo a reminder—justice was not a performance.

He paused for just a moment at the edge of the fountain, feeling the icy spray as the wind shifted. In his pocket, his phone buzzed with texts from Sara and Hunter, his own children—words of encouragement, prayers for strength. He closed his eyes, letting their invisible arms wrap him up, even as he heard Donna's voice in his memory:

"Wherever you go, don't go alone."

He opened his eyes to the crowd: adversaries, allies, the simply curious, and those who hungered for scandal as much as truth. Every headline in the city seemed to have his name stamped across the top:

JUDGE JACKSON DEFIES DA

JUDGE WHO CHALLENGES THE SYSTEM

HERO OR HAZARD?

He tightened his grip around the folder of decisions, court orders, and handwritten notes from the girl whose future he had just helped save. Underneath, the chess piece—his lucky talisman—brushed his palm softly, grounding him.

Inside, the courthouse was alive with the murmur of anticipation. He could see it in the way the guards stood a little straighter, the hurried steps of paralegals, the wide, wary glances of local politicians skirting the edges of the crowd. The energy was electric—volatile, dangerous. But he walked through it with his head high and shoulders squared, the fire in his gut burning clearer than ever: if not him, then who?

Outside his chambers, a pair of teenage boys in too-large hoodies lingered, nervously glancing through a sheaf of paperwork. Dallas caught their eyes as he passed, pausing.

"You two lost?" he asked, his tone gentle.

They shifted, their bravado paper-thin. One stammered, "We heard about… the new program?" He lifted a flyer, the bold letters of JACKSON JUSTICE INITIATIVE glowing under the hall lights.

Dallas's voice softened, his gaze warm. "You're in the right place. Wait here. Somebody will show you where to go." As he stepped forward, he heard one of them whisper: "That's really him?"

For a moment, the armor of the robe felt less like protection, more like acceptance. He breathed in the hope these boys carried like fragile glass.

Roman waited for him in the chamber—arms folded, the city's headlines spread out on Dallas's desk like a police barricade. The air between them was sharp with tension, but Roman's concern wasn't simply for the case—it was for the man behind the nameplate on the door.

"You've stepped into the storm now, Dallas," Roman said, the hard edge of worry in every syllable.

Dallas shrugged off his coat, letting it fall over the back of his chair. "You warned me to play it safe."

Roman shook his head, lips pressing into a reluctant, proud smile. "I warned you to be careful, not cowardly. But you don't know any other way, do you?"

Dallas leaned against the desk, eyes on the headlines. "No. And if this robe means anything, it should mean taking the blow for somebody who can't."

There was a beat of silence before Roman replied. "The program is working. The girl's mother wrote you a letter. Want to read it?"

Dallas nodded, taking the folded paper. The words were shaky, but the message was clear. Thank you for seeing my child.

He read it twice. Then again, more quietly.

With the trial of the year underway—a high-profile corruption case involving city contractors and abuse of power—the pressure mounted. Dallas presided with steady control, but every objection, every evidentiary ruling, every narrowed look from the defense was another point on the scoreboard of public scrutiny. He could feel the stares from the gallery: activists, students, skeptics, a few quiet faces from Fairview group home—kids, now adults, peering at the man who once shared their bed frame or their breakfast table.

One morning during recess, Donna arrived with a thermos of soup and an envelope.

"You need to eat. And you should open this," she said, voice brisk but lined with concern. "Letters from some of your first youth diversion graduates. They're rooting for you."

He held the envelope for a long moment, tracing the signatures—some tall and neat, some a scrawl—and let the memories come. "You told me once that broken kids can become judges," he whispered.

Donna grinned. "And that you still need soup to survive a marathon."

They laughed—the sound fragile but real, punctuation against the storm of the day.

Evenings were the hardest. Dallas would return home late, the weight of the day pressing down until even the comfort of soft lamplight felt distant. He'd sit at his kitchen table, going over court notes with trembling fingers, his robe slung over the back of a chair like a weary ghost. Some nights he called Sara or Hunter, his voice thick with exhaustion, sharing his doubts and hopes not as a judge, but as their father.

On other nights, sleep would not come. He'd take the battered chess piece from his desk drawer, running his thumb along its edges, and stare out the window at the restless city.

"Are you proud of me, Mom?" he'd whisper to the darkness, the memory of Donna's embrace anchoring him through the long vigil until dawn.

The second week of the trial, headlines hit harder.

Controversial Ruling, Protest Planned at Courthouse.

JACKSON JUSTICE INITIATIVE UNDER FIRE.

Judge's Compassion: Crosses the Line?

As he arrived that morning, protesters gathered beyond the police tape—some holding signs reading "Kids Deserve Chances," others shouting for "Law and Order." Between them, Dallas saw the faces of three kids from Fairview, there not to accuse but simply to watch. He paused, catching the gaze of one—a girl named Erica, who gave him a small, brave nod.

Inside, a meeting with city leaders became tense.

"How far will you take this?" demanded one councilman, his tone spat like a challenge.

Dallas answered with the cool integrity he had ground into every part of himself: "As far as our youth have to walk before someone sees them. As far as it takes for blind justice to see the whole person."

The room buzzed with resistance, but Dallas did not back down.

The Jackson Justice Initiative's progress unfolded not only as headlines or statistics, but through transformations felt in every room, meeting, and story that Dallas encountered. Nights at the downtown rec center became a recurring mosaic of gratitude, vulnerability, and courage, as teens faced personal crossroads and learned that showing up, again and again, could re-write a future that once felt set in stone.

Dallas's honest answers resonated deeper than any legal ruling, challenging young people to keep striving even in moments of uncertainty. Roman's encouragement and Donna's quiet strength anchored him through both victories and skepticism, forging a leadership rooted in community rather than solitary heroism. The Initiative's rise, marked first by press coverage and then by city funding, sparked shifts within neighborhoods: more kids claimed seats in classrooms and at tutoring clinics, fewer arrived at detention centers, and local partnerships flourished with the help of volunteers—former group home youth, retired police, and dedicated educators.

The program's statistical impact mirrored its emotional depth. National restorative justice programs, similar to Dallas's, regularly report lower recidivism: some show a decline from 27% to as little as 13%, with significantly higher rates of victim and community satisfaction. Beyond numbers, Donna's parent advocacy and Roman's legal work fostered healing not just for individuals, but for local families and networks—a transformation built not from spotlights, but from circles of support, trust, and hard-won hope. Through every season, Dallas witnessed the living proof that survival, wisdom, and steadfast leadership together can redefine the fabric of justice and belonging.

And Dallas? He remained both the face and the backbone of it all. In court he was fair, unflinching, and just as hard on himself as on anyone else. On weekends, though, he'd sit in circles with the kids—sometimes playing chess with a nervous twelve-year-old, sometimes quietly listening as another teen admitted, "I thought nobody saw me." He'd just smile back, honest and tired:

"I see you. I know who you are. I was you."

In those moments, the heavy robe didn't feel like armor at all. It felt like history—personal, collective—and, finally, hope.

One late afternoon, Dallas walked through the now-familiar courthouse lobby, where flyers for the JJI program shared space with wanted notices and adoption posters. A mural hung near the entrance, painted by the teens—chains breaking into birds across a background of storm clouds, a judge's robe waving like a flag.

He paused before it, smile gentle, eyes shining, letting the city's noise wash over him. He wasn't just bearing the weight of the robe.

He was lifting it, too—for everyone who might wear it after him.

And somewhere, as dusk settled on the courthouse, the world seemed to exhale. The story wasn't finished. There would always be new cases, new doubts, new headlines. But for one man, one city, the scales had shifted—if only a little—toward justice rooted in mercy, and power made strong by compassion.

In the hush that followed, Dallas stepped inside his chambers, slipped off the robe, and let himself rest. The day would come again—but for now, he allowed hope to be enough.

Chapter 9: Truth on Trial

———————————— • ————————————

Dallas sat at the head of the conference table, city lights smeared beyond the windows. The tense hum of debate filled the room—voices circling data and doubt, coffee cooling in forgotten cups, the folder with the Jackson Justice Initiative at the center like a beacon for critics and dreamers alike.

He glanced at Roman—steady at his side; Donna, just behind, quietly watchful, the steadfast ballast of his life.

On the table, the court administrator slid an envelope forward. "An anonymous complaint," she said carefully. "It references your brother's trial."

The word echoed—brother. The gravity in Dallas's chest was sudden, familiar.

Childhood Flashback from Fairview

Flashback: At age seven, Dallas sat alone on the playground at Fairview Group Home, the chill of fall translating into the sting of isolation. Word had spread—he learned he'd received a complaint from a staff worker about intentionally ignoring the rules, and whispers passed among other staffs. He felt the ache of being misunderstood, the uncertainty of standing alone. Yet, as he watched other children form easy groups, Dallas remembered the advice from one of his caring caretaker: "You have to stand firm when you're alone. Even if it hurts, that's when you know you're strong." He wiped his tears in private and refused to hide from recess or avoid the classroom, even as glances lingered. Day by day, he practiced resilience—speaking up for himself, apologizing when needed but holding to his truth, and reaching out to classmates despite setbacks. By week's end, he'd weathered the solitude, learned to trust his own voice, and discovered that courage grows strongest in moments of loneliness and challenge.

In the attack of doubt swirling through the conference room, Dallas recalls that seven-year-old courage—the conviction to face pushback, trust his resilience, and move forward, no matter how others judge him. The early lesson at Fairview becomes the wellspring of strength now, shaping the man who faces critics and stands for justice, anchored by the endurance of his childhood self.

Back in the present, Dallas doesn't flinch as he reaches for the envelope. "Did they specify a case?" he asks.

"No, but it's tied to your brother's trial," the administrator replies, her expression taut with the knowledge of what they've all risked for change.

Roman stiffens—a flash of old anger in his jaw. "It was by the book," he says, voice adult and hard. But Dallas can see, for a flicker, the nine-year-old who once took every punishment so Dallas wouldn't have to.

Donna's fingers still on the tabletop. "They see power shifting," she says, her tone fierce if you know where to listen. "They want things to stay broken."

Dallas's voice is even. "Let them look. I'm not backing down."

Flashback: The first night Dallas arrived at Fairview—soft-bodied, scared, clutching a bag of clothes too big for him. Arnold, skeptical of everyone, wordlessly shoved over half his dinner roll. Later, unable to sleep, Dallas found Arnold reading comics under the covers with a flashlight. "If you get up before sunrise, you get the hot water first," Arnold whispered, with a lopsided grin. "I'll wake you."

After the meeting, the hallways emptied much too slowly. Dallas lingered, returning handshakes, nodding at detractors, promising more data, more transparency, more accountability. When the crowd finally dispersed, he paced the marble floors, exhausted but unable to leave. Evening janitors trundled past with bins and mops, a silent ballet to the city's unseen labor. In the shadowed corridor, Roman pressed a file into Dallas's hand.

"Ethics complaint," Roman said, voice tense. "Anonymous. Says you overreached. Cites your brother's trial. The old allegations."

Dallas didn't flinch. He peeled the envelope open, read the terse, unsigned lines: Improper conduct. Failure to recuse. Favoritism. His chest ached—a rage cold and quiet, too familiar. "They're not stopping," he murmured.

"They see the change," Roman replied, eyes hard. "They want to break you before it gets rolling any further."

Donna joined them, her arms folded but face bright with purpose. "You stood for kids nobody stood for. Some people make money or keep power by keeping things broken."

For a moment, Dallas let the warmth of their faith steady him. He remembered nights at Fairview—white-knuckling sheets, vowing to outlast every bully, every broken adult. Even then, he'd known some storms could only be survived by standing still and refusing to fall.

He spent that night alone with the report, details of cases—real, desperate, raw—laying open across his desk. Each file was a story that had once begun with hopelessness and now, because of small acts, might end differently. He swallowed the ache, thinking of the kids he used to be, the ones lost between foster placements and intake forms, invisible until they weren't even children anymore.

Sleep came in fragments. Dreams tangled: flashes of the bench, his mother's voice, the courthouse morphing into an orphanage, headlines smearing and sharp. He awoke before dawn, washed in gray light, resolve settling in his bones like cooling steel.

The ethics inquiry was swift. No drawn-out drama—just a row of impassive faces and files. The panel's head, a judge Dallas admired but barely knew, read from prepared notes. Questions were hard, sometimes humiliating. Dallas answered simply, honestly, refusing to hedge or grandstand.

"Did your relationship with Roman Jackson influence your conduct in his trial?"

"I recused myself the moment a conflict could arise. I have documentation and witnesses."

"Do you deny that community outreach has colored your public role?"

"I hope it has. This city needs public servants who are more than bureaucrats."

A younger member pressed harder. "And if it costs you your seat?"

Dallas's hands were steady, his voice quieter but sharper. "Then I did something worth losing it for."

They adjourned, silent and stone-faced. Dallas walked out into the hall, the carved faces of former judges staring down from their sepia portraits, long lines of history where only a few had ever dared break with convention.

Donna and Roman were there—their relief tenuous, their defiance ready. Donna cupped his cheek, eyes shining but tiger-bright. "You gave them nothing they could use. That's enough. Come home. Eat."

He resisted, at first. Needed to walk the city, feel the pulse without cameras. Needed to know who still believed. Outside, a line of youth volunteers—some former defendants—stood silent vigil on the courthouse steps, holding signs ("CHANGE THE SYSTEM, NOT THE KIDS" and "JJI GAVE ME A FUTURE"). Dallas walked through them, pausing only once, to shake the hand of the smallest boy, whose wide eyes shimmered with something like trust.

That night he let Donna cook, even as headlines unfurled in new bursts—calls for resignation, calls for awards, editorials tugging him in every direction. At dinner, Roman grumbled about politicians but kept refilling glasses and passing bread. The conversation was easy, laughter surfacing despite the storm outside. For a while, Dallas let himself be just a man at his mother's table, not a judge at a crossroads.

Day by day, the city's temperature swung hard. Some called Dallas a "radical in a robe" and called for investigations at higher levels. Some city council members offered guarded support, while youth groups held rallies outside the courthouse: music, poetry, protest, hope, and anger all mingling in the cold morning air.

Reporters prowled, looking for cracks—would his team cave? Would past mistakes surface? Donna weathered them with calm; Roman fed the hungry ones facts and nothing more.

Dallas returned to every meeting, every town hall. He sat with parents until the hour grew unreasonable, until the janitors stacked chairs and the coffee went cold. He listened to their doubts and their pride, to stories retold so many times they had become worn and polished, like stones rolling in the same riverbed. He didn't interrupt. He nodded, took notes, promised to follow up—even when he didn't yet know how.

The next day, he walked into another gymnasium, another echoing auditorium heavy with suspicion. He presented outcome data, even the numbers that hurt. He didn't soften the edges or spin the failures. Transparency had become his shield, his confession, and sometimes his only defense.

He hosted a live-stream Q&A, reading aloud the hard messages flooding the comments feed—"You care more about criminals than law-abiding families!" "You'd never understand if it were your child!"—and answered with stories. He spoke of the cycles he'd broken: the teenager who'd written from prison to say thank you, the father he'd watched reunite with his son after ten years apart, the woman who now mentored girls she once recruited into chaos. For every message of hate, there was a name, a face, a stubborn miracle that kept him going.

But at night, when the cameras shut down and the auditorium lights dimmed, doubt seeped back in. Privately, he worried—about budgets, policies, optics. But mostly, he feared that change came one soul at a time, and maybe that was too slow for a city losing patience. In one such moment, Donna found him in his office, slumped and silent, his tie loosened, the city noise rising in a low, pulsing hum from the streets below.

"You think I'm right?" he asked, voice barely audible. His eyes didn't lift from the scattered reports on his desk—ink smudged by the heel of his hand, a coffee ring bleeding into a margin. "Because some nights, it feels like I'm just… rearranging the rubble."

Donna crossed the room and switched off the harsh fluorescent light, leaving only the city's amber glow spilling through the window. "I think you're the only one still brave enough to stand in it," she said softly. "That has to mean something."

He exhaled, long and raw. Outside, a siren wailed, distant but familiar—part of the city's endless heartbeat. For the first time that week, he let himself close his eyes and imagine what peace might sound like.She squeezed his hand. "Yes, I do. But it's not about right. It's about not letting them make you smaller. You see them—their pain. You won't stop. That's why you wear the robe, Dallas. Even when it burns."

He nodded, finding his footing again.

Dallas received the ethics board's letter—an unmarked envelope, ordinary among bills and circulars. Alone at his desk, he broke the seal with unsteady hands, the silence of the office pressing in. The verdict was clear and brief: "No violation found. No suspension." Sighing in a rush of relief, his shoulders shook, all the months of scrutiny and sleepless nights finally letting go.

That afternoon, after so much waiting, Dallas headed for the courthouse steps where tension lingered—rows of supporters holding signs alongside critics waving banners, the line between praise and protest as sharp as the autumn wind. His footsteps echoed, steady and deliberate, on the stone stairs, drawing the gaze of cameras arrayed in hungry anticipation. Questions cut through the air, each flash stinging his eyes, but he straightened his coat against the wind, jaw set.

He spoke, not seeking vindication but offering vision—a purpose honed in adversity. "I became a judge to serve people. The robe isn't armor—it's obligation. I will keep fighting for justice that sees the whole person. For courts that heal, not just punish. I'm not backing down. I won't—because to retreat would mean betraying those we're meant to serve."

His voice carried over the restless crowd, firm and measured amid the swirl of opinions. For Dallas, the letter wasn't the end—it was permission to press forward, carrying the scars of the ordeal as proof that integrity demanded resilience, and justice true to its name was worth every fight.

Final flashback: Dallas, arms crossed on the window ledge, staring out into the dusk, the echo of Arnold's voice a steady drum—"Play for both of us." In the present, he straightens his robe, squares his shoulders against the city's night, and steps into the future, playing for everyone who's still waiting for their turn.

A wave of cheers swept the crowd, joined by skeptics' scowls. But Dallas saw the future in the upturned faces of the young, the weary, the hopeful. He stood tall—not immune to the cost, but more certain than ever that sometimes, the trial of truth is the greatest legacy a person can claim.

Chapter 10: Blood Tells the Truth

———————— • ————————

The courthouse was standing-room only. The air thrummed with anticipation—a low, electric charge that ran beneath the coughs, whispers, and shuffles of a hundred people waiting for Dallas Jackson's verdict. Rain streaked the tall windows, throwing restless shadows across the tile. City lights bled softly through the storm, painting trembling reflections on the marble floor. This building had always been a theater of reckonings—its echoes full of pleas, confessions, and silent bargains—but never had the stakes felt so personal, so generational, a history pressing down from the gallery to the benches.

Behind the rail, Donna sat close beside Roman—a family, once splintered by addiction, abandonment, bureaucracy, and brutal luck, now drawn together by a fragile thread of healing and one quiet, desperate hope. Donna's hands twisted nervously in her lap, a wedding band spinning round and round on her finger. Roman's jaw was clamped shut, eyes fixed forward but trembling at each whispered name. The hope between them, unspoken and raw, nearly shone in the air.

Dallas took his seat on the bench, the ancient wood creaking with the weight of ritual and expectation. His spine straight but heart wild, he felt the robe settle heavy on his shoulders, a burden stitched with every judgment he'd ever made. Each breath summoned memories: Roman's mischievous, crooked smile on their last night at Fairview, the cold symmetry of cots lined up under humming lights, his own promise whispered through the dark—"We'll be brothers, no matter what happens, no matter who's listening." Those words echoed now as a vow and a weapon against despair.

He scanned the courtroom—attorneys with faces tight as masks, bailiffs impassive at their posts, the Miller family clinging to one another on the left-hand pew, the defendant's mother on the right nervously twisting her ring, knuckles paper-white. In the center, a boy, barely twelve, watched with haunted hope, chin tucked, hands clenched. Dallas saw a flicker of himself in that boy—the dread of not being seen, the wish that this moment could mean a new beginning.

The prosecutor spoke—legal phrases rising and falling like distant thunder—but Dallas's focus drifted, his mind slipping down corridors lined with truths and regrets. Each argument, each plea, layered atop the unvoiced histories in the room. He weighed not just the facts, but the future rippling out from this decision, a verdict that could fracture or heal. All around, anticipation pulsed, not just for justice, but for absolution—a reckoning measured in second chances and silent prayers.

Flashback: Age seven. Dallas, smallest kid in the home, trailing Arnold (not yet Roman) down the cafeteria line, copying every move. Tray trembling, he sits opposite Arnold. "You'll get used to it," Arnold says, breaking a roll and pressing half into his palm. "Someday, maybe someone will pick you for good." Dallas only nods, trying and failing to look brave.

The prosecutor recited the facts in clipped tones, painting the defendant's failures in blocks of evidence, and Dallas nodded, but his mind drifted. In every sentence, Dallas heard another sentence—a line of children, shuffled from foster family to foster family, carrying file numbers, always waiting to be chosen. He wondered if anyone could understand how the law could wound just as much as it healed.

He focused, letting his training take over, but the pain was familiar: every law he ever recited had been written over memories like these.

Every time he struck a gavel, he heard in his mind the click of a closing group home door, and the silence that lingered after Arnold was gone.

Flashback: Dallas, alone for the first night after Arnold's adoption. Staring up into the ceiling vents, clutching Arnold's comic book with its torn cover. A well-meaning caseworker tries to tuck him in. "He'll write," she promises. Dallas turns his face to the wall. He knew the lie: in Fairview, goodbyes were mostly for other people.

As the defense attorney began to speak, her tone softer, Dallas leaned in. The words were not new—explanations, apologies, the context of poverty, addiction, the long shadow of a family history broken long before the law intervened. But what caught Dallas was the defendant's voice, wavering, exhausted, stripped bare: "I just wanted somebody to come back. No one ever does."

He felt every heartbeat rattle in his ribcage. How many times had he wanted someone—Arnold, Donna, even a stranger—to come back for him? How long had he measured hope by the number of days since a goodbye?

Now, as rain hammered the courthouse, he realized this was not just a verdict. It was an inflection point in a lifetime of verdicts, both spoken and silent.

He cleared his throat. "This court," Dallas said, "recognizes guilt, but also the architecture of burdens—how pain can build walls between us and the futures we deserve. Sometimes, blood tells the truth. But so does what we choose—to forgive, to hope, to make family of strangers when the world would split us apart."

He spoke into the silence, making a ruling both with the law and with the story he had lived: the defendant would serve time, yes— rehabilitation and community service—but the sentence would be designed to reconnect, not destroy. "In this court, we remember what justice forgets—that lives do not begin or end with a single choice, but with every chance to come back again."

The gavel struck, thunder rolling outside as if to mark the moment.

* * *

Back in his chambers, Dallas felt the wind slow. The office was nearly dark; only city glow and the lightning's blade illuminated the shelves, the diplomas, the one faded Polaroid of him and Arnold—faces squashed together, smiling on a cracked step at Fairview.

The DNA results sat on his desk, folded in thick paper, heavy as stone. He turned it over in his hands, piecing memories together. He saw, all at once, the boy he had been—frightened and small, the heartbreak of being left behind—and the man he was, with the power to change what it meant to be family.

Flashback: Adoption day, years ago. Arnold in a pressed shirt beside a new family's minivan. Dallas watches from an upstairs window, pressing his forehead to sun-warmed glass. Arnold spots him—raises a hand, smiles with that old bravado. Dallas mimics the wave, refusing to cry until the car rounds the corner and he is finally, impossibly, alone.

A tap at the door startled him. Donna appeared, rain on her shoulders, red-rimmed eyes searching his face. Neither spoke for a moment. Dallas handed her the letter, every gesture suspended in the stillness broken only by wind and rain.

Donna read. The truth shimmered out—a quiet, aching Yes. She covered her mouth, a sob escaping, and then she hugged Dallas, the paper sandwiched between them, proof that hope had not lied.

"How do I tell him?" Dallas asked, voice ragged.

Donna shook her head. "Show him. Love him the way you always have. Fate isn't enough, Dallas. Family is chosen, too."

The evening unfolded around a dinner table—just Dallas, Donna, Roman, the scent of roasted garlic and warm bread, the flicker of candles at war with the storm outside.

For an hour, it was just laughter, gentle teasing, talk of work and lives lived through courtrooms and kitchens alike. Roman imitated a pompous attorney, Donna howled, Dallas actually smiled. The cheese burned under Donna's broiler, and no one cared.

After dessert, Donna brought out an old photo album. Hands trembling, she flipped to a page where ink-smudged footprints pressed up against a brittle hospital ID. Roman's brow creased. "Where did you get this?"

Donna's voice broke. "From the day you were born. They let me hold you for five minutes before they took you. I kept the proof. I never stopped believing you'd come back."

Roman's breath hitched. Dallas offered the napkin—creased, drawn with the checkerboard they'd sketched under bedsheets at Fairview.

"Do you remember?" Dallas asked.

"Every square," Roman said, his arms suddenly around them both. "I kept trying to find it—find us," he confessed, his voice muffled against Dallas's shoulder. "Even when I didn't know how."

Tears fell—silently at first, but then openly, freedom in the pain and joy mixed together. The candles guttered, the storm rolled on, and the three of them, once so separate, became family by admission, by blood, by old longing finally answered.

They talked deep into the night: of lost years, missed birthdays, Dallas's cold adoptive home, Roman's struggle to fit into the world outside the system, Donna's years of recovery. Each story closed a distance, every confession a small piece of healing.

"There's nobody else I'd want as my family," Roman said, voice thick. "Not anymore."

Donna took both their hands, squeezing tight. "The world tried to keep us apart. And it lost."

The next morning, the courthouse returned to its usual rush—phones ringing, doors slamming, lawyers in frantic search for a last signature or file. But inside Courtroom 1, Dallas and Roman stepped in together—silent, unannounced, just present.

Staff felt the difference—something changed, something solidified. No title needed, no speech required; the connection was visible, a kind of calm at the heart of the daily storm.

Dallas took his seat at the bench, Roman observing with all the composure of a colleague and all the secret pride of a brother newly found. Today, verdicts were handed down not out of habit but out of deep, lived understanding.

Flashback: The last day in Fairview. A staffer calls Roman's name; he hugs Dallas so fast it's nearly missed. "Play for both of us," Roman whispers. Dallas, too stunned, nods. "I will," he says—and, for all the years apart, he never really stopped.

After adjournment, Dallas met Roman's eyes across the room—an unspoken promise now made flesh and spirit. They would never be disconnected again.

The world would go on—still unfair, still slow to learn. But for Dallas, for Roman, for Donna, the search was over. The missing pieces had come home.

And in that realization, in that shared smile, a new story began—of second chances not just for the kids in the courthouse, but for everyone brave enough to hope again.

Chapter 11: Full Circle

———————— • ————————

The courtroom doors opened—slow, deliberate, their aged hinges singing a note of warning into the high-ceilinged hush. A shaft of morning light slashed across the black-and-ivory checkerboard of polished tiles, and for a moment, dust twirled like dancers in the golden air—a quiet spectacle before chaos and judgment. Dallas Jackson entered—his gait measured, disciplined after years spent crossing battlefields and borders. He held his spine impossibly straight, a habit from Fairview days, yet the scars earned in silent corners pressed against his fresh-laundered shirt: reminders that courage is sometimes quieter than fear.

Every step Dallas took felt like a declaration. No longer the thin, retreating boy who'd survived one small-town cruelty after another, nor the patrolman haunted by flashes of loss and violence, he crossed the room as a judge practicing mercy and restraint. He scanned the benches—lines worn smooth by thousands who'd come seeking either absolution or punishment—and found a kindred loneliness in every surface.

The docket appeared routine at first: procedural hearings, complaints echoing old family resentments, a minor possession case with a boy whose hands shook as he clung to his public defender's words. Dallas, ever vigilant, marked the boy's silent plea beneath a mop of hair—he recognized fear that wore through generations.

But then, an anomaly—a file with a name pulsing atop it in stark, typewritten letters:

State vs. Jake Cooper.

A chill drifted up Dallas's spine. He touched the folder, recalling the ways trauma shape-shifts, returning when least expected. The name bruised his memory: Jake, his adolescent nemesis, whose cruel laughter and jeering stings raced through Dallas's neurons even years later. High school snapped into focus—locker banks echoing with slammed doors, Dallas braced for the next humiliation, his braces glinting, sleeves chewed and damp with nervous sweat. Jake, relentless, always ready with a shove and a sneer.

Dallas closed his eyes, grounding himself—breathing as military training and therapy instructed, through the ache, into the present.

Donna entered, her clerk's badge swinging gently with each purposeful step. Rain pixels sparkled on the windows; coffee steam curled above her mug. Years of addiction and recovery had transformed Donna—her pain now transmuted into compassion, her sense of order near-religious. She set out the files precisely, her hands deft and steady. Her gaze rested on the prosecution table, where Roman—her son—stacked notes with military precision.

Roman's jaw bore a fresh scar, livid and unspoken. Donna's heart skipped; the injury called up every guilt and every failure she'd cataloged as a mother. It reminded her of a day, long ago: a crowded hallway, teachers yelling, Roman bleeding but defiant, Jake's name like poison in the mouths of witnesses.

She reached for Roman now, her touch hesitant but resolute. "Did something happen in school?" she asked, voice thinning against the weight of old pain.

Roman stared at the file, the old wound mirrored in his eyes. "A fight. Some kid—Jake—pulled a knife." The words fell like verdicts. Donna's grip trembled, desperate for understanding but unwilling to unravel.

Roman presented the case with unwavering focus, laying out facts with the steely calm learned from watching too many verdicts fall. He held the room's attention the way a field medic commands those in shock—a survivor, not just a prosecutor.

Dallas presided, reciting statutes almost by muscle memory. But inside, his old wounds stirred, tracing the psychology of cruelty cultivated in hallways and homes. Was there ever real justice for heartbreak seeded in childhood? He remembered Jake cornering him near the lockers, words slashing deeper than any blade: "You think anyone's coming for you? Not in this school. Not in this world." Each trial since had been a response to that promise—Dallas's vow to stand for those forgotten.

He steadied himself: This proceeding would not be revenge disguised as justice. It would be an act of transformation—a crucible to break the chain of suffering, turning bitter inheritance into hope.

During recess, Donna pressed a folded note into Dallas's palm. "The scar on Roman—it's Jake. I saw it. I needed you to know." Dallas folded the note into his jacket, understanding instantly—there would be no vengeance, only the demand for compassion.

The trial unfolded quietly, tension thick as steam. Dallas met Jake's gaze as he took the stand—older now, the bravado drained, empty eyes fixed somewhere between regret and resignation. As testimony unraveled, the air in the courtroom sharpened, every whisper and shuffle heightened by the stakes.

After closing arguments, Dallas rendered his verdict. Not just punishment but a prescription for growth: Jake would serve time, yes, but the sentence also mandated counseling, restitution, community service—resources meant to break cycles, not reinforce them. "Justice is not about who we were," Dallas intoned, voice nearly breaking, "but who we choose to be—starting now."

The gavel fell—soft, almost a blessing rather than a rebuke. The doors closed behind Jake, and a new silence filled the courtroom—less the aftermath of battle, more the breath before new beginnings.

Donna, Roman, and Dallas lingered, the possibility of healing palpable between them. They left together, the past no longer a chain, but a circle—where every scar, every failed rescue, every hard-won forgiveness bent toward redemption.

Flashback: Jake cornering Dallas near the lockers. "You think anyone's coming for you? Not in this school. Not in this world." Dallas trembling, heart pounding, every cruel echo becoming a future promise: I will become someone who comes for the forgotten.

This trial, Dallas resolved, would not be about revenge. It would be about the power to break the chain—to transform poisoned inheritance into healing. "Today," he whispered to himself, "we prove brokenness doesn't have to last forever."

During recess, Donna pressed a folded note into Dallas's palm. "Roman's scar—it's from Jake. I remember it. I saw it happen. I needed you to know." Dallas tucked it close to his heart, no words needed—she understood, just as Roman did, that knowing the truth didn't demand vengeance but demanded compassion.

The trial ended quietly. Dallas looked into Jake's eyes—now older, hollow, the bully burned away, remnant of lost potential. He rendered a verdict not just for the crime, but for the cruelty that shaped both their histories. Jake would serve time—but with a focus on rehabilitation, with mandated counseling, with opportunities to break free from the legacy of pain. "Justice is not about who we were," Dallas intoned, "but who we choose to be, starting now."

As Dallas struck the gavel, the echo was softer than usual—less a final blow, more a gentle closing of a long, unfinished story.

The courtroom emptied; the hush left behind brimmed with possibility. Donna, Roman, and Dallas lingered, gathered near the bench—a family remade by resilience, gathering up the messy threads of the past.

Flashback: Donna, lost to addiction, watching social workers walk her children away—first Roman, then Dallas, then silence. Her decision later—phone calls, rehab meetings, her hands trembling each time she said the word "mother."

Now, as clerk, she watched Roman—confident, purposeful. She felt the old ache soften: "I thought I'd lost you both. But here you are."

Roman took her hand, silent solidarity in their shared pain. "We came back," he answered. "Full circle."

Together, with Dallas, they left the courthouse as the rain tapered off. Each step down the hall felt lighter—a ritual of release, finally possible.

Epilogue: Full Circle: Revisited

Rain drummed a slow, meditative tattoo on the courthouse windows as Dallas Jackson settled back in his chair, robe folded across his lap, hands at rest for the first time in years. The office, usually a hive of hurried consultations and ringing phones, felt different tonight—quieter, softer, but rich with the imprints of countless struggles and triumphs. The dim glow of lamplight softened the shelves stacked with law books and the well-worn chessboard tucked in the corner. The room hummed with echoes—laughter, tears, victories, and losses—each memory a small act of grace or defiance.

But tonight, the silence wasn't empty.

It was earned.

Donna and Roman sat together nearby, going through albums and relics: the checkerboard napkin from Fairview, the battered black chess knight passed between hands in silence years before, the Polaroid faded to time but clear in meaning. Three souls, once shattered apart, were now linked across a table set for hope.

Dallas had seen many reunions in his courthouse—some trembling, some angry, some short-lived—but nothing could have prepared him for this. The way Donna's hands trembled as she touched the edges of a faded photo. The way Roman's eyes softened every time he caught Dallas staring, as if rediscovering his brother all over again. The way Dallas felt a strange new tether pulling at his heart, one that anchored him not toward the past, but toward a future he never imagined he deserved.

Flashback

A letter, crumpled from countless readings, Dallas's name scribbled on the front in uneven penmanship.

Dear Dallas, I hope you're doing good…

Roman, in an unfamiliar new room, writing by a night-light, every word a lifeline thrown across the gulf of separation. Donna, years later, thumbing through a shoebox filled with these notes, hoping something—love, destiny, pure stubbornness—would one day knit their family back together.

The rain deepened outside, a steady, cleansing rhythm.

Dallas looked through rain-laced glass at the city, light fractured in rivers across the dark. The courthouse, once a fortress and sometimes a cage, felt newly transfigured—a place of sanctuary, of beginnings, not just endings. He thought of every child who'd stood before him, frightened or angry, carrying the weight of stories no one else wanted to hear. He thought of every parent clawing their way back from failure; every sibling who'd learned too early the fragility of belonging.

He thought of himself.

He thought of the boy he was told he'd never outgrow.

His greatest verdict, Dallas knew, was not measured in gavel strikes. It was the way ordinary grace multiplied—through small, stubborn acts of courage and forgiveness. Acts that echoed louder than the courtroom microphones, louder than the past anyone once tried to trap him in.

He whispered softly, his words threading out through the drizzle onto empty streets.

"We cannot change where our story starts, but we choose, again and again, where it ends. We choose love, justice, and the power to break the cycles the world gives us."

He stood, shoulders lighter.

"Let's go home," he said—not to an address, but to Donna and Roman—the faces that held his future.

As they stepped into the echoing corridor, music drifted faintly from an upper floor—someone rehearsing a violin, another employee singing to herself, a young lawyer laughing with a bailiff over an inside joke. The world Dallas once believed indifferent was, after all, stitched together with moments like these. Moments where life insisted on gentleness.

Monday Morning

The rain eased off. The morning air smelled like fresh stone and possibility.

Dallas moved through courtroom halls, a living thread woven into the warp and weft of justice—no longer a cage, but a cathedral. His steps sparked memory upon memory with every echo:

Flashback: Young Dallas, anxious in the Fairview dayroom, staring longingly at the front gate. A volunteer once told him, "Sometimes the only way out is through." He repeated those words until they became armor.

He had walked through.

And somehow, impossibly, there was more road ahead.

Cases came and went: a minor possession charge, a squabble between neighbors, the usual shuffle of daily grievances and hopes. But then, the next defendant—a gaunt man in orange, head bowed, scars of living visible in every shrug—brought Dallas full circle.

Jake Cooper.

Once a bully, now another soul spilled onto the floor of the justice system.

Dallas paused, letting himself remember—shoved books, cruel nicknames, muttered threats back in school, and the raw shame that followed him home. He remembered the sting, the humiliation, the quiet tears he hid in the back stairwell.

And yet, as he watched Jake's trembling hands, the whole story unfolded: every cruelty a defense, every threat the echo of a childhood spent with no safe place to land. Abuse breeds fear. Fear breeds anger. Anger lashes out at whatever stands closest.

For the first time, Dallas saw Jake not as the monster from middle school, but as the wounded boy behind the noise.

Flashback:

Dallas, hiding in the library, tracing chess moves onto scrap paper, promising himself he would never treat anyone as badly as he'd been treated. Loneliness and hope, twin gods of his growing up.

He granted Jake probation instead of jail—mandating therapy and meaningful service, a chance to make different choices.

The gavel fell—a sound not of vengeance, but of reprieve.

Jake looked up at him, eyes wet. "Why?"

Dallas didn't hesitate.

"Because someone once gave me a chance when I didn't deserve it either."

Jake nodded, swallowing hard—an old wound finally given room to breathe.

Donna's Discovery

Donna, working the morning docket, couldn't take her eyes off the prosecutor. The jagged mark near his eye, a tilt of his smile, the resonance in his voice—so hauntingly familiar it stirred something deep and primal. "Could it be?" she thought. Her heart raced.

Between cases, she scribbled a note and brought it to Dallas:

"Please see Prosecutor Arnold in chambers. Emergency."

After court, in his office, tension crackled as Dallas and Donna waited. In came Arnold, rain still on his shoes, calm yet wary. Donna's hands shook as she reached for him, too afraid to touch"Who is your mother? Were you adopted?" she asked, her voice a whisper.

"My mom is Anne. I was adopted at seven," Arnold answered, eyes darting, uncertainty flickering.

Donna pressed on. "You were born at Memorial Hospital. You had a birthmark like this." She pointed, tears now free. "Your name was Roman Arnold."

Arnold's world spun. He called his mother, voice trembling. "Was I born as Roman Arnold?"

A soft voice on the phone: "Yes, sweetheart. Yes, that was you."

Donna erupted into tears, years of wanting and not daring to hope pouring out. "I found my baby," she wept, grasping him like he was light and air.

Dallas, eyes wide, stepped back—memories colliding: childhood chess games in the group home, a best friend who changed his life, a deep, unspoken ache for family.

"You… you're my brother," he choked. "You taught me chess. You were my hero, Arnold—Roman. My real brother."

In that instant, the room grew small, history and fate coiling together. The three embraced—Donna, Roman, Dallas—a fragile, fierce tangle of arms and joy and tears.

A New Life Together

They went home that night, not as the judge, the clerk, and the prosecutor—but as a mother and her sons. Over a humble dinner, stories poured out—Donna told of the lonely years and every failed attempt to search; Roman spoke of wondering why nothing quite fit, and Dallas relived every promise, every night spent hoping someone would remember him.

They toasted the chess piece, the napkin, the faded Polaroid—relics of a time now rewritten into legacy. Roman, fiddling with the chess knight, laughed softly. "You know, I always wanted a brother. I just didn't expect to get him in the courtroom."

Donna squeezed their hands, her eyes shining. "My babies," she whispered, "you found each other through every storm."

Flashback:

Donna, years earlier, lighting a single candle on a kitchen counter, praying quietly, "Give them each what I could not. Give them family, even if it's not me."

Now, against all odds, she had both.

Sunrise

The next morning, as dawn broke over the city and shafts of gold spilled across marble floors, Dallas walked through the courthouse with Roman and Donna by his side. The halls seemed softer, more forgiving. He stopped at the mural of birds and open hands—painted by youth from the Initiative, a reminder that hope is a daily decision.

Outside, the world was waiting—but inside, Dallas was, at last, at peace. He had remade a legacy from broken pieces. He had chosen, every day, to answer cruelty with justice, shame with mercy, loneliness with love.

He turned, looking at Roman and Donna, all the words not needed in the warm silence between them.

"Let's go home. Start again."

The courthouse was empty, but their footsteps rang with assurance, echoing into the city—proof that the story didn't end in pain, but in return, in family, in the hard-won freedom of belonging.

Full circle.

At last.

One Month Later

The reunion didn't simply shift the atmosphere in the Jackson household — it shifted everything.

What began as late-night conversations turned into morning routines: coffee cups clinking, shared breakfasts, Roman dropping by before work, Donna humming gospel songs while packing baked goods for the courthouse staff. Their once-fractured family was slowly forming its own rhythm, hesitant but hopeful, like a choir learning the harmony of new notes.

For Dallas, every morning felt like stepping into a world he had watched from afar but never fully entered. There were moments he still caught himself stopping in doorways, staring at Donna and Roman laughing over crossword puzzles and thinking:

Is this real? Are they really mine?

Sometimes his chest tightened — joy and grief intertwined, two threads wrapped around each other. He had so much love now, but also so much time lost.

Roman noticed these pauses, these quiet internal storms. One night he placed a gentle hand on Dallas's shoulder.

"We can't get the years back," Roman said, "but we can fill the ones ahead."

Dallas nodded, swallowing hard. It wasn't forgiveness he needed — it was permission to be loved.

Healing the Years Between Them

Family therapy began every Thursday evening after work. They sat together in a warmly lit office full of lush plants and soft jazz music.

The therapist, Dr. Imani Rhodes, had a way of thinning walls with simple questions.

"What did you need back then?"

"What do you need now?"

"Where does the pain show up in your body?"

"How does your voice sound when you talk to someone you trust?"

Donna struggled the most at first. She clutched tissue after tissue as she confessed the shame, the addiction, the mental health battles, the choices she wished she could erase.

"I abandoned them," she whispered one evening. "Twice. Once when I lost them, and again when I convinced myself they were better off without me."

Roman reached for her hand. "You didn't abandon us. You lost your way. But you're here now."

Dallas took a long breath. His heart cracked open in slow inches. "I thought… if my own mother couldn't keep me, I must not have been worth keeping."

Donna broke — not in despair, but in release. She slid off the couch and wrapped her arms around him, sobbing into his shirt.

"My baby," she whispered. "You were never the problem. Life was."

They stayed there, tangled in old wounds and new healing, until the therapist gently guided them back to their seats.

It would not fix everything at once.

But it cracked open the door to healing.

Community Ripples Begin

It didn't take long before people at the courthouse noticed something different about Dallas — a shift in his posture, a gentleness threading through his uncompromising sense of justice. He was still firm, still brilliant, still surgical with his words, but there was more space in him now. More understanding.

The story of his reunion with Roman and Donna — whispered in hallways, repeated in conference rooms — began circulating quietly. Staff exchanged knowing smiles. Clerks brought casseroles and congratulatory cards. The bailiff joked that the courthouse felt like a Hallmark movie.

But something deeper was happening beneath the surface.

People began approaching Dallas differently.

A young public defender asked if he could help her create a mentorship program.

A social worker mentioned wanting to start a trauma-informed court day.

A probation officer asked about restorative justice circles.

Dallas found himself saying yes — not out of obligation, but out of a newfound mission.

His reunion hadn't just healed him — it ignited something.

A purpose.

A calling.

A responsibility.

One evening he gathered everyone in a small courtroom and proposed an idea that simmered in him for weeks:

The Fairview Initiative.

A program named after the place where he and Roman once lived — a bridge between the community, the courthouse, and the youth most at risk of falling through the cracks. It would offer:

- mentorship
- therapy
- job readiness
- addiction support
- parent restoration
- and restorative justice practices

A second chance for kids who reminded him too much of himself.

The room erupted in applause.

For the first time, Dallas wasn't just healing his past.

He was changing someone else's future.

Three Months Later — Expanding the Circle

The Jackson family was no longer meeting only on Sundays. They were showing up at each other's lives the way families do when they realize time is precious.

Roman helped Dallas repaint his living room.

Donna brought over homemade meals almost daily.

Dallas took Donna to her doctor appointments, something she had always done alone.

They attended therapy together, worship together, and sometimes sat in silence together.

One evening, Donna brought a long-forgotten tin box from her attic.

Inside were scraps of their childhood:

A lock of hair.

A tiny bracelet.

A hospital card with smudged footprints.

A list of names she once dreamed of giving them.

Roman sorted through each item with reverence.

Dallas stared at the hospital card — his tiny footprints stamped in fading ink.

"How did you keep this?" he whispered.

"Because I never stopped loving you," Donna said. "I just didn't know how to come back."

The words softened something rigid inside him. He didn't forgive her instantly, but he understood her in a way he never had. Trauma spoke many languages; hers had always been silence.

That night, he hugged her longer than usual.

The Community Responds

As the Fairview Initiative grew, donations began arriving from unexpected places.

A retired teacher offered to tutor.

A local pastor volunteered his church basement for meetings.

A business owner sponsored youth internships.

Parents signed up for support groups, some for the first time in their lives.

Kids who once sat in holding cells now sat in art classes.

Teens who once fought on street corners now learned to box safely in supervised programs.

Youth who were dismissed as troublemakers now gathered around tables discussing their dreams.

The courthouse began to feel like a bridge, not a barrier.

One afternoon, a teenage boy named Mateo stood in front of Dallas, eyes wide with emotion.

"You don't know me," he said, "but you saved my life. My case got sent to the Initiative instead of jail… and I'm passing all my classes now. My mom said she can sleep at night again."

Dallas swallowed hard. "I'm proud of you, Mateo."

"Can I… can I hug you?" the boy asked.

They embraced, and a photographer for the county captured the moment quietly from the doorway.

That photo went viral.

The caption read:

"Judgment does not always mean punishment."

A Moment of Reflection

One crisp autumn evening, Dallas visited the Fairview group home — the place where he'd once felt both trapped and protected. The building had been repainted, and a new playground stood where the cracked pavement once stretched.

Roman stood beside him, hands in his pockets.

"Feels different than I remember," Roman said.

"It does," Dallas agreed. "But I think we're different too."

A group of kids ran past them, laughing — one wearing a backpack too big for his shoulders, another carrying a notebook full of doodles. A staff member waved from the porch.

Dallas felt his heart turn warm and unfamiliar.

This was the place he once prayed to escape.

Now it was the place he prayed others would escape from too — but with support, not abandonment.

"We survived this," Roman said quietly. "We really did."

Dallas nodded. "And look how far we made it."

Roman smirked. "Mom said she wants family pictures next week. Matching outfits."

Dallas groaned. "God help us."

They both laughed, the kind of laugh only survivors share — one that tastes like freedom.

Donna's Turning Point

Donna had started working part-time at a nonprofit that helped mothers recovering from addiction reunify with their children. She sat in circles with women trembling with hope, fear, shame, and longing.

She shared her story — not as a professional, but as a mother who knew the depth of regret intimately.

"I lost my children," she told them, "and I thought that meant I lost God's grace too. But God still found me. And my sons did too."

Women cried. Women hugged her.

Women asked her how she learned to forgive herself.

She always answered honestly.

"I haven't finished forgiving myself. But I wake up every morning and try."

Her honesty made her something rare in that space: believable.

Her story spread through the community, not as gossip, but as hope.

A Turning Point for Dallas

One night, after a long day in court, Dallas sat alone in his office staring at the chessboard. The black knight — the same battered piece Roman once used in Fairview — sat in the center.

He lifted it gently.

Every scar on the piece felt like a scar on him.

He remembered the nights he sat in the dormitory, placing chess pieces in imaginary tournaments, trying to think like a champion instead of a statistic.

Now, he was not only a champion of his own life

He was becoming a champion of others.

He set the knight down firmly.

"I'm not done," he whispered.

Six Months Later — The First Annual Fairview Dinner

The Fairview Initiative grew faster than anyone expected. What started as a single mentoring circle inside a courthouse conference room blossomed into a full-fledged network of programs. There were counseling sessions, job training clinics, fatherhood classes, art therapy workshops, and conflict resolution seminars.

People came not because they were ordered to,

but because—for the first time—they felt seen.

To celebrate the progress, the Initiative held its first annual dinner at the community center gym. The space was transformed with string lights, rented tablecloths, and dozens of posters showcasing the artwork of participating teens.

Dallas stood near the entrance with Roman and Donna, each equally stunned at the turn-out.

"Look at this," Roman murmured, scanning the room. "A year ago, none of this existed."

Donna gripped both their arms, tears shimmering. "You boys did this."

"No," Dallas corrected gently, "we did this."

A young girl approached them shyly—no older than thirteen, dressed in a hand-me-down blazer.

"Judge Jackson," she said quietly, "I want to say thank you. My brother… he got into that art program after his case, and now he's doing better. He's happier."

Dallas crouched down to her eye level. "What's his name?"

"Eric." She smiled. "He made one of the paintings over there. The one with the birds."

Dallas turned toward the mural-sized canvas: three dark silhouettes of boys standing beneath a sunrise, birds soaring above them. The symbolism struck him with unexpected force.

Three boys.

A sunrise.

A beginning.

His throat tightened.

"It's beautiful," he whispered.

She nodded proudly. "He said it's about how you helped give him wings."

Dallas blinked rapidly. "Tell him… tell him he gave himself wings. I only opened the window."

The girl giggled, ran back to her mother, and whispered excitedly.

Donna touched the center of her chest. "You're changing lives, baby."

Dallas inhaled, deeply humbled. "We all are."

Before the dinner ended, Dallas gave a short speech. He wasn't a man prone to long public talks, but tonight the words came naturally.

"When I was young," he began, "I believed that broken beginnings meant broken futures. But what I've learned—what we've all learned—is that healing doesn't happen alone. It happens in community. It happens when people show up."

He looked at Donna and Roman.

"At one point, I didn't believe I had a family. Now I have two brothers standing beside me—one by blood, one by destiny. And I have a mother who fought her way back through storms most people never survive."

Donna began crying softly.

"This initiative," Dallas continued, "isn't a courthouse program. It's a living reminder that cycles can break. Kids can rise. Families can be rebuilt. And hope—real hope—can take root in the places we least expect."

The applause shook the gym.

It was the kind of applause that doesn't just honor someoneIt believes in them.

Roman's Rising Purpose

While Dallas became the face of the Initiative, Roman found himself stepping into something he never anticipated: mentorship.

He began leading weekly chess groups for young boys—some from the courthouse, some from broken homes, some simply needing a space to breathe. The club met in a circle of tables at the community library.

Roman didn't teach chess the way most instructors did.

He taught it the way he had learned it at Fairviewas survival, strategy, and storytelling.

"Every piece," he explained one afternoon, "has strengths and weaknesses. Like people. Like us. The trick isn't to be the strongest piece. It's to understand how to move with purpose."

One boy—Jason, age eleven—stared at the chessboard with arms folded tightly across his chest.

"I always lose," he muttered.

Roman leaned forward. "So did I. But losing is what teaches you to see the board."

Jason looked up, confused.

"See it how?"

Roman tapped the knight—the same battered piece he carried for years, the one he always kept in his pocket.

"You start by noticing your options. Then you choose your future."

Jason stared at the piece, eyes widening.

"You can borrow it," Roman said softly. "Only if you want to."

Jason held it like something sacred.

In that moment, Roman realized what Dallas had discovered months earlier:

Healing was contagious.

Donna's Second Chance

Donna had always known she wanted to help people. What she didn't know was that the community wanted her.

Her raw honesty, her transparency, her quiet resilience—it drew people to her like a lighthouse on stormy waters. Soon she was asked to speak at recovery centers, then women's shelters, then local churches.

One evening, she was invited to share her story at a mother-daughter conference. The room was filled with women who held pain behind carefully painted faces.

Donna stepped up to the podium with trembling hands.

"I spent years lost in addiction," she began. "It took my children from me. It took my health, my dreams, my hope. I thought my story ended there."

A hush fell over the audience.

"But God whispered that I wasn't done. And my sons… they found me again. They saved me without knowing they saved me."

Women cried openly.

Teenage daughters clutched their mothers' hands.

Afterward, a young woman approached Donna.

"My mom is in recovery," she said, voice cracking. "Do you think someone like her could—could really rebuild with me?"

Donna took her hands gently.

"Baby, if there's breath in her lungs and love in her heart, she can rebuild anything."

The girl sobbed, folding into her arms.

Donna held her as if she were one of her own.

A Crisis at the Courthouse

One rainy afternoon, chaos erupted in the courthouse lobby. A mother who had lost custody of her children collapsed in hysterics after her hearing. Security panicked. Staff shouted. People stood frozen.

Dallas rushed forward, kneeling beside the woman.

She shook violently. "They took my babies—they took them—they took them—"

Dallas held her hands firmly.

"Look at me," he said, voice low but steady. "You're not alone. Not today."

Her sobs softened into whimpers.

"You hear me?" he repeated. "This is not the end of your story. We will get you help. We will get you support. You can fight for them. You can rise."

She leaned into him, shaking.

When paramedics arrived, they asked Dallas to step aside.

The woman reached for his hand.

"Please don't forget me," she whispered.

He shook his head. "I won't. And I won't let you forget yourself."

The incident shook Dallas more than he admitted.

It reminded him of Donna—of the day she lost everything.

Of how close she came to never returning.

That evening, he sat at the kitchen table with Donna and Roman.

"We need a crisis team at the courthouse," Dallas said. "Mental health intervention. A safe space. Trained responders."

Donna nodded immediately. "I'll help."

Roman said, "Tell me where to sign."

Within months, the courthouse established a dedicated Family Stabilization Unit—the first of its kind in the county.

Healing wasn't just happening in homes and programs.

It was happening inside the very system that once failed them.

A Night of Truth

One evening, after a long day of work and a modest dinner at Donna's house, Dallas found himself lingering after Roman left.

Donna was washing the last plate when she noticed him staring into an old family photo on her wall: a picture of her at nineteen, holding a baby that could have been Roman or Dallas.

"You look like you're thinking hard," she said, drying her hands.

Dallas swallowed. "Do you ever wish things were different?"

Donna stepped closer. "Every day. But wishing don't change the past, baby. Only living does."

He nodded, but something still sat heavy on him.

"You don't regret finding me?" he asked quietly. "Finding us?"

Donna's eyes softened to a tenderness that nearly unraveled him.

"Oh, Dallas," she whispered. "Finding you saved me. You brought me home to myself."

He broke then—tears filling his eyes as he took her into his arms.

For the first time, he allowed himself to believe it:

He wasn't a burden.

He wasn't a mistake.

He was a miracle.

And so was she.

The Seed of a Legacy

The Fairview Initiative received a federal grant.

The courthouse crisis unit became a statewide model.

Donna's story inspired a documentary team to approach her for an interview.

Roman's chess club doubled in size and received a county award for youth empowerment.

And Dallas?

He became something he never expected to be:

A symbol.

A symbol of resilience.

A symbol of second chances.

A symbol of systems reimagined, not abandoned.

But he was also something far more precious:

A son.

A brother.

A man choosing love without fear.

One Year Later — The Courthouse Garden

The courthouse grounds had always been a place of tension. People paced between hearings, lawyers rehearsed arguments, mothers cried, fathers prayed, and children fidgeted on benches they didn't understand.

But now, something new existed there:

The Fairview Garden.

What began as a small patch of soil outside the west entrance grew into a full community garden maintained by youth in the Fairview Initiative. Herbs, flowers, vegetables—everything flourished under hands that once trembled with fear or anger.

A sign stood at the entrance:

"Where healing takes root."

— Dedicated to all who rise again

Dallas walked through the garden on a quiet morning, the sun still yawning across the horizon. Dewdrops clung to petals like soft glass. Volunteers watered beds in silence, a peacefulness wrapped around them.

Roman joined him moments later, coffee in hand.

"Can you believe we used to be in holding tanks inside this building?" he said with a half-smirk.

Dallas exhaled. "Feels like a different lifetime."

"Maybe it is."

A group of teens waved at them from the far side of the garden.

"Judge Jackson! Mr. Arnold! Come see the peppers!"

The brothers approached, laughing as one boy held up a bright red pepper in triumph.

"Look, it's bigger than my hand!"

"That's because you planted it," Dallas said. "You chose to give it time, attention, patience."

Another boy chimed in, "Like you and your brother?"

Roman laughed. "Something like that."

The garden had become more than a symbol.

It was a declaration:

People grow where they are nurtured.

A Major Case That Changed Everything

The year wasn't without challenges.

One case in particular tested Dallas in ways he hadn't expected.

A teenage boy named Malik faced charges for armed robbery. He was sixteen, terrified, and carried trauma so thick it clung to every movement. The system wanted to try him as an adult.

But Dallas saw something else.

He saw a boy who flinched at loud noises.

A boy who apologized too quickly.

A boy carrying bruises that were too old and too deep.

During court, Malik's voice shook as he said, "I wasn't trying to hurt nobody. I just… I couldn't pay rent. My mom got laid off. My brother's sick. I thought it was the only way."

The prosecution wanted jail time.

The public roared for punishment.

But Dallas knew punishment without restoration only deepened cycles.

He stood before the judge, center of a courtroom buzzing with expectation.

"Your Honor," he began, "I'm not here to argue innocence. Malik made a mistake. But if we only punish him, we create another adult with no support, no options, no hope. If we intervene—truly intervene—we save a child from becoming a statistic."

The judge frowned. "You're recommending full diversion?"

"Yes," Dallas said firmly. "And placement in the Fairview Initiative."

The courtroom murmured loudly.

Dallas continued, "This young man is not a criminal. He is a child carrying the weight of adult survival. Let us lift that weight—not add to it."

The judge deliberated for several long minutes before granting the request.

Malik broke down in tears.

After the hearing, Dallas found him sitting on the steps outside the courthouse.

"Why'd you do that for me?" Malik asked.

Dallas sat beside him. "Because someone did it for me. And because you matter."

Malik wiped his face. "I wanna do better."

"You will," Dallas said. "And we'll be here to help."

This case became a turning point for the county.

A shift in ideology.

A statement that childhood pain doesn't have to become adult crime.

A Letter from the Governor

Months later, a sealed envelope arrived in Dallas's courthouse mailbox. The return address made him freeze.

Office of the Governor.

Inside was a formal letter, written with sincere tone:

"Your leadership has sparked statewide interest in restorative justice practices. We are considering adopting the Fairview Model as a statewide program. Your personal story and professional integrity have inspired many. We would like to schedule a meeting to discuss implementation."

Dallas sank into his chair.

Roman burst into the office minutes later after hearing the news.

"You're going statewide?" he demanded.

"No," Dallas murmured. "We are."

Roman hugged him hard. "I'm proud of you, man."

Donna, upon hearing the news, immediately burst into tears.

"My son… making laws? Helping children across the state? God, you do work miracles."

The Fairview Initiative wasn't just growing.

It was becoming a blueprint.

A Visit to Donna's Past

To move forward, they had to heal backward.

One quiet Saturday, Donna asked Dallas and Roman if they could accompany her somewhere. She wouldn't say where.

They drove to a small, sun-faded apartment complex on the outskirts of the city. Donna walked slowly, breathing shakily.

"This is where… everything fell apart," she whispered. "This is where I lost you."

Roman took one of her hands.

Dallas took the other.

She stood in front of the building as if standing before a grave.

But after several minutes, her breathing steadied.

"This place used to haunt me," she said. "But I'm done letting it."

She turned away.

"I have my boys now. I have a second chance."

They walked her back to the car, arms linked.

For the first time in decades, Donna took control of her own story.

Roman's New Identity

Roman had always carried quiet strength — but now it was becoming a purpose.

He earned certifications in youth counseling, conflict mediation, and trauma-informed coaching. He spent weekends attending workshops and nights studying until dawn. The chess club grew so popular that libraries and schools requested satellite programs.

People began calling him "Coach Ro."

He laughed at the nickname but secretly loved it.

One evening after club, Jason — the boy who borrowed Roman's chess knight months before — pulled him aside.

"I won my first tournament," Jason said proudly.

Roman grinned and hugged him.

"That's incredible!"

Jason handed him the knight.

"I want you to have it back."

Roman shook his head. "No, buddy. That's yours now. You've earned it."

Jason's face lit up.

"Does this mean… I can be a coach one day too?"

Roman crouched to the boy's height.

"You can be anything. And I'll help you get there."

In that moment Roman realized:

For years he thought Dallas was the hero.

But he had become one, too.

Donna's New Role in the Initiative

The Initiative leaders approached Donna with an offer:

Director of Family Restoration & Support Services.

She laughed at first, thinking they couldn't be serious. But they were.

She was the bridge between lived experience and professional guidance — and no one could speak to the realities of family loss and reunification like she could.

During her first team meeting, she looked nervous until Dallas squeezed her shoulder and whispered, "Just speak from the heart. That's your superpower."

So she did.

"Families don't break because of lack of love," she said. "They break because life gets heavy. My job is to help parents carry that weight."

A round of applause filled the room.

Donna was officially, finally,

a leader of healing — not shame.

The Anniversary of Their Reunion

A year after their courthouse reunion, they celebrated with a small dinner at Donna's home — mismatched plates, homemade food, soft gospel music.

Roman brought flowers.

Dallas brought dessert.

Donna lit a candle.

"To healing," she said.

"To family," Roman added.

"To the ones we were and the ones we've become," Dallas finished.

They ate, laughed, cried.

Old wounds felt lighter.

New memories began stitching themselves into the fabric of their lives.

After dinner, Donna showed them a scrapbook she'd been making — a collection of images from the past year: the garden, the chess club, the courthouse crisis unit, family therapy, the Initiative's dinner, and countless candid moments of them simply living life together.

On the final page was a picture of the three of them standing under the courthouse mural of open hands and birds.

Beneath it Donna had written:

"Love didn't arrive late.

It arrived right on time."

A Community United

By the end of the year, the county experienced:

- a 36% drop in juvenile recidivism,
- increased school attendance among Initiative participants,
- higher parent engagement rates,
- and fewer emergency removals.

Families were healing.

Youth were thriving.

Systems were shifting.

People credited Dallas, Roman, and Donna — but each of them insisted it was the work of many hearts.

Still, the community began referring to them affectionately as:

"The Jackson Trio of Hope."

They hated the nickname.

They pretended to groan whenever it was used.

But secretly, each of them cherished it deeply.

A Moment of Peace

One evening, after a particularly long day, Dallas and Roman returned to the Fairview Garden. Fireflies flickered softly. The air smelled like lavender.

Roman nudged Dallas. "Look at us."

Dallas smiled softly. "Who would've thought?"

"Mom," Roman said simply. "She always believed."

Dallas looked up at the sky, stars scattered like promises.

"Yeah," he whispered. "She did."

They stood in the garden for a long time — two brothers, whole at last.

One Year Later — A New Beginning

Spring arrived like a promise.

It swept through the city with gentle winds and sunlight that clung to windowsills like gold. The courthouse grounds were newly planted with flowers donated by volunteers from the Initiative. The same families who had once come through its doors seeking mercy now returned with seedlings, topsoil, and hope.

Dallas arrived early that morning, a thermos of tea in his hand. He paused at the stairs, looking at the vibrant purple blossoms lining the walkway.

"Morning, Judge Jackson!" a voice called.

He turned to see Mateo—the boy who once hugged him in the hallway, the same young man who credited Dallas with helping him turn his life around. Now he wore a campus sweatshirt, books tucked under one arm.

"Got into Miami Dade Honors Program!" Mateo announced proudly.

Dallas' heart swelled. "I knew you would. I'm proud of you."

Mateo grinned. "My mom said you should come over for dinner again. She's making birria tacos."

Dallas laughed. "Don't threaten me with a good time."

Mateo hugged him quickly before running off. Dallas watched him go—another life that refused to follow statistics.

There were hundreds like Mateo now.

Hundreds.

And each one reminded Dallas that generational cycles didn't break through punishment—they broke through compassion, accountability, and opportunity.

The Expanding Initiative

The Fairview Initiative had grown beyond the courthouse and community center. Partnerships formed with:

- schools
- juvenile divisions
- addiction recovery centers
- small businesses
- foster agencies
- faith-based organizations
- trauma-informed therapists
- vocational training programs

The Initiative had become a movement.

One afternoon, the mayor requested a private meeting with Dallas.

"You've changed the landscape of youth justice," the mayor said, leaning forward at her desk. "People see hope again."

Dallas blinked at the praise. He never pursued recognition—only impact.

Still, hearing those words stirred something inside him.

"We want to allocate permanent funding," the mayor continued. "Not just grants. We want the Initiative to become institutionalized."

Dallas nodded slowly. He'd seen programs die the moment leadership changed. Permanent funding meant survival. Growth. Reach.

"It means more families healed," he said quietly.

"It does," she agreed. "And we want you at the head of it."

Dallas felt a ripple of humility and overwhelm. "I don't want to be a face on a billboard," he said. "I want real results."

"That," she said, "is why we need you."

Donna's Breakthrough

Donna's work at the recovery center became her lifeline.

After a lengthy application process, she earned her Peer Support Specialist Certification, meaning she could officially counsel women navigating addiction and reunification. Her journey—once marked by shame—had become her greatest qualification.

One of her proudest moments was the day she stood before a graduating class of women who had completed the center's full recovery program.

"You remind me of myself," she said, voice trembling. "All that regret, all that confusion, all that fear… but I promise you, if healing can find me, it can find anyone."

The women cried with her.

They embraced her.

They thanked her.

But the moment that broke her completely was when a young mother— barely twenty-one—approached her with a toddler on her hip.

"Miss Donna… I got my baby back," she whispered.

Donna touched the child's cheek gently.

"You did the work," Donna replied. "You fought the storm. I'm just proud to have walked beside you."

That night, Donna sat on her porch under dim string lights and wept— not from sorrow, but from the overwhelming, holy relief of being useful. Being redeemed.

Being whole.

Roman's New Calling

Roman had always been the quiet one, the steady one, the observer. But the chess club had awakened a fire in him he hadn't known he possessed. He began taking night classes in youth counseling, slowly pursuing his Master's in Social Work.

"I want to do for others what someone did for me," he told Dallas one afternoon.

The brothers sat in a café with mismatched chairs and hand-painted mugs. Sunlight streamed in through the windows, casting warm stripes across their table.

"You're good at this," Dallas said. "Better than you think."

Roman smirked. "You're biased."

"No," Dallas said, shaking his head. "I've scanned a thousand case files. I've seen a thousand stories. But I've never met anyone who sees kids the way you do."

Roman swallowed hard at the compliment. Words like that still felt foreign against his skin.

"I want to open a youth center," he finally said. "A permanent one. Not just a club. A space where kids like us don't have to feel invisible."

Dallas leaned back. "Then let's build it."

And they did.

Within six months, they secured a building and donations. Volunteers painted walls, local artists designed murals, and Roman personally built the chess room—complete with dozens of boards, inspirational quotes, and a wall dedicated to former Fairview youth who had gone on to achieve their dreams.

At the entrance, engraved on a metal plate, were the words:

"Choose Your Move."

Below it:

Dedicated to the children who fight to rewrite their stories.

The News Feature

A local reporter caught wind of the Jackson family story—of the mother who reunited with her sons, the brothers who transformed the justice system, and the Initiative reshaping the city.

The feature aired one Sunday evening on the largest local network.

It included:

- archival footage of Fairview
- interviews with Donna
- highlights of the Initiative
- scenes of Roman teaching chess
- Dallas in the courtroom granting restorative sentences
- mothers reunited with their children
- teens who had avoided jail
- a montage of healed families

But the moment that left viewers sobbing was the one filmed silently—Dallas, standing alongside Donna and Roman at the mural of birds and open hands, gazing at the artwork that symbolized their entire journey.

The narrator's voice said:

"Some stories begin in brokenness, but they don't have to end there."

The feature went viral.

Within a week, emails poured in from across the country:

- judges asking for guidance
- teachers requesting mentorship programs
- parents sharing stories of reunification
- producers asking if the family would consider a documentary

But the message that touched Dallas most came from a man he hadn't spoken to in 15 years:

Jake Cooper.

"Judge Jackson… thank you. I'm clean now. Working at a barbershop. I'm rebuilding. Thank you for giving me a chance I never gave you in school."

Dallas breathed deeply and sent one line back.

"Everyone deserves redemption."

The Reunion Cookout

Donna insisted on hosting a massive family cookout to celebrate one full year of restoration. She invited cousins, neighbors, church members, coworkers, and half the Initiative staff.

The backyard filled with voices and laughter, the smell of grilled food drifting through the summer air. Children played tag, adults shared stories, and music hummed through speakers.

At one point, Donna grabbed a microphone with a dramatic flair only she could pull off.

"I just want to say," she began, swaying slightly as everyone turned toward her, "that God didn't just restore me—He restored us. And I'm proud of my boys. Both of 'em."

Roman shook his head shyly. Dallas laughed.

Donna pointed the microphone at Dallas.

"This one right here… he's stubborn as all outdoors, but he's got a heart that won't quit."

Everyone cheered.

Then she pointed to Roman.

"And this one… my quiet storm. The one who never forgot what love feels like, even when the world tried to take it from him."

Roman covered his face as the crowd roared in affectionate teasing.

Donna's voice cracked.

"I thought I had lost everything. But God brought them back. And He gave us more—this community, this mission, this second chance."

Tears streaked her cheeks.

Dallas hugged her.

Roman joined.

And for a moment, the yard grew still, people quietly witnessing a family reborn.

The Hallway Conversation

Later that night, after the guests left and the air cooled, Dallas and Roman stood on the front porch staring at the moonlit street.

"You think we're doing enough?" Roman asked.

Dallas considered the question.

"No," he admitted. "But the world's too broken to ever do 'enough.' We're doing what we can. And that's more than most."

Roman nodded slowly. "I used to think our childhood ruined us."

Dallas exhaled. "I used to think that too."

"But now…" Roman said, eyes softening, "I think it prepared us."

Dallas turned to him.

"For what?"

Roman looked upward.

"For this."

One Year Later — A New Kind of Anniversary

The Jackson family marked the one-year anniversary of their reunion not with fanfare, but with a quiet dinner in Donna's living room. The table was dressed with a simple white cloth, three candles, and a home-cooked spread of everything they used to dream about during the hardest years: turkey wings with rice, cornbread, macaroni pie, collard greens, and peach cobbler cooling on the window sill.

Roman lifted a cup of sweet tea.

"To surviving," he said.

Donna shook her head softly. "No, baby. To living."

Dallas raised his glass last. "To choosing each other."

They clinked glasses, and for the first time in a long time, the sound didn't echo against loneliness.

It sang against belonging.

After dinner, Donna brought out three sealed envelopes.

"What's this?" Dallas asked.

"These are letters you boys wrote to yourselves when you were young," she said softly. "I kept them in my Bible. I didn't feel worthy of opening them. But I think it's time."

Each son hesitated—because each letter held a version of themselves they had buried deep.

Roman opened his first. His handwriting wobbled across the page:

Dear Roman,

I hope when I grow up, I'm not scared anymore. I hope I can protect my brother. I hope I get a family.

He pressed the letter to his forehead.

"I didn't protect you," he whispered to Dallas.

Dallas shook his head. "Rome… you protected my spirit. You taught me chess. You made me believe someone cared."

Tears ran silently down Roman's face.

Then Dallas opened his.

His letter was shorter.

Dear Dallas,

I hope someone loves me one day.

Please let there be someone.

Please.

He closed his eyes, exhaling a shaky breath.

Donna touched his hand. "I love you, baby. I always did."

Dallas leaned his head back against the couch, overwhelmed.

Healing wasn't always loud.

Sometimes it sounded like soft sniffles in a dimly lit room.

The Fairview Center Opens

That spring, after months of construction and countless grants, Phase 2 of the Fairview Initiative opened:

The Fairview Resilience Center.

A full community complex — classrooms, therapy suites, a performance hall, and a glass-walled atrium lined with photographs of youth who had transformed their lives.

Dallas stood at the podium for the ribbon-cutting ceremony. Reporters lined the back. Community leaders filled the seats.

Donna and Roman stood proudly behind him.

He cleared his throat and began:

"When I was 12, I sat in a group home wondering if anyone would ever fight for me. Today, I stand here knowing that the boy I used to be would be proud — not because I became a judge, but because I found my family again and found a purpose bigger than myself."

Applause swelled.

"This building is not a monument," Dallas continued. "It is a promise. A promise that no child walks alone. A promise that justice is not siloed to courtrooms. A promise that healing is community work."

He glanced at Donna, who was wiping tears.

"A promise," he finished quietly, "that broken beginnings can still lead to beautiful futures."

The crowd rose to their feet.

As the ribbon fell, kids ran inside laughing, taking in the space like it was a new world.

Donna whispered in his ear, "You built what I prayed for."

But Dallas whispered back:

"Mom… we built it."

A Crisis That Tests the System

The new center drew praise — but it also drew skepticism from those who believed justice meant punishment, not prevention.

One day, a teenager named Khalil, who had recently joined the Initiative, was arrested during a violent altercation at a basketball court. The news spread fast. Headlines questioned whether the program was "too soft." Commentators demanded Khalil be charged as an adult.

Dallas's stomach twisted as he watched the footage — Khalil throwing punches, pain written across his face. But he also saw something others didn't:

Fear.

Desperation.

A boy cornered.

At the hearing, the courtroom was electric with tension.

The prosecutor recommended charges.

The defense begged for mercy.

The gallery buzzed with opinions.

Khalil stepped forward, shaking. "I messed up," he said. "But I don't wanna go to jail. I'm trying… I swear I'm trying."

Dallas studied him — the quiver in his lip, the clench of his fists, the familiar panic. He remembered being that age. He remembered feeling as if the world offered two doors: survival or destruction.

The entire room held its breath.

Dallas's gavel hovered.

"This court," he said finally, "believes in accountability. But this court also believes in redemption."

A murmur swept the room.

"So here is my ruling: Khalil will enter the Fairview Resilience Program full-time. His participation will be monitored weekly. His progress will determine his future."

Gasps echoed.

"But let me be clear," Dallas added, locking eyes with him, "this is your last chance. Not because you're unworthy… but because you are worthy of change."

Khalil broke into tears.

The ruling went viral — hailed as groundbreaking by some, criticized by others. But for Dallas, the moment reaffirmed something sacred:

Justice without humanity is merely punishment.

Justice with humanity is transformation.

A New Tradition — "Family Friday"

At Donna's request, the Jackson trio began a weekly tradition. Every Friday after work, no matter how exhausted or overwhelmed, they met for dinner.

Some nights were loud and filled with laughter; some nights were quiet and contemplative; some were tearful as they unpacked old trauma.

But every Friday, without fail, they were together.

One night, Donna brought out a long folder.

"These," she said, "are the documents I kept from when you boys were taken. I couldn't throw them away."

Roman and Dallas exchanged a look — one of trepidation and readiness.

Donna opened the folder. She shared old court papers, case notes, intake forms from the group home, social worker observations.

It was painful.

It was raw.

But it was necessary.

Roman held her hand while she cried.

Dallas rubbed her back gently.

"Mom," he said, "you don't need to punish yourself anymore. You survived. We survived."

Donna nodded slowly.

"It still hurts."

Roman kissed her forehead. "That means you're healing."

They burned the papers in a small fire pit in the backyard — a symbolic release of decades of shame and grief.

Donna whispered to the flames:

"Thank You for letting me get my babies back."

A Visit to an Old Ghost

Years after they left Fairview, the old group home remained a ghost in their memories. But Dallas suggested that confronting ghosts was part of healing.

So they went.

The building had been renovated into a transitional youth center, but the bones were the same. The halls echoed with the faintest traces of childhood fear and hope.

Donna walked through the rooms with trembling fingers tracing walls that once separated her from her sons.

"I failed you here," she whispered.

"No," Roman said, stepping closer. "The system failed all of us."

Dallas added, "But look at us now."

They toured the new rooms — bright murals, beanbag chairs, shelves of donated books.

A small boy approached Dallas nervously.

"Help with homework?" he asked.

Dallas smiled. "Yeah, buddy. I got you."

As he leaned over the workbook, Roman snapped a picture — the same angle as a faded Polaroid from years before, but now with grown men and second chances.

Donna stood behind them, tears streaming silently.

Healing wasn't a moment.

It was a journey.

And today, the journey felt holy.

A Glimpse Into the Future

A local university partnered with the Fairview Initiative to create scholarships for former foster youth. One of the first recipients, a girl named Tiana, sent Dallas a letter:

Judge Jackson,

Thank you for fighting for kids like me. I don't know how my life will end, but because of this program, I know how it can begin.

Dallas kept that letter framed on his desk.

Roman's chess club produced two county champions — one of them the boy he gave his knight to.

Donna became a beloved figure in several recovery circles.

The Family Stabilization Unit reduced recidivism by 40% in the first year.

Their healing had become contagious.

And the community was breathing easier.

One Year Later — A New Tradition

The Jackson family didn't just reunite—they built a tradition of staying together.

Every Sunday evening became "Family Reset."

Donna cooked. Roman brought dessert. Dallas brought board games, though most nights they didn't make it past the first round before the conversations took over.

Some Sundays were filled with laughter—stories from childhood, memories of Fairview, playful arguments about who was the better chess player. Other Sundays were quieter, filled with moments where someone revealed a piece of pain they hadn't dared share before.

One evening, Donna surprised them both with a framed picture she kept hidden for decades: a photograph of young Dallas and Roman as toddlers, sitting in a plastic kiddie pool in a rundown backyard. Both boys were smiling—big, toothless, unburdened grins.

Dallas stared at it for a long time.

"Why didn't you show us this before?" he asked softly.

Donna touched the frame, her fingers trembling slightly.

"Because it hurt too much. I thought… if I pretended the memories weren't real, maybe my mistakes weren't either."

Roman placed a hand over hers. "But we want them. All of them."

Dallas felt something shift inside him—a piece of the broken past quietly sliding into place.

"Frame more," he told her. "All the ones you have."

Donna smiled. "I will."

The photo became a cornerstone on Dallas's mantle—a reminder not of what was lost, but of what survived.

Roman's Breakthrough

Roman's work in the Initiative brought him face-to-face with boys who reminded him of himself at twelve—eyes guarded, shoulders tight, hearts walled off. But one boy, in particular, challenged him more than any other.

Jayden.

Age 15.

Anger simmering beneath the surface like a storm waiting to break.

Jayden never smiled.

Never laughed.

Never accepted help.

Every chess session ended with him flipping the board or storming out.

One afternoon, after a blowup where Jayden shoved a table and cursed loudly, Roman followed him outside.

"Stop following me," Jayden snapped.

Roman leaned against the wall calmly. "Fine. I'll just stand here."

"You don't get it," Jayden spat. "You had your family come back. No one's coming back for me."

Roman exhaled slowly. There it was—the truth behind the anger.

"Come sit," Roman said gently. "Just for a minute."

Surprisingly, Jayden did.

Roman pulled out the battered black chess knight—the same one from Fairview, the one that had survived all their moves and all their losses.

"I carried this piece through everything," Roman said. "Not because it made me strong, but because it reminded me I was still playing the game."

Jayden frowned. "What does that even mean?"

"It means," Roman said, "your story isn't over. Not if you keep moving."

Jayden stared at the knight. Then he broke—silent tears rolling down his cheeks as he pressed his palms into his eyes.

Roman didn't touch him; he just sat beside him, letting the moment breathe.

After several minutes, Jayden whispered, "Do you think someone like me can change?"

Roman answered without hesitation.

"I don't think—I know. Because I was you."

That was the day Jayden stopped running.

It was the day Roman fully stepped into purpose.

Donna's Journey Toward Peace

Donna's recovery wasn't linear.

She still attended meetings.

Still worked with her sponsor.

Still fought the occasional whisper of self-doubt.

But she no longer carried her burdens alone.

One afternoon, she stood on the small stage of a women's recovery conference, looking out at nearly a hundred faces. She held a microphone with steady hands.

"I used to think healing meant forgetting," she said. "But healing means remembering—and choosing differently anyway."

The crowd nodded, many crying softly.

"I used to think being a mother meant perfection. But being a mother is really about perseverance."

Her voice broke.

"I lost years with my boys. Years I can never get back. But God gave me the strength to fight for the years ahead. And my sons gave me grace I didn't deserve."

Donna stepped off the stage to a standing ovation.

Afterward, several women gathered around her, hugging her, whispering stories of their own battles.

One woman, barely thirty, took her hands. "I didn't think I had another chance."

Donna squeezed her firmly. "Baby, as long as you're breathing, you've got another chance."

It became her slogan—repeated in shelters, meetings, courtrooms:

"As long as you're breathing, you've got another chance."

Dallas's Quiet Transformation

Dallas, once known for his steely composure, found himself changing in subtle but profound ways.

He didn't just resolve casesHe dug into the roots.

He asked the questions no one else asked.

He pushed for restorative practices, mental health evaluations, community service alternatives.

Other prosecutors teased him at first.

"You going soft, Jackson?"

"You creating a therapy court now?"

"You trying to be Oprah in a robe?"

Dallas simply smiled.

"I'm trying to stop cycles," he answered.

He didn't need validation.

He had vision.

And soon, even his critics couldn't ignore the impact:

Reduced recidivism.

Safer neighborhoods.

Families choosing counseling over chaos.

Teens choosing art, boxing, or school over street corners.

One late evening, a janitor tapped his door.

"Judge Jackson? I just wanted to say… my nephew was in your program. He's different now. Thank you."

Dallas nodded, touched beyond words.

After the man left, Dallas leaned back in his chair, staring at the ceiling. Something inside him was expanding—gratitude layered with purpose, peace layered with responsibility.

He whispered to no one:

"I'm not done yet."

A Test of Strength

Healing is never a straight line.

And the Jackson family learned that deeply when a crisis hit their own home.

Donna received a call one evening:

Her younger sister, Terri, had relapsed.

Terri was brought to the emergency room unconscious.

Dallas and Roman rushed to the hospital, Donna shaking between them. The waiting room felt like a cruel echo of her own past—its sterile lights, its loneliness, its uncertainty.

When the doctor came out, Donna stood up so fast she nearly fell.

"She's stable," he said gently. "But she'll need long-term treatment and strong family support."

Donna collapsed into Dallas's arms, sobbing.

"It's happening all over again," she cried. "I can't lose her. I can't lose someone else."

Dallas held her tightly. "We won't let that happen."

Roman nodded. "No one gets left behind. Not anymore."

They stayed through the night, taking turns sitting beside Terri's bed.

When Terri finally woke up, her eyes filled with shame.

"I messed up," she whispered. "I'm so sorry, Donna."

Donna took her hand. "You're breathing. That means you got another chance."

Terri wept softly.

In that moment, the Jackson family realized something powerful:

Healing didn't just belong to them.

It belonged to everyone their story touched.

And they were strong enough now to carry others through storms.

The County Calls

Months later, the County Board requested a private meeting with Dallas.

He expected a policy proposal.

Or maybe an inquiry.

Or maybe a complaint.

What he didn't expect was a full roundtable of officials applauding him as he entered.

The Chairwoman stood.

"Judge Jackson, your work with the Fairview Initiative has caught the attention of the state. We want to fund a pilot project in every county. We want you to oversee the rollout."

Dallas blinked.

"You… want me to lead a statewide restorative justice program?"

"We want you to change the way the justice system works," she said.

He sat in stunned silence.

A year ago, he was a man quietly battling ghosts.

Now the state wanted him to help rewrite the future.

Dallas nodded slowly.

"Then let's make history."

Roman's Big Step

Inspired by Dallas's leadership, Roman applied for a scholarship to pursue a Master's in Social Work.

He wrote his personal statement at the dining room table while Donna chopped vegetables for dinner and Dallas worked on briefs nearby.

When he finished reading it aloud, Donna had tears running down her cheeks.

"You boys," she whispered. "Y'all turned your pain into power."

A month later, the letter arrived.

Roman was accepted—with a full scholarship.

Donna shrieked so loud the neighbors thought something happened.

Dallas lifted Roman in a hug so tight they nearly toppled over.

Roman whispered, voice cracking, "I'm doing this because you believed in me."

"No," Dallas said firmly. "You're doing this because you chose to rise."

Seeds of a Bigger Legacy

By the end of the year:

- The Fairview Initiative expanded to three cities.
- Donna launched a podcast on recovery and motherhood.
- Roman started teaching court-ordered classes for young men.
- Dallas was invited to speak at a national restorative justice conference.

Their impact wasn't a ripple anymore.

It was a wave.

A wave that carried families, youth, courts, and entire communities with it.

A wave that newspapers began calling:

"The Fairview Effect."

It was the kind of movement that producers notice.

The kind that inspires documentaries.

The kind that becomes film-worthy.

And it all began with three broken people choosing each otherChoosing healing — Choosing a second chance.

One Year Later — A New Rhythm

Life settled into something none of them had ever known before: stability.

Not perfection.

Not fairy-tale harmony.

But stability — the kind that grows from showing up day after day, even when it's hard.

Dallas still rose before dawn, sipping coffee in silence as the city stretched awake beneath the skyline. But now, mornings often included a text from Roman:

"Breakfast at Mom's?"

Or a message from Donna:

"I made pancakes. Get here."

Sometimes Dallas went. Sometimes work pulled him in early. Sometimes he arrived just early enough to grab a plate, kiss Donna's cheek, and run out the door.

But no matter what, they stayed connected — through shared meals, therapy sessions, family nights, and the constant thread of recommitting to each other.

The fear of losing it never quite went away.

Trauma rarely leaves without scars.

But the love overpowered the fear more days than not.

A Courtroom That Breathes Different

The courthouse had changed.

People whispered about it in the elevators, in break rooms, in the cafeteria line. There was a shift — subtle, then pronounced — in the energy. More compassion. More discretion. More curiosity instead of judgment.

Dallas wasn't the only force behind it, but he became the anchor.

He implemented training on trauma-informed prosecution.

He created partnerships with shelters and mental health centers.

He ensured every juvenile case included a holistic evaluation.

He pushed back on unnecessarily harsh sentencing recommendations.

And lawyers followed his lead.

Not because they feared him but because they respected him.

One morning, while reviewing files, a young prosecutor named Marissa knocked softly on his door.

"Judge Jackson… can I ask you something?"

Dallas smiled. "Of course."

She stepped in nervously. "I have a case. A teenager. Seventeen. Caught breaking into a store. No prior record. He said he was hungry. His mother is sick."

Dallas leaned back. "What does your gut tell you?"

"That he needs help," she said. "Not jail."

"Then help him," Dallas said simply. "The law is not a hammer. It's a scale. Don't let fear tip it."

Marissa exhaled a breath she'd been holding for weeks.

"Thank you," she whispered.

These were the ripples.

This was the legacy beginning to take shape.

Roman's Breakthrough

Roman's chess program became a county staple.

Each week, he sat with kids who reminded him painfully of himself — angry, uncertain, brilliant, fragile. Boys who had been told they were problems instead of possibilities.

One of them, a foster child named Aaron, had a habit of flipping the chessboard every time he felt cornered. The staff considered removing him from the group.

Roman refused.

After one particularly rough session, Roman sat across from him on the floor — the chess pieces scattered everywhere.

"You think you're broken," Roman said gently. "But you're not."

Aaron looked away. "I'm just tired of losing."

Roman nodded slowly. "Me too. But every time I lost, I learned where the board was weakest — and where I was strongest."

Aaron blinked, confused. "What do you mean?"

"You're not losing," Roman said softly. "You're discovering."

For the first time, the boy's breathing steadied.

He helped Roman pick up the pieces.

Two months later, Aaron won his first match.

Roman called Dallas that night, breathless with pride.

"Bro… you should've seen him."

Dallas smiled through the phone. "I know exactly how that feels."

Donna's Healing

Donna's transformation was ongoing — sometimes soaring, sometimes quiet, sometimes painful. Recovery rarely moves in a straight line, but Donna held onto her sobriety with tenacious grace.

She attended meetings religiously.

She helped other mothers fight for reinstatement.

She built friendships she'd never had before.

She even enrolled in night classes to earn her certification in peer counseling.

But the greatest shift came from within.

One afternoon, she stood in front of a mirror, staring at her reflection — older, stronger, softer. A woman who had crawled back from the edges of devastation.

For a long time, she whispered to the mirror:

"You deserve this chance. You deserve this family."

And slowly, she began to believe it.

A Painful Conversation

Healing doesn't erase memories.

It reveals them.

One evening, the three sat around Donna's kitchen table. A thunderstorm rumbled outside, wind rattling the windows.

Dallas turned to Donna, voice trembling with vulnerability.

"Why didn't you come for me sooner?"

Donna closed her eyes — a mother's worst question, asked by a child who lived its answer.

"I was ashamed," Donna whispered. "I thought… if you saw me the way I was, you'd run from me. And I didn't want to ruin what little life you might've built."

"But I needed you," Dallas said. "I still do."

Donna reached for his hand.

"And I'm here. I'm here until the last breath leaves my lungs."

Roman placed his hand over theirs.

A triangle of forgiveness.

A constellation of belonging they built themselves.

A Living Memorial

Months later, the Fairview Initiative unveiled a mural on the side of the community center — a massive, breathtaking tribute painted by youth participants.

At the center was a boy standing at a crossroads, a broken chain falling from one wrist, a glowing chess knight in his hand. Behind him, two figures — a mother and a brother — reached out, guiding him toward a horizon filled with color.

The mural was titled:

"Full Circle."

When Dallas saw it, he stood completely still.

The artist, a sixteen-year-old with shy eyes, approached him.

"We based it on your story," she said. "I hope that's okay."

Dallas swallowed thickly. "It's perfect."

Roman stared at the chess knight and laughed softly. "They even got the scratches right."

Donna wiped tears with her sleeve. "My babies… look at what your story is doing."

The unveiling drew hundreds.

Local news filmed.

Community leaders spoke.

Kids cheered.

But the moment that sealed it — the moment that made the mural a living memorial — happened when an elderly man approached Dallas.

"I lived through segregation," he said. "I saw systems break people. But I never thought I'd see the day when a judge built systems to heal them."

Dallas placed a hand over his heart.

"Thank you, sir."

"No," the man said, gripping his shoulder. "Thank you."

The Night Everything Changed

A year after their reunion, Donna hosted a family barbecue in her backyard — music, laughter, kids playing tag, neighbors dropping by with desserts.

At sunset, Roman brought out the old Polaroid camera that Donna had kept all those years.

"Let's take a real family picture," he said.

They stood together — Donna in the middle, her sons on each side.

But before Roman clicked the shutter, Donna grabbed their hands.

"Wait. One more thing."

She looked at both of them with a mixture of pride and awe.

"I prayed for this before I even knew how to pray. You two… you saved me. You saved each other. And now you're saving this whole city."

Dallas felt tears sting his eyes.

Roman exhaled shakily.

Donna smiled the softest smile they had ever seen.

"Let's capture this moment before we blink and it becomes memory."

The flash went off.

It wasn't just a picture.

It was a resurrection.

One Year Later

The first year after their reunion wasn't a straight line.

It was a loop—grief and joy circling around each other, old habits flaring and then softening, tiny ruptures followed by intentional repair.

On the anniversary of the day Donna found out who Roman really was, she invited everyone to a small park near her apartment. It wasn't anything grand—no catered food, no balloon arches—just a grill, a few folding chairs, and a worn picnic blanket that had seen better days.

Roman arrived first, carrying a cooler.

"You brought enough to feed the whole city," Donna teased, peeking inside.

"You said 'light snacks,'" he said. "You're the one who taught me that means too much food in this family."

Dallas came a few minutes later, still half in work-mode, jacket folded over his arm, tie loosened. He paused for a moment, watching them from a distance. The scene could have been from someone else's life: a mother fussing over the grill, a brother organizing plates, music playing low from someone's phone.

"Hey, stranger," Roman called out, waving him over. "You gonna stand there looking sentimental or help me carry this table?"

Dallas shook his head, smiling as he joined them.

They ate grilled chicken and corn, potato salad and Donna's sweet tea that was always a little too sweet. They argued about music and movies. They made fun of the way Dallas still over-pronounced legal terms. They reminisced.

Then Donna disappeared into her car and came back holding a small box.

"I've been waiting a year to do this," she said, suddenly shy.

Inside were three matching bracelets: simple leather bands with a small metal plate on each. Stamped into the metal were three words:

"We made it."

Roman picked one up, turning it over. "When did you—"

"I ordered them the week after we found out," Donna said, voice thick. "I didn't know if we'd… stay this close. I was scared. But y'all kept showing up. So I figured… it's time."

Dallas fastened his around his wrist. The leather felt warm from the sun.

"Mom," he said quietly, the word still new enough to make her eyes glisten, "this is… beautiful."

Roman slipped his on too. "Now we're official," he said. "Family membership bands."

Donna laughed, swatting at him. "Y'all always been my babies. This is just proof."

They took a photo—Donna in the middle, her sons on either side, each of them holding up their wrists, the metal plates catching the afternoon light.

Later that night, after the park emptied and the last of the dishes were washed, Dallas sat in his car staring at the bracelet. He traced the words with his thumb.

We made it.

He knew they hadn't arrived at some perfect destination. There were still days when old hurt echoed too loud, when guilt weighed heavier on Donna, when Roman questioned his place between two mothers, two histories.

But "we made it" didn't mean it's over.

It meant:

We survived long enough to build something new.

Anne and Donna

A few months after that first anniversary, Roman asked Dallas for a favor.

"I want you there," he said nervously. "When they meet."

"Are you sure?" Dallas asked.

"Absolutely not," Roman said. "But I think it's time."

"They" were Anne and Donna.

The woman who raised him, and the woman who gave birth to him.

They agreed to meet in a quiet coffee shop halfway between their homes. Donna dressed carefully, smoothing her blouse three times before they walked in; Anne arrived with a manila envelope tucked under her arm, like she'd brought paperwork for court.

When they sat down, there was an awkward stretch of silence—three women and two sons who didn't quite know how to sit in the same frame.

Anne broke it first.

"You must be Donna," she said, voice soft.

"Yes, ma'am," Donna replied, hands clasped tight. "Thank you… for taking care of my baby when I couldn't."

Anne's eyes filled. "He was never just your baby or mine," she said, glancing at Roman. "He was always his own person. We both just carried him through different storms."

Roman reached for both their hands, bridging the table.

"I wouldn't be here without either of you," he said. "No more guilt. No more blame. Just… thanks."

They talked for over two hours. They cried in turns. Anne confessed the fear she'd always carried—that one day Roman would resent her for not being his "real" mother. Donna confessed the fear that he'd never want to know her at all.

By the time they left, the manila envelope sat open on the table. Inside were pictures from Roman's childhood—the first day of kindergarten, his high school graduation, the day he passed the bar.

"You should have these," Anne told Donna. "They're your memories too."

That night, Dallas watched as Donna sat at her kitchen table, laying the photos out in a careful line. Her fingers brushed each image as if she could step inside it and hold the younger version of her son.

"I missed so much," she whispered.

Dallas sat beside her. "You're here now," he said. "That's what matters."

She nodded, tears slipping silently down her cheeks.

"God gave him two mothers," she said finally. "It took me a long time to see that as a blessing instead of a punishment."

Three Years Later — Numbers and Names

Three years into the Fairview Initiative, the numbers started to turn heads.

Juvenile re-offense rates dropped.

School attendance climbed.

Emergency mental health calls at the courthouse decreased.

More cases were diverted to restorative programs instead of jail.

Reporters wrote articles.

Politicians asked for tours.

Researchers asked to collect data.

But the numbers were never what mattered most to Dallas.

The names did.

Names like Mateo, who graduated high school and started community college.

Names like Jason, who now volunteered as a junior chess coach.

Names like Eric, whose sunrise painting became the official symbol of the Initiative.

On the third anniversary, the community held a block party—music, food trucks, kids running around with face paint. The mural of birds and open hands that once lived inside the courthouse lobby had been replicated on the side of a building downtown, thanks to a local arts grant.

Dallas stood with Roman and Donna, watching toddlers chase bubbles in the street.

A woman approached him with a toddler in her arms.

"Judge Jackson?" she asked.

He recognized her face—the woman who had collapsed in the courthouse lobby years earlier.

"Of course," he said. "How are you?"

She smiled, eyes glowing. "I'm in my third year clean. I've got shared custody now. This is Malik." She bounced the toddler gently. "He knows his mama stayed."

Dallas swallowed hard. "I'm proud of you."

"No," she said. "You saw me when I didn't see myself. That changed everything."

Malik reached for Dallas's robe sleeve.

"Hi, little man," Dallas said, tickling his hand. "You keep your mama smiling, okay?"

The woman nodded. "I will. We will."

As she walked away, Donna slipped her hand into Dallas's.

"You see?" she said quietly. "You're giving people the second chance I needed."

He looked over at her. "You got your second chance too."

She smiled sadly. "Yeah. In ways I never dreamed I would."

Private Struggles, Public Strength

It would be easy to pretend everything turned rosy and smooth, but real healing doesn't work that way.

There were still rough days.

There was the night Roman and Dallas exploded into an argument over a case—Roman prosecuting, Dallas overseeing. They clashed over a sentencing recommendation, old wounds hiding in new disagreements.

"You always have to fix everything," Roman snapped.

"And you always think mercy means being naïve," Dallas shot back.

They didn't speak for three days.

Donna finally called them both. "Get over here," she ordered. "Now."

They arrived at her apartment, each convinced they were right.

She sat them at her kitchen table like they were sixteen again.

"You think I prayed y'all back into my life so you could act like enemies?" she demanded. "Apologize. Right now."

They both started to speak at once.

"Not to me," she interrupted. "To each other. This family went through hell to find its way home. You will not burn it down because your egos got tired."

Silence settled over the room.

"I'm sorry," Dallas said first. "I let the job speak louder than my respect for you."

Roman nodded slowly. "I'm sorry too. I still get scared I'll disappear if I'm not the toughest voice in the room. You don't deserve the fallout from that."

They didn't solve everything that night. But they chose, again, not to walk away.

Healing wasn't a single decision.

It was a habit.

Five Years Later — The Building with Their Name

Five years after the Fairview Initiative launched, they cut a ribbon in front of a new building.

A real home.

The Jackson–Arnold Center for Youth Justice & Healing.

The name had caused a fight. Dallas wanted to call it something neutral. Roman argued that their story was the very reason people had given money in the first place. Donna just wanted them to stop arguing.

In the end, the board insisted.

"You didn't just start a program," the director told them. "You started a movement. People need to know where it came from."

The center had classrooms, counseling offices, a meditation room, a daycare, and a rooftop garden where kids grew vegetables and wrote their own affirmations on smooth stones. There was a small wing dedicated to families affected by addiction.

Donna led weekly groups there.

"Welcome," she would say. "You're not broken beyond repair. You're broken open for something new."

On opening day, kids ran through the halls like it had always belonged to them.

Roman gave a short speech.

"I grew up in a place where we counted down the days until we aged out," he said. "Now we're building a place where kids can count up— to their goals, their dreams, their futures."

Dallas stepped up next.

"Systems don't change because we wish it," he said. "They change because people inside them refuse to repeat the same harm. This center is a promise: we will not give up on any kid, any family, any story— even when it looks like the ending was written."

He thought briefly of his younger self, staring out of a group home window. Of Donna, alone in a kitchen with a single candle. Of Roman, writing letters by night-light.

Then he looked out at the crowd.

"We're proof that endings can be rewritten," he said. "Every day, in every room, we will keep doing exactly that."

Ten Years Later — A New Generation

Ten years after that rainy night in the courthouse when the epilogue of his life began, Dallas woke to a strange and familiar sound.

"Uncle Dee! Uncle Dee! You're gonna be late!"

A small whirlwind burst into his bedroom—a girl with wild curls, cartoon socks, and a plastic tiara tilted on her head. This was Nova,

Roman's daughter, who had long ago decided Dallas was "Uncle Dee," whether he liked it or not.

"I cannot be late for a princess," he said, sitting up, feigning panic. "What did I forget?"

"You promised to come to Career Day!" she said. "You said you were gonna tell them about being a judge and how you help kids and how your robe is like a superhero cape."

He laughed. "I said it's not a cape. That's how rumors start."

She crossed her arms. "You lied?"

He held up his hands. "Okay, okay. I'll be there. I just need coffee and, you know, pants."

"Adults are weird," she muttered, spinning out of the room.

At the school, he stood in front of twenty second-graders, his robe hanging on a hook beside him. He explained what a judge did using words they understood.

"I make decisions," he said. "But the best part of my job is helping people find better choices for their lives. Especially kids."

A boy raised his hand.

"Did you ever get in trouble when you were a kid?" he asked.

Dallas smiled. "I didn't always feel like I belonged anywhere. Sometimes that made me angry. Sometimes it made me quiet. I didn't always act the way I should."

"What happened?" another girl asked.

"I met people who believed I could be more than my worst days," he said. "That's what I try to be for others now."

Nova beamed from her spot on the rug, as if she owned the whole story.

Afterward, as they walked through the hallway, she slipped her small hand into his.

"Do you think I could be a judge one day?" she asked.

"I think you can be anything you want," he replied. "Judge, artist, astronaut, chef…"

She frowned. "What if I want to be all of them?"

He chuckled. "Then we'll need a bigger business card."

Legacy in Motion

The Jackson–Arnold Center had expanded to three locations. The crisis unit model had been replicated in neighboring counties. A state bill— informally called the Fairview Bill—passed, ensuring that all juvenile courts in the state had access to diversion programs and mental health resources.

Dallas had testified in front of lawmakers, Roman at his side.

"Some of you see numbers on a page," Dallas had told them. "I see kids who look like the boy I used to be. We can either keep punishing hurt… or we can start healing it."

It wasn't easy. There was pushback. There were headlines. There were moments when old philosophies clashed with new approaches.

But the work kept going.

Donna, now affectionately called "Miss D" by half the community, was a kind of quiet celebrity at the center. Young people approached her for advice. Older women approached her for courage.

"Do you ever stop feeling guilty?" one mother asked her one evening.

Donna took her hand. "No," she said honestly. "But the guilt stops driving the car. It just rides in the backseat while you move forward."

Fully Full Circle

On the tenth anniversary of the Fairview Initiative, they hosted a commemorative event back where it all began: the courthouse.

The mural of birds and open hands had been restored and expanded. Now, if you looked closely, you could see three small figures standing at the bottom of it—stylized silhouettes of boys facing a rising sun.

One of them held a chess piece in his hand.

The atrium was filled with people: program graduates, families, staff, judges, social workers, old volunteers, new donors, children running under chairs.

Dallas stood near the edge of the crowd, watching as a young woman took the stage.

"My name is Tiana," she said into the microphone. "When I was fifteen, I was angry at everyone. Angry at the world. Angry at my mom. Angry at myself."

She glanced down, steadying her breath.

"I came through this courthouse in handcuffs," she continued. "But instead of going to jail, I was sent to the Fairview Initiative. They gave me therapy. They gave me a mentor. They made me go back to school." She smiled faintly. "And they didn't give up on me. Even when I tried to make them."

The audience listened, rapt.

"Next month," Tiana said, voice shaking, "I start my first semester of law school. I want to be a public defender. I want to stand next to kids who feel like I felt and tell them: 'You're not the worst thing you've ever done.'"

Applause thundered through the hall.

Dallas's eyes burned.

Roman stepped to his side, nudging him. "You did that," he said.

"We did that," Dallas corrected.

A hand slipped into Dallas's other one.

Donna.

She was older now. Time had etched new lines into her face, but there was a light in her eyes that hadn't been there when they first reunited.

"You proud?" she asked softly.

"More than I can explain," he said.

They stood like that for a long moment—mother in the middle, sons on either side—watching a future they'd never imagined unfold right in front of them.

One Last Visit

Later that evening, after the event, Dallas drove alone to the place he hadn't visited in years.

Fairview.

The building had been renovated again. The chain-link fence replaced by a garden. The old concrete courtyard now had benches and a small fountain. There were bright murals instead of peeling paint.

He walked the perimeter slowly, memories pressing in from all sides.

The boy who stared out this window,

the teen who traced chess moves on the edge of his mattress,

the kid who wondered if anyone would remember himthey all walked beside him.

He sat on a bench facing the entrance and closed his eyes.

"You made it," he whispered to his younger self. "We made it."

He thought of Roman—writing letters in the dark.

He thought of Donna—praying over a candle.

He thought of every child whose case file once looked like a lost cause.

He pulled the leather bracelet gently, feeling the metal plate against his wrist.

We made it.

A group of kids spilled out the front doors, supervised by a staff member. They looked at him curiously—just another man in a suit, sitting on a bench.

One of them—a boy with braids and a stubborn tilt to his chin— paused.

"You work here?" the boy asked.

"No," Dallas said. "I used to live here."

The boy blinked. "For real?"

"For real," Dallas said. "Now I work at the courthouse. I help run some of the programs for kids who come through there."

The boy shifted. "Is it better than here?"

Dallas thought for a moment. "It's different," he said. "But I'll tell you this: this place doesn't have to be the end of your story. It can be the beginning."

The boy studied him for a second, then nodded.

"Okay," he said. "I'll remember that."

He ran off to catch up with the others.

Dallas watched him go, a soft smile tugging at his mouth.

Home

That night, the family gathered at Donna's house for dinner.

Anne came too. So did Roman's wife and Nova. The table was crowded with food and stories. Someone had brought a cake with 10 YEARS written in frosting.

At one point, Donna raised her glass.

"I want to say something," she said.

The table quieted.

"I used to think my life was proof that some people just don't get happy endings," she began. "But sitting here, looking at all of you… I realize I was wrong."

She looked at her sons, at her granddaughter, at the women who shared motherhood with her in different ways.

"I don't have the ending I imagined," she said. "I have one I never even knew to ask for."

Her voice wavered.

"This family is not perfect," she continued. "We argue. We mess up. We have scars. But we keep choosing each other. Over and over again. And that, to me, is what healing looks like."

She lifted her glass higher.

"To second chances," she said. "To cycles broken. To the kids we were and the people we became."

Everyone echoed her.

"To second chances."

Dallas looked around the table, his chest full.

For so long, he'd chased justice like a finish line. Now he understood it was something else entirely—not a moment, but a movement. Not a verdict, but a way of living.

Later, as the dishes were cleared and laughter spilled into the hallway, he stepped out onto the small balcony for air. The city lights glittered around him. Somewhere in the distance, sirens wailed, a reminder that the work was never truly "done."

But he felt no despair.

Only resolve.

Roman joined him, leaning against the railing.

"Think we did alright?" Roman asked.

Dallas exhaled slowly. "I think we did more than alright."

They stood in silence for a while, listening to the murmur of family inside.

"You know," Roman said, "if someone made a movie out of all this, no one would believe it."

Dallas chuckled. "They'd say it was too much. Too convenient. Too… hopeful."

"Guess real life still gets the last word then," Roman replied.

"Yeah," Dallas said. "It does."

Behind them, the sliding door opened.

"Boys!" Donna called. "Come take this picture! Y'all always running from the camera."

They turned.

Donna stood in the doorway holding her phone, framed by warm kitchen light. Nova tugged at her shirt, trying to get into position.

Dallas glanced at Roman.

"Ready?" he asked.

Roman shrugged. "Been ready."

They stepped back into the glow of the living room.

Together.

Donna held up the phone.

"Say 'we made it,'" she instructed.

They laughed.

"We made it," they replied in unison.

The picture captured more than faces. It caught years of pain, thousands of choices, countless small mercies and stubborn hopes—all of it held inside a single, ordinary moment of togetherness.

If anyone had looked closely, they might have noticed the matching bracelets on their wrists, the way their bodies leaned slightly toward each other, the ease in their smiles.

The story that began in broken places did not end there.

It ended here:

In a modest living room full of noise and love,

with a family that refused to let the past have the final say,

and a man who finally understoodHe was never just judged by what he'd survived.

He was defined by what he chose to build from it.

Full circle.

And still moving forward.

Dedication

<hr>

To all who have served—my fellow veterans, whose courage and sacrifice taught me not only discipline, but the power of resilience and belonging.

May this story honor your service and the strength found in community and purpose.

To the curious minds shaped by the studies of sociology and psychology, whose pursuit of understanding has inspired me to look beyond appearances and reach the heart of every story.

To my family, friends, mentors, and every reader—

Thank you for believing, challenging, and helping me write beyond the limits of judgment.

This book is for the dreamers, the doubted, the determined, and those who rise above every label—

Let your journey be your greatest verdict.

Cheurlie Pierre-Russell

Contact the Author

Cheurlie Pierre-Russell would love to hear from her readers!

To connect, collaborate, or request event appearances, please use the information below:

Email: j3russellbooks@gmail.com

Official Website: www.j3russellbooks.com

Social Media:

Facebook: @RussellBook

Instagram: @JudgeMeNow.Film

Youtube: @JudgeMeNowbook